Praise for the Ca

CW00880982

Wow! A rea

"How to start? Right from the off this is a truly explosive read and it doesn't disappoint as it continues on. The action grips from beginning to end and the confrontations between the main human characters and the Rabid is fast, furious and bloody. An adrenaline-fuelled rollercoaster adventure that simply roars along at pace leaving you as breathless as the combatants in the story. I loved it, the military parlance is entirely in keeping with the storyline and for even those with a rudimentary understanding of the military, it shouldn't present any problem in following the story as it unfolds. I for one can't wait to get stuck into the follow-up."

Wonderful book

"I very much enjoyed reading this book. In fact, I read the whole book at one time, could not put it down."

A book full of suspense, action and emotion. A brilliant read, couldn't put it down!

"This book has it all. It was thrilling, scary with humour and raw emotion thrown into the mix. The characters were relatable and very well written. My favourite by far was Andy and Emily's father/daughter relationship, you could really feel what they were going through. I was hooked from the start and couldn't put it down, a definite sign of a good read. I'm really looking forward to the next book in the series and highly recommend everyone to give this book a read, you definitely won't regret it. Well done Lance!"

Great read!!

"Very easy to follow and a good pace can't wait for more!!!"

Lance Winkless was born in Sutton Coldfield, England, brought up in Plymouth, Devon and now lives in Staffordshire with his partner and daughter.

For more information on Lance Winkless
and future writing see his website.

www.LanceWinkless.com

By Lance Winkless

CAPITAL FALLING
CAPITAL FALLING 2 – DENIAL
CAPITAL FALLING 3 – RESURGENCE

THE Z SEASON –

KILL TONE
VOODOO SUN
CRUEL FIX

Visit Amazon Author Pages

Amazon US - Amazon.com/author/lancewinkless

Amazon UK - Amazon.co.uk/-/e/B07QJV2LR3

Why Not Follow

Facebook www.facebook.com/LanceWinklessAuthor

Twitter   @LanceWinkless

Instagram @LanceWinkless

Pinterest www.pinterest.com/lancewinkless

BookBub www.bookbub.com/authors/lance-winkless

ALL REVIEWS POSTED ARE VERY MUCH APPRECIATED,
THEY ARE SO IMPORTANT, THANKS

CAPITAL
FALLING 2
DENIAL

Lance Winkless
25/5/2022

Lance Winkless

This book is a work of fiction, any resemblance to actual persons, living or dead, organisations, places, incidents and events are coincidental.

ISBN: 9781697798142

Published by Lance Winkless
www.LanceWinkless.com

Chapter 1

In a rage, Molly slams her hand down on the door handle and pushes the office door open with a force she barely knew she possessed. She immediately releases the handle, letting the heavy door fly inwards, and it does fly, through 180° until it inevitably crashes into the closest object behind it.

Doctor Rees's bicycle absorbs the majority of the door's kinetic energy; some is transferred to the wall against which the bike was balanced, but the bike absorbs the most. The bike turns that energy into sound in the form of a loud crash, and into motion, by twisting and falling from its perch on the wall and back against the door, pushing it back towards Molly.

The bike ends up in a heap on the floor with its front wheel jutting out from behind the door and sticking up into the air, its spokes clicking as it revolves—as if they would continue for eternity.

The door is now half-closed again with the bloody bike stuck behind it, but that doesn't deter Molly. She again forces the door open further by shoulder-barging both the door and the bike as far as she can, back into the wall.

"This whole operation is totally unacceptable," Molly barks, her rage undiminished following her fight with the door and the bike. "We were assured these outside contractors would be fully trained professionals, but they are a bunch of clowns, amateurs, I am sure some of them are fresh out of school!"

Stephen Rees springs back in his leather chair as his head whips up from the pile of documents on his desk, a pile he is struggling to get through. His eyes were just starting to glaze over but the sudden crash and resulting commotion from Molly bursting through the door has shocked him out of his near slumber.

"How can you agree with this!" Molly barks again, red-faced.

"By all means come in, Lieutenant, but you will stand to attention when you address me." Major Doctor Stephen Rees demands from behind his desk, now wide awake.

"Yes Sir," Molly says, immediately standing rigidly to attention in reflex as some of the wind is taken out of her sails.

"Please continue," the Major tells Molly, who is red in the face and looks like steam might be about to burst from her ears.

"Sir, we cannot let this continue. These people clearly don't know what they are doing or what they are dealing with. They are not taking nearly enough care disassembling the equipment and moving it, and we are about to start preparing the cold storage assemblies ready for transport. I don't need to tell you what the result could be if even one of those is damaged and containment is lost! This should be a military operation, Sir," Molly finishes.

"I understand your concern, Lieutenant, but we have our orders and I expect you and your team to carry them out, to oversee and ensure the safety of this operation."

"Sir, I can't." The Major cuts her off.

"Molly," the Major says calmingly, "I totally understand what you are saying and I'll be honest with you; I completely agree. I had a long video call with the General and his assistant at 0630 and told him the same, but the General didn't agree and gave me a direct order to continue with the operation and get it complete with the resources allocated. Now we both know it's wrong and that the budget shouldn't outweigh the safety but I'm afraid it does, so let's get this done with what we have. Once complete, at least it will mean those vials will be either destroyed or stored in the new facility and out of this old place. They should never have been here in the first place."

"But Sir," Molly tries again.

"You have your orders, Lieutenant."

Molly's head drops slightly as she says, "Yes Sir," rather sheepishly.

"Carry on, Lieutenant, oh and remember, as I said in this morning's briefing, if I am needed in the lab to oversee any part of the operation, don't hesitate to inform me." Major Reese says, quickly adding, "My door is always open."

The joke brings the slightest hint of a smile across Molly's face as her stand to attention hardens again. She salutes her superior officer, colleague and friend. She then turns to re-engage her fight with the bike. This time, however, she fumbles to get the bike back upright and back into its space, balanced against the wall behind the door.

As peace breaks out between Molly and the bike, she hears, "Thank you, Lieutenant," from the Major whose head is already down, returned to his mountain of paperwork as she leaves the office, closing the door behind her.

The door clicks shut, and Molly moves across the sterile hospital-like corridor to the wall opposite, where she places her forehead against the wall, resting it while she gathers herself.

Budget-cutting and saving money has been an integral part of her experience in her six years in the British Army, but it just seems to be getting worse and worse. Budgets get tighter, corners are cut, manpower diminishes, equipment gets older and no matter who or how loudly they protest, nobody listens. That is until something goes seriously wrong and even then, action is only usually taken if the media picks up on the incident and some politicians career might be in jeopardy.

Sighing to herself, Molly is positive that the Major is just as frustrated as she is; she has known him long enough, and he knows the dangers of this operation at least as well as she does, but no matter how much shouting and screaming she does, his hands are tied, just as hers are.

Molly lifts her head off the wall, straightens her back, then turns and marches down the brightly lit corridor back towards the laboratory and storage facility.

The ten-minute walk goes in a flash, her mind working as she deliberates the operational plan and safety measures that she and the Major have put in place. Almost surprised to find herself at the security entrance, she presses her thumb onto the security pad, the magnetic locks release and Molly pushes through the hissing doors and back into her domain.

Chapter 2

The cold storage facility situated next to the laboratory seems strangely unfamiliar to Molly now, even though she has spent an inordinate amount of time here over the last four and a half years. She is used to it being a quiet area, where only she and a very select few of her colleges have access.

Soft blue lighting and a cold atmosphere always gave her the feeling, she was somehow in the arctic and the usual stillness and silence certainly gave you pause to imagine you were there.

A crunching noise puts pay to any remaining reminiscing, as the three-wheeler electric forklift's solid black tyre crushes something it shouldn't into the concrete floor before the driver slammed on its brakes.

"BE CAREFUL!" Molly again shouts at the top of her voice, for what seems like the hundredth time in the last hour. Not that she is sure if the driver or any of the other contractors listen to her now, or on any of the other ninety-nine times she has shouted it into the bubble helmet of her Biohazard suit. They are all probably sick of her shouting it and bawling other orders at them; for all she knows, they have turned the volume down on their radio earpieces to get her voice out of their heads.

Second Lieutenant Brian Simms, Molly's assistant whom she can see and hear through her earpiece is having

5

the same running battle on the opposite side of the facility to her. *Oh God, let this be over*, she thinks.

The temperature inside her suit seems to be rising by the minute, the suit's built-in temperature control is struggling to cope, only adding to her frustration and bad temper. The only slight relief is the small amount of cool air entering the suit from the pipe attached to the back it, which is in turn connected to the air supply on the wall behind her.

The suit is struggling to regulate the temperature probably because of Molly's raised heartbeat and body temperature but mainly because this normally cool, secure storage facility has had a large hole cut into the wall away to her left. The hole is where the loading of the transport trucks is taking place.

The new loading bay is sealed airtight with two airtight thick plastic sections; the trucks reverse up to the outer opening and the back of the truck is sealed into the opening. And only when it is completely sealed into the opening, the second section's seal is broken and is opened to allow the forklift access to the back of the truck to load. Even though the opening is airtight, it doesn't stop the majority of the heat from the hot day outside getting in. This gets worse when the back doors of the truck are opened up, the sun beating down onto the roofs of the trucks and the heat seems to billow out of them and into the storage facility. When the truck is full and all the refrigerated storage assemblies are plugged into the on-board power source, the truck doors are closed, and an air conditioner kicks in to cool the truck for its journey.

Molly still finds it surprising that the hole was cut into the wall of this area for the temporary loading bay, which is the most sensitive and secure area of the whole facility. She wasn't consulted about this part of the moving plan and was only informed of this hairbrained idea two days before the work actually began and the wall cutting started. The only consolation to this security breach is that there is now a company of heavily armed soldiers from the London

Regiment now stationed in the area on the other side of the wall twenty-four hours a day until the operation is complete.

On the opposite side of the room, Brian is directing three of the contractors as they push and pull the next storage assembly into place, ready for the forklift to pick up. The four large castors with grey rubber tyres fixed to the bottom of the assemblies make it possible to move these assemblies by hand, but they are very heavy, and it is by no means easy. The men straining to move them must be even hotter than Molly and Brian, cocooned in their orange biohazard suit enclosures as the rubber wheels squeak, rolling slowly across the light blue painted concrete floor.

Finally, the assembly is in a position Brian is happy with and he gives the three men a double thumbs up with his plastic gloved hands. Two of the men walk away relieved, with their hands on their hips; they head to take a breather whilst the third, a young lad named Olly, puts his arm up onto the assembly, his hooded head dropping against it to also take a breather.

Molly hears a lot of heavy breathing coming through her earpiece and says, "Well done," to the three men, but gets no acknowledgement from any of the three in return.

The driver of the forklift has been waiting patiently, perched up in his seat behind the wheel of the forklift; as he awaits the next assembly to be in position ready for him to lift and for Molly to give him the go-ahead to proceed. As usual, however, Molly waits; she gives the three men who pushed the assembly time to get their breath back, listening through her earpiece for the heavy breathing to die down. The last thing she wants to do is to rush this operation, even though she wants it to be over as soon as possible. So, she waits until she is satisfied that everyone is recovered and ready to proceed.

A few minutes pass. Olly has moved away from the assembly and the heavy breathing in her earpiece has diminished. And so, Molly decides to proceed with getting the latest assembly loaded onto the truck.

She looks over to Mark, the driver, who seems to have anticipated her go-ahead because he is already leaning forward and reaching for the ignition key to switch on the forklift's almost silent motor. Nevertheless, Molly says, "Okay to proceed, Mark," into the hidden microphone in her suit helmet and raises her hand, showing Mark he is clear to proceed, with a raised thumb.

Mark selects forward and the forklift almost glides over to the assembly. He takes care to position his forks before they slide under the assembly until they are fully inserted, at which point he applies the handbrake. The three men who pushed the assembly into place converge around the forklift and the assembly with a strap, to secure the assembly to the forklift. One end of the strap is hooked onto the cage of the forklift and then wrapped around the assembly until the other end is hooked onto the other side of the cage. The strap is then ratcheted until it is tight, securing the assembly to the forklift so it cannot fall off, in case Mark has to take some evasive action while moving.

Reverse is selected and the forklift arches backwards in Molly's direction, comes to a stop and then starts to move forward towards the rear of the waiting truck. Two of the men are a short distance either side of the lifted assembly, following, ensuring there are no unforeseen obstacles or hazards for the forklift to run into, while Olly is walking in front checking for the same. This might be complete overkill because there isn't anything for the forklift to run into unless it veers seriously off course and drives into a wall, but Mark's forward view is impaired by the assembly on his forks so the method is set and stuck to.

Molly and Brian watch unconcerned as the forklift moves around, making its way towards the truck, Molly has even started to think about getting the next assembly ready for lifting as she looks at the rear of the forklift moving away from her.

Suddenly, her earpiece is filled with heavy breathing, quickly followed by coughing but she can't tell who it is coming from; she is just about to shout *halt*, when it squawks into her ear. She is beaten to it by Brian and the two men either side of the forklift.

Without warning, Olly collapses straight down onto the concrete floor and into the path of the oncoming forklift. Brian is first to shout *halt* by a split second, as his hands and feet tingle with adrenaline as he sees Olly collapse. The two men either side are shouting the same as their arms shoot up into the air for Mark to see. Mark—whose mind, if the truth is told, had started to wander slightly to the 'date' set up for tonight with a woman he has had his eye on for some time—presses the brake pedal far too heavily.

The forklift snaps to an instant stop and in the same instant, the assembly slips forward on the forks, towards to end of them, carrying on its journey as the strap on one side inexplicably falls to the floor.

Molly takes a sharp intake of breath through her open mouth, her eyes wide as she sees the assembly slipping towards the end of the forks, its own momentum carrying it almost halfway off the forks. For a moment, the assembly comes to a stop.

Panic now courses through Brian's veins as he sees the assembly slip forward. It comes to a small stop but then starts to tilt, as he realises nothing can stop gravity now; the forklift's load is past the point of no return and is going to fall and crash to the floor. There is going to be a bio release into this room—he has no doubt about that now, but that isn't what is making him panic. He has trained for such circumstances; the room is sealed and everyone in the room is contained in their protective suits.

Brian's panic is caused by Olly; he has fallen directly underneath the heavy, tilting assembly. Brian moves as fast as his suit will allow to grab Olly's arm, which is closest to him, just as the assembly's tilt gets faster and starts to go into freefall. Brian pushes back with all the strength he has in his legs, pulling Olly's arm as hard as he can, dragging him as far from the point of impact as possible.

The deafening crash as the assembly hits the floor is immense and reverberates around the room, but probably more chilling is the sound of smashing glass. The front of the assembly has a glass door, smashed for sure, but Molly is more worried about the glass vials contained inside, *if even one of those has broken,* she thinks, frozen to the spot.

Re-gathering herself, her training kicking in; she turns around and hits her hand onto the large red button that is on the wall behind her with EMERGENCY also in red, printed above it. Immediately, a shrieking alarm sounds and red lights start to flash around the perimeter of the room. She also knows the airtight entrance door will now be locked, alarms will be sounding throughout the rest of the building and automatic text messages will have been sent to all key people associated with this facility. An image flashes through her head of Major Rees scrambling from behind his desk two floors up.

Flat on his back, still gripping Olly's hand and panting heavily into the transparent Perspex of his suit helmet in front of his face, Brian tries to remember if he heard the assembly hitting the floor. Then all at once, he registers red lights flashing on the wall above him and the alarm sound accosting his ears. Brian releases Olly's hand and somewhat gingerly gets to his feet, almost afraid to look over to Olly; did he manage to pull him out from beneath the impact or is Olly horribly crushed under the heavy assembly?

Forcing himself, Brian looks down at Olly and a wave of relief passes over him as he sees Olly flat on his back, head and body intact; his gaze moves down to his two legs as the relief grows stronger.

Brian then notices three orange-clad men jostling hurriedly around the assembly as if they are trying to lift it and Molly rushing over to join them. He can't understand what they are trying to do, and he is about to tell them to stop, that they will never lift it and that precautions need to be taken before they try and move it when he sees the reason for the urgency.

For a second, Brian foolishly thinks he is looking at tomato sauce spilt on the painted blue floor, but it is blood pooling around the edge of the assembly and around Olly's right arm, which has been crushed, like a tomato, from halfway down his lower left arm and right under the now immovable assembly. It is small consolation that Olly seems to have passed out, saving himself from the pain, at least for now!

Molly shouts at the men to stop trying to move the assembly, that they need to prepare and do it properly, but they don't listen. She pulls on Mark's arm, telling him to stop, but at first, he tries to brush her off. Eventually, he calms slightly and then surrenders and moves back. As he does so, the other two men also give up and move away. Molly quickly goes around to check on Olly. She sees straight away what has happened to his arm, which is shocking enough but she is far more concerned with the fact that his suit has been breached—and to make matters worse, so has his skin! She stands, her mind racing, calculating the best course of action; the protocol for this situation is to get everybody into decontamination immediately, but how can they if Olly's arm is stuck? She knows she should still do that and leave Olly here, for now, get decontaminated, then reassess and consult with her colleagues. If she decides to do that, she seriously doubts whether the three contactors would just leave Olly here? She knows what she has to do.

Molly turns, "Mark?" At first, he doesn't respond; he is probably in shock. "Mark," she shouts, making sure she is heard over the alarm.

"Yes," he finally replies through her earpiece.

"What tools do you have with you, I need a knife or a saw?"

"We have both with us." As he says it, Molly sees in his eyes that he knows what she is planning to do.

"You're not cutting his arm off, no fucking way," Mark says, sounding like he might be sick at any moment.

"It is too dangerous to move that," she says pointing at the assembly, "it is face down and possibly still contained, we have to get to decontamination now and get Olly medical attention. So yes, I am cutting his 'fucking' arm off. Get me the knife now!" As Molly finishes, Olly's body jerks violently, briefly convulsing, and they all see it. "NOW, MARK."

Mark turns and runs towards the contractor's kit.

"Brian, seal the inner curtain on the loading bay," Molly orders.

Brian immediately moves towards the curtains; as he approaches them, he can see silhouettes moving on the other side of the opaque plastic. He trusts that the soldiers outside will follow their orders and not unseal the outer barrier to see what the emergency is, even if they think they can help.

Molly bends down to see if she can determine Olly's condition; she looks at his young face through the Perspex, but he still appears to be passed out, whether it's for the same reason he collapsed or as a result of the accident, she doesn't know. He is frothing at the mouth and his lips are dark red. She looks closer, checking: SHIT, he isn't breathing. Has his airline failed somehow, is that why he collapsed? She makes a split second, calculated decision and reaches for his suit zipper and pulls it all the way up, letting air in. Contaminated air or not, his suit was breached anyway. Molly yanks and pulls, struggling to get Olly's suit off as far as she can, determined to get his head out. She can't breathe air into his lungs because of her suit but there must be something she can do.

One of the other contractors gets on his knees, helping Molly. Together, they get Olly's one arm and head out and as soon as they do, Olly starts violently convulsing again, but this time it is not briefly. His body jerks and spasms violently, as if it has 20,000 volts of electricity coursing through it. Molly and the contractor try and hold him down, but it doesn't stop; it is so violent that his arm that was trapped under the assembly is ripped free, skin, bone, suit and all. Suddenly, Olly's eyes snap open, the convulsing stops, his head twists—and opening his mouth impossibly wide, it wraps around the contractor's arm nearest to him and he bites down with so much force, his teeth rip clean through the suit as if it was orange peel, and through the arm's flesh, taking a whole chunk out.

The man screams inside his suit and falls backwards. Molly, stunned, also falls backwards, scrambling away. She sees Olly seem to spring to his feet, his legs sliding out of his suit in the same motion; he is then instantly attacking the second contractor before he knows what is happening. Olly grabs him with the hand that is still attached, his bloody stump helping the hold as he swings his head towards the neck of the contractor. But as his teeth go to bite, the contractor's head turns, and the teeth bounce off the hoods Perspex front. Olly goes to bite again but again hits Perspex.

Mark arrives back on the scene and struggles to comprehend what is happening; he sees Olly fighting with one of the three contractors in their orange suit, the other two down on the floor, one of whom seems to have injured his arm. It then dawns on him; Olly is out of his suit and up. How the hell did that happen and why are they fighting?

Mark drops the knife and goes to break up the fight. Olly has his back to Mark and is frantically trying to attack the other person. Mark grabs Olly's shoulders and drags him off. The other person loses his balance and falls to the floor facing the knife, and to Mark's shock, Olly starts to attack him. *What's wrong with him? He doesn't look well.* Mark struggles to process. A searing pain hits Marks shoulder where Olly's teeth bite into him.

Brian reaches what he is pretty sure is Molly and starts to help her up; as they get to their feet, they see the contractor who was just attacked by Olly also get up and he has the knife in his hand. At first, they both think he is going to attack Olly who is now on top of Mark, but he doesn't, he just runs for the loading bay and the sealed curtains.

Both Molly and Brian break forward, Brian slightly in front, chasing after him. *If he gets through that seal, who knows what the catastrophic consequences could be, but he is nearly at the first sealed curtain!*

"STOP," Molly shouts in desperation, hopelessly. "STOP, DON'T GO OUTSIDE! IT ISN'T SAFE."

Molly sees him break through the first curtains' sealed enclosure all too easily, Brian almost upon him—and then Brian has him. Brian jumps onto his back but as he does, the arm holding the knife goes up and they both hit the second seal as they fall. As they go down, the knife slices a long, curved slit into the protective plastic, the top of which flaps open in the summer breeze.

"No!" Molly either says or shouts, too shocked to know as she sees the soldiers outside in the bright sunlight raise their rifles and open fire, filling both Brian and the other man with bullets.

Molly can't believe what she is seeing as both men's bodies jerk with the numerous bullets entering them. She sees one of the soldiers giving the cease-fire signal, but not all of the soldiers see it because one of them is aiming at Molly and begins to fire!

Molly dives to the side just in time for the bullets to miss her, but the bullets continue their high-velocity trajectory and hit one of the long thin black oxygen bottles chained to the far wall of the storage room. The bottle explodes in a bright flash and with a tremendous BOOM, and fire immediately breaks out.

Molly only has one option, to get to the decontamination room and lock the door behind her. She gets to her feet, hoping against hope that the soldiers won't fire on her again as she rises. If they do shoot, she doesn't hear the shots and they don't hit her as she runs as fast as she can towards the room.

Molly just raises her hand to the door handle when she is knocked off her feet sideways and onto her back, hitting the floor hard. Someone is on top of her. She panics and tries to scramble to get up, but the person is too heavy; eventually, she gains focus and stares into the black eyes of Olly, smoke billowing above his head from the fire. He is pushing her shoulders down with his arms, a hand on one shoulder and a stump on the other.

Her panic is uncontrollable as she tries to break free of Olly's grip, but she can't. She tries to resist as he lowers his head deliberately, his infested red mouth opening wide. It touches her suit and then she feels the pain slicing into the side of her neck.

Chapter 3

I join the white-coated young woman from the medical staff who has just woken me, outside the cage. As I exit, I can't help but hover outside while the cage door is re-shut to look at Josh and Emily as they sleep with Stacey close by, hoping I am back before they wake. Before I go, I give Catherine, who still looks half asleep, a reassuring smile followed by a feeble wave which she returns as I leave.

"This way, Captain Richards," the medic instructs.

The quarantine cages now flow past on my left side, as we follow the path we entered by and every one of the people locked inside them is asleep. It seems that I am the only one cursed enough to be woken at this hour. Maybe it is a bit of payback from Colonel Reed for my 'misdemeanours' yesterday.

Whatever the reason the Colonel decided to wake me, my head is very heavy, my joints are aching, and my vision is still slightly blurry; what I would've given for a few more hours of shut-eye.

The young medic leads me out and towards the large office which had about five military personnel in it when we arrived, and far from the office being deserted at this time in the morning, there are actually more people in there now. I see them through the bank of windows along the front of the office. There are at least ten people in there, with about an even split between people in military uniforms and medical white coats; at least some of the white coats will be military personnel too.

As we enter the office, a slight hush ascends over the room, with almost everyone looking over, sizing me up, the new addition to their space.

I am led towards the back of the brightly lit room and towards a desk that only has a phone on it, its receiver out of its cradle and lying ominously on the desk.

The medic picks up the receiver and puts it to her ear. "Hello… I have Captain Richards," she says and then points the receiver at me.

"Captain Richards, please hold for Colonel Reed," a young-sounding man tells me.

Colonel Reed unsurprisingly keeps me waiting so my eyes wander around the room, taking my turn to do a bit of sizing up. The medic who fetched me has sat behind a desk close by and is reading some paperwork through glasses I can't even remember if she was wearing a minute ago; 'damn', I do need to wake up!

Most of the people are moving around the room from desk to desk looking at different documents, having discussions with each other about the documents and then moving on. My guess would be that they are going through test results for the people in quarantine, but I cannot be sure. I wonder if the rest of our results are in there somewhere, circulating around, although I am not overly concerned about any of our results. The medics seem to be the ones seated at a desk mostly and it is the people in military uniform who are moving from desk to desk, checking, discussing and then moving on.

"Richards?" The unmistakable gravelly voice of Colonel Reed blasts down the phone line and into my ear. He normally calls me by my first name, at least since our new 'business' relationship?

"Good morning Colonel, thank you for the early morning call," I say sarcastically.

"A pleasure, I hope you enjoyed your bit of R & R, because it's more than I've had," he retorts.

"How can I help you?" I say getting to the point.

"Debriefing at 0515. Captain, you will be picked up at 0500. I hear they have shower facilities there so make yourself presentable, understood?"

"Affirmative, Colonel," Reed hangs up the phone, cutting me off halfway through me saying, *Colonel. I was expecting a debrief.* So, there was no point protesting, even if the Colonel was so blunt.

I put the phone down and walk the short distance over to the desk where the medic sat before I arrived. She looks up. "Captain Richards?" she says, looking over the top of her glasses.

"Hi, I need to use the shower, can you point me in the right direction, please?

"Certainly," she says, getting up.

We head out of the office and take a right turn, walk up a short corridor where she points down another corridor on the left and tells me they are just on the left, while she still points.

"Thanks, I have a meeting, I don't suppose there are any clean clothes around are there, I forgot my overnight bag?" I joke, looking down at my blood-stained clothes.

"There are clean towels and a laundry bag with various clothes in it, in the changing rooms. See what you can find in there, they are clean too, but I'm not sure what's in there," she says, smiling a little at my joke.

"Thanks, are those the test results you are going through, in there?" I venture to ask.

"That is one of our tasks, Sir, but I cannot comment further," she says with conviction.

"Okay, I understand, thanks for your help."

"No problem, good luck with your meeting."

"Thanks," I say again as she turns back towards the office.

After my five-minute shower—which I would have made last for an hour if I'd had my choice, it felt so good—I leave the changing rooms feeling far more *with it*, having found a black t-shirt and black fleece to put on, if nothing else in the laundry bag.

I assume I am going to be picked up at the same entrance we came in through so that's where I go, back past the door to the quarantine area, resisting the temptation to pop back and let Catherine know what is happening. There is something I need to do before I go, however, and take a left turn into a room farther down the corridor.

Snapping off the tie, fastening my locker closed, I'm relieved to see my Sig lying where I left it and quickly pull off the fleece, hang it over the locker door and pull on the Sig's holster. I rummage around in the locker, insert my knife into the holster, slide my belt back on, get my phone (which is dead) and get my other bits and pieces. At the bottom of the locker is my body armour and inside it, nestling in the inside pocket is a magazine for the Sig, which I must have 'forgotten' to surrender. Finally, I retrieve the Sig and push the magazine home, glancing over my shoulder as I do so to check no one is watching. It feels good to have the gun in my hand again but I slide it into its holster and quickly put the fleece back on and go.

As soon as I get to the dingy waiting area by the outer doors, I decide to get some fresh air in the remaining two minutes that are left until my pick-up is due at five.

19

Unfortunately, the air outside isn't as fresh as I'd hoped; there is a definite whiff of smoke in the air, but it'll do. The two young squaddies stationed outside in the dawn light are startled as I exit and quickly pull themselves together, to stand to attention.

"At ease," I tell them, reminiscing back to my time on guard duty, which seems a lifetime ago now.

They both relax, and a cigarette appears in one of the lad's hands as if from nowhere; that he must be well versed in hiding at a moment's notice.

"Those things will kill you," I half joke to the closer boy in a military uniform.

"If the Zombies don't first, you mean," he says, trying an unconvincing joke. The poor lad looks worried to death. They both do.

"The Zombies haven't killed you yet, soldier, so do your jobs and watch each other's backs, they haven't won yet," I tell them both, trying to instil some confidence.

They both look at each other, unsure of what to say.

I turn to look over at the dawn rising over Heathrow Airport, the banks of helicopters a short distance away looking almost like sleeping insects, still in shadow, waiting for the sunlight to hit them and bring them back to life. The airport isn't as busy as it was last night, some ground staff are still around, the odd vehicle going in and out of the hangar to my right. And the air traffic is thinner, heavy transport planes still landing and taking off, but in smaller numbers.

Just as I am about to look at my watch to see if my pick-up is late, a pair of headlights appear down by the beginning of the hangars, I look at my watch anyway and see that it is three minutes late.

The Defender pulls up and the driver, a middle-aged man in an orange high-vis jacket, asks me if I am Captain Richards, through the open window. Hearing, 'Captain,' the two lads on guard duty quickly stand to attention again and salute as I get into the passenger seat.

"Stay alert," I tell them as we pull off.

The drive only takes a few minutes and is uneventful. There is a bit of small talk with the driver, who I learn has worked at Heathrow for seventeen years and has no family to be worried about, but mostly I take in my surroundings as we drive.

The part of the airport I see is covered with military vehicles, various types of planes, helicopters, as well as banks of tanks and personnel carriers all around. Heathrow seems to have been taken over by the military entirely and my driver confirms that virtually the whole airport is.

As we pull up outside a nondescript back door to another large building, I take a few seconds to 'burn' the route back to the quarantine area into my brain, just in case.

We both get out of the Defender and walk up to the door where the driver picks up the lanyard hanging from his neck by his belly and swipes it through a slot sticking out to the side of the door; the door clicks and he pulls it open.

"This is where I leave you," the driver tells me. "Straight up the stairs to the third floor, then go through the door and down the corridor to the right, and you will see a reception desk there, okay?

"Thanks, and good luck," I reply.

Reaching the reception desk slightly out of breath from the stairs, I report in. As I do, a tall, handsome man in uniform gets up from a chair the other side of the reception desk and approaches, saluting as he reaches me.

"Captain Richards, I'm Lieutenant Winters. Please follow me; I will take you to the Colonel."

We go past the reception desk towards tall glass windows that overlook the airport and one of the runways. We turn left and follow the windows for some distance. The sun is now up and I take the chance to look out over the packed airport as we go. I have to admit I am in awe of the view of the hardware assembled and I'm certain it will be on the move sooner rather than later.

We arrive at what seems to be a conference room, but the long glass-walled side has all the blinds closed so I can't be sure. There are a few people milling around outside it, with more sitting down, the majority of whom are dressed in high-ranking uniforms. My guess would be that this is where any plans are being finalised and the briefings and orders are being given out.

"Please wait here, Captain." The Lieutenant says, before making his way over to the door leading into the conference room.

As he disappears, I look closer at the other people stuck on the outside with me, checking to see if I recognise any of them. I don't, so I start milling about with them and wait. A few people go into the room and a few come out. And still, I wait, some staying nearby whilst others leave. All who leave do so with purpose, obviously to go carry out their orders.

Time moves on, and I eventually take a seat at 0545, realising I won't be there when Emily wakes up if she hasn't already. I take comfort knowing Josh is with her, but it then strikes me that I actually don't know that for sure; how can I? I've been gone for an hour and a quarter, a fact that makes me very edgy. Josh could be anywhere now, as could Alice; they are still serving soldiers and could be back with their units or have been given new postings with another unit. In fact, the more I think about it, the more likely it is. *When's this bloody debriefing!*

Finally, at 0553, the Lieutenant emerges from the door and thankfully heads my way.

"Sorry for the delay, Captain, please follow me."

I get straight up and do exactly that in some futile attempt to speed things up.

"Please take a seat where I show you, Captain, and wait until you are called upon," the Lieutenant instructs during the short walk to the entrance.

The room is indeed a conference room and when I enter, it is dark, the only light coming from the open door that is soon closed and from two large TV screens. The room is a rectangle, the blinds are closed, blocking the windows that would be overlooking the runway, along with the blinds I was looking at from outside that cover the long glass wall.

The Lieutenant shows me to one of the empty seats, which run straight against the blinds on this wall. He picks up a thick pile of folders from the seat to my left before he sits on it, putting the folder on his lap. In front of me is a large oval table with about twenty-five seats around it, all occupied. And past that are the two TV screens which are showing some drone video footage of some of the devastation in London. I can't make out anybody seated around the table because they are all facing away from me, unmoving, looking at the screens.

It suddenly dawns on me what area of London we are viewing and my stomach fizzes when the drone flies over the Orion Building. The triangular building is unmistakable; I can even make out our exit hole that we blew into the roof!

"Thank you, that'll do, lights please," an authoritative male voice says from a central position on the other side of the table.

As the chairs on the other side start to swivel around to face the table, the lights come on and someone turns the TV screens off.

Now able to see the people assembled—at least those on the far side of the table who are now facing me—I recognise more than a few of the faces, all of which are looking gravely in my direction. There is a mix of mid- to high-ranking officers scattered around the table, and I immediately see two Generals, a Brigadier and two Majors I have worked with. Colonel Reed is away to my left and looks as serious as ever halfway down the table. The centre of the table, however, is overrun with politicians, some I've met, the others I have seen on the television. And sitting in the very centre of the table right opposite me are the Home Secretary and the Defence Secretary. I now realise I recognise the voice of the man who gave the instruction to turn the lights on; it is Gerald Culvner, the smarmy Home Secretary.

"Is this the retired Captain that led us a merry dance yesterday, Colonel Reed?" As soon as Gerald Culvner finishes his sentence, the urge to get up, go around the table and break his nose is hard to resist, but I do.

"It is the Home Secretary," the Colonel says.

"So, Captain," the Home Secretary says, leaning back in his chair but unfortunately not falling out of it. "The Colonel tells me that you insist any information Sir Malcolm would have had about this virus would be on his computer, which we have drawn a blank with... or in his safe in the Orion Building. Please elaborate."

Again, suppressing my urge, I get up and address the table. "I am afraid I cannot elaborate much; I was unaware of Sir Malcolm's previous posting connected to this virus until the Colonel told me over the phone yesterday. I am unaware of him keeping any files connected to that time or related to the virus. I merely told the Colonel that if he had indeed kept any files, they would either be on his work computer or in his safe."

The Home Secretary thinks for a second and then asks, "And why are you sure that's where they would be?"

"As I told the Colonel, Sir Malcolm did not take work home with him."

"Well we have the computer, which we have hacked into and there is no information on it, so according to you it must be in his safe?"

"No, I did not say that. I said, if he kept files, they would be in one of those places," I say bluntly.

"And why didn't you get the safe as you said you would, Captain?"

"Because the safe was secured to the floor, the building was infested with these Rabids, or Zombies, whatever you want to call them, and they were about to break through to our position... and it was too dangerous to try, especially with the personnel and equipment we had. Would you have had the receptionist or my young daughter cover our position while we tried to break the safe free?" I tell him, my anger growing.

"Thank you, Captain." He says dismissively as he looks away and turns to talk quietly into the ear of the Defence Secretary next to him.

Now I am about to boil over and give him a piece of my mind, but before I do, Colonel Reed, probably seeing it, takes my attention and speaks.

"Thank you, Andy, please wait outside. Lieutenant Winters will come out and see you shortly."

Taking the opportunity to get out of that fucking room and leave that tosser behind, I go back out to the waiting area, heading straight over to the windows to try and calm down.

As I look out, I wonder why he got under my skin so quickly; it's not as if I haven't dealt with idiots like that many times before. Perhaps it's because I'm still a bit tired or because I'm worried about where my children and I go from here?

Having calmed down and taken a seat again to wait for the Lieutenant, I notice a few phone chargers plugged into the wall close by, so I shuffle along the seats to see if there is one that fits my phone. There is and my phone is soon plugged in and powering on.

Just as the phone has started, the Lieutenant emerges from the conference room. This time, he doesn't come straight over to me, but starts talking to a female RAF officer. This gives me a chance to check my phone; have Stacey's parents tried to contact me? It would be a surprise if they have to be honest after what we saw in their office building yesterday, but I hope. My heart sinks a little even more for Stacey, to see that there are no messages or missed calls from either Jim or Karen. Poor Stacey.

The only activity of any consequence is a pile of messages and missed calls from Josh and Emily's Mum, Jessica. To be fair to her, she does seem frantic, if not late; the first time she tried any contact wasn't until just gone midnight.

Not bothering to listen to the numerous voicemails she has left, instead, I go direct and click her number, glancing at my watch as I do, wondering what the time will be wherever she is in the world if it is nearly 0630 here? Whatever the time is, I am pretty sure she will answer for a change because her last message was only twenty minutes ago.

"Andy, thank God, are the children safe?" she answers immediately and frantically.

"Yes, they are safe. We made it out to Heathrow Airport. It was close, but we made it to safety," I tell her. It still seems strange hearing her voice, even after so long.

"Let me speak to them—is Josh there?"

"They aren't here right now; I've only just managed to get my phone on."

"Where are they then?" She nearly shouts at me.

"They are safe, Jessica, I have had to leave them for a while to try and sort things out, I will be back with them shortly, I hope, and I will get them to ring you."

"You've left them? Are you serious?" she says, getting hysterical.

"Calm down, Jessica, I don't think you are in any position to judge. Where are you anyway?"

After a moment of silence, she does calm down slightly. "In Sri Lanka, me and Dylan found some cheap flights, so we took them."

Dylan, for Christ sake, I think to myself, *I haven't heard of him before, probably some long-haired hippy.*

"Are you planning on coming back?" I ask her.

"How can we?" she asks, getting upset, "All flights are cancelled, everywhere, people are stranded all over the world!"

Her news doesn't come as a big shock; even though I hadn't thought of it, it makes sense for governments to close airspace with this type of threat. Nobody is going to want this virus on their doorstep.

"Oh, I didn't know that," I tell her.

"You didn't know? How could you not know that? Where have you been?"

"It's a long story and I haven't got time to tell it now, Jessica." I see Lieutenant Winters coming my way.

"I've got to go, Jessica, the kids are safe for now and I will get them to phone you as soon as I can. I am sure they will fill you in with what has gone on, okay?"

"Okay Andy, please keep them safe, I will get back as soon as possible." She is starting to cry now.

"I will, Jessica, goodbye."

Just as I hang up the phone, the Lieutenant gets to me.

"Sorry to have kept you waiting, Captain, shall we make arrangements to get you back to your children?"

"By all means, Lieutenant, lead on."

As we walk back the way we came, he doesn't mention anything about the meeting I have just had in the conference room or anything else for that matter, but I try to probe him.

"How long has that meeting been going on for?" I ask casually, starting with a relatively unimportant question.

"I am sorry, Sir, but I am under orders to not discuss any aspect of that meeting." The Lieutenant informs me bluntly. He then continues, "I have been instructed to tell you that the Colonel will want to see you again before very long, I will make arrangements for you to be collected when needed; is that acceptable?" he finishes as we get back to the reception desk.

"Do I have a choice?" I ask.

"I don't think so, Sir. Now if you'll excuse me, I will call for your transport back to your children," he says as he goes over to the reception desk, looking slightly confused.

Upon his return, the Lieutenant has me worried for a second when he tells me that my children have been moved, but seeing the concern on my face, he quickly tells me that it is good news. Both my children and the rest of the group I arrived with are out of quarantine and in fact, we're now in the same building, in the food hall here in Terminal 5 of the airport. He then waves over one of the young Privates who are stationed all around this area and instructs him to escort me down to the food hall.

As we travel on the long walk through Terminal 5 of Heathrow Airport, the Private and I—who I learn is named Jason—have quite a long talk. He is Scottish, which is plain from his accent and he travelled through the night last night with his Brigade of over four thousand troops from Maryhill Barracks near Glasgow. They were apparently crammed into three trains and it took just over five and a half hours to arrive in London, he tells me that he managed to get some sleep on the train, but not much.

Once we are acquainted, I ask him how the rest of the country is reacting to what is happening and he tells me the brutal truth.

He tells me the whole country has gone into meltdown; when the news first broke, every shop and supermarket in the country was cleared out of food and other essentials in a matter of hours by panic buyers, which was basically everybody. After the food ran out in the shops, the looting took over. Anywhere that might have had food was looted—warehouses, restaurants, schools and even a few hospitals. The government eventually declared Martial Law over the whole country at around six o'clock last night and ordered a curfew from seven-thirty, but both have been quite ineffective because there aren't enough police to enforce either and the military is here in London trying to contain the outbreak.

Unfortunately, he carries on, telling me that riots erupted late last night in the centre of Birmingham around the conference centre there, which is supposed to be the new temporary Parliament. The rioting spread to a few other major cities like Liverpool and Sheffield but fortunately, most of the rioting died down late last night.

"Jesus," I manage to say, but he hasn't finished.

The country has also gone into financial meltdown, he tells me, the bottom having dropped out of the stock market before it was suspended indefinitely at one thirty yesterday afternoon. That caused the bottoms to fall out of the stock markets across Europe and New York, all of which have also been suspended and the rest of the world has followed suit as they were due to open. Nobody is expecting the banks to reopen today, or any business to open for that matter.

"Bloody hell, Jason, it sounds like the virus has crippled the country before it's even spread!"

"I'm afraid it looks that way, Sir. Apparently, other countries are already saying that and that it's lucky it happened here because it's an island… Bastards!"

"Bastards indeed. They don't know us very well; we've been down before but never out!"

"Too right, Sir, they don't know us at all."

Chapter 4

Things go quieter for a while as I try to get my head around the distressing things Jason has just told me about what has happened—and is happening—to the country. Seeing first-hand what has happened to London so far has been appalling enough, and I suppose I was kidding myself if I didn't think London suffering as badly as it is doing wouldn't have dire ramifications for the whole country.

Jason snaps me out of my dark thoughts, thankfully.

"All but there now, Sir; the escalator down to the Food Hall is just around here."

Hearing that lifts my mood. I'm looking forward to getting back to the group and I pick up my pace behind Jason.

We exit the confines of the large but enclosed walkway into an area overlooking the cavernous Departure Lounge of Terminal 5.

It's like we have entered another world, gleaming shop and boutique signs sparkling all around, and I'm nearly fooled into pretending some exotic destination for us all is within reach. But before that dream goes any further, the closed shop shutters, dead departure boards and muted atmosphere drag me back to reality.

Nevertheless, I can feel my children, Catherine, Stacey, Dan and the others close now, which is good enough for me.

Jason is still leading the way, which I am impressed by considering he hasn't been here long. Yet he seems to know his way around this massive building, heading now towards the escalator that goes down to the Food Hall level.

"You seem to know your way around, Jason."

"My belly is leading the way, Sir." *I should have known,* I think to myself, laughing.

We get to the top of the escalator, which doesn't move and has turned into one long metal staircase, reaffirming the fact that there will be no flights to anywhere exotic today from this building.

Walking down an unmoving escalator is not as easy as you might think; the steps are wider and taller than an actual staircase, the polished metal surface seems slippery underfoot and the rubber handrail sticks to your hand rather than letting it glide, so we go down steadily. There was a sign to the stairs at the top, but at least climbing down this escalator gives us a panoramic view of the lower Departure Lounge and most of the Food Hall.

The lower area is busy enough with people moving about and sitting at tables eating, but again this is no normal scene for the Food Hall. A large majority of the people are dressed in uniforms; the green uniforms of the Army, dark blue Navy and sky-blue RAF uniforms are all around and mingling together, most ranks too.

My eyes search for anyone from the group, trying to pick out Josh's blond hair or Emily's small stature, but I'm struggling to see any of them, and as we near the bottom I'm starting doubt they are here. *Maybe we are in the wrong building?*

"DAD!" Emily's voice shouts out from my left, and my head spins and I see her running towards me, leaving Josh, who is thankfully still here and Catherine walking behind her. I get off the escalator just in time for her to jump into my arms, and we squeeze each other tight.

"How's your morning been, Em? Sorry I had to leave early and wasn't there when you woke."

"Don't worry Dad, it's been okay, I wasn't worried, Catherine told me you had a meeting and we weren't in there for much longer after I woke. We've just had a massive breakfast."

"Lucky you, I'm absolutely starving," I tell her.

"How did you get on?" Josh asks, as he and Catherine catch up with Emily.

"Oh, you know how those things are," I tell him, "a lot of waiting around for a five-minute briefing with a-holes. They didn't tell me anything, but I'm sure they are about to take some kind of action."

"Dad, I know what an a-hole is, I'm not stupid," Emily scolds me.

"Sorry Em, I know you're not stupid." We all smile. "Where's Dan and the others?"

"They are over the other side; we have a table there," Catherine says, pointing. "Have you eaten yet?"

"No, I'm famished," I tell her. "Oh God, sorry. This is Jason," I say turning to the young Private who has been standing patiently just behind us. I put Emily down and introduce him to the others. "Have you got to get back to your post or do you want to get some brekky with me?"

"I'll get a quick bite. It would be a shame to come all this way and not fill up, but if you don't mind, I'll leave you to it. Sir, I've just seen some mates?" Jason says indicating over his shoulder to a group of young squaddies.

"Of course, carry on Private and thanks for the escort." Jason stands to attention and goes to salute me, but before he does, I offer him my hand which he takes and shakes vigorously, and then he is gone, lost in the crowd of uniforms.

We make our way across the Food Hall, Josh and Emily leading the way, Emily turns and sniggers before saying something to Josh, and I've no doubt that it's because Catherine has taken my hand in hers; Emily finds it very amusing and entertaining.

As we go, I clock where the breakfast is being served off military-issue serving tables, and I eye the length of the queue. The only place with food in the whole of this massive lounge, that will be serving anytime soon. The multiple restaurants and takeaways are all standing idle, even if their kitchens may have been made use of.

As we walk, I'm constantly checking the faces of the people in uniforms to see if there is anyone I know, who I might be able to get some intel from, but I don't see anyone. It seems like the Army has moved on in the five years since I resigned.

Emily runs ahead to where Stacey, Dan, Alice, Lindsay and Stan are sitting at a more secluded table against a wall and under the hangover of the floor above.

As she gets close to them, I hear her shout, "We found Dad," and they all look around at us coming towards them.

"Nice fleece, we must stop shopping in the same place," Dan jokes, as he gets up and gives me a slap on the back greeting.

"Didn't they have it in your size?" I joke back, and Dan feigns offence. "How is everyone?" I ask more seriously as I move around behind Stacey and put my hand on her shoulder.

Everyone one else seems to be as well as can be expected but Stacey, unsurprisingly, is quiet, seated next to her phone that has a wire leading from it to a plug socket on the wall. I sit in the empty seat next to her.

"How are you holding up?" I ask her, taking her hand.

"I don't really know, Andy, I'm not sure it has sunk in yet, I was still hoping there might have been a message from Mum or Dad when I got my phone switched on again earlier."

"So, did I Stacey, but I'm afraid there wasn't anything, so try and stay strong, I know it's hard." I try to soothe, but there isn't much I can say. The poor girl has just lost her parents. "Have you eaten?" I ask her.

"Some, but I wasn't really hungry."

"As long as you've had something, it will help you keep your strength up," I tell her, squeezing her hand.

"Has anyone got any news or heard anything this morning?" I ask everyone.

"We've got nothing really," Dan replies, "They told us we were clear of the virus and let us out, and we had quick showers. Then they took our phone numbers and dropped us here. I've had a walk around and tried to gain some intel but I don't think anyone here knows what's going on?"

"I didn't learn much this morning. I was taken to a meeting of the top brass and politicians. The Home and Defence Secretaries were both there, as was Colonel Reed, viewing drone footage of London which included the Orion building, but they just asked me questions about Sir Malcolm and his safe. I told them what we know and I was then asked to leave. I know that Colonel Reed wants to see me again shortly but that is all I have," I tell the group.

"I can guess what the Colonel wants," Stan starts, but I shoot him a look and look down at Emily. Stan stops mid-sentence and thankfully, Emily doesn't seem to register what he was saying.

"Do you think we are allowed to leave here?" Lindsay asks, "my Mum wants to drive down from Oxford to pick me up?"

"I don't see why that will be a problem, I'm sure we can get that arranged," I tell her. "Have you had any contact with your superiors, Alice?"

"Nothing, Andy, I'm going to have to report in."

"Can you hold off for a while until we know what is going on?" I ask her.

"I suppose so, for a while."

"You'd better get some food down before the Colonel wants you, Boss," Dan says.

"Yes, you're right," I say getting up, "you stay here with Stacey, Emily, okay?"

"Yes, okay Dad."

"Come on Josh, you can show me where the food is," I tell him as I go back around the table to where he is still standing, giving Catherine's arm a squeeze when I pass her.

Josh and I make our way over to the food, I know full well where it is, but I need to speak to him without Emily around.

"What about you; have you had any contact with your unit?" I ask him, anxious about his reply.

"No, nothing, I was surprised when they dropped me and Alice here with everyone else, I thought we would be back on duty by now."

"Yes, I thought about that when I was gone and was half expecting it. I was relieved to see you when I got back. I think the best thing to do is say nothing, let them come to

36

you," I tell him, but have a feeling deep down that it won't be that simple.

"Dad, I stayed with Emily while you were gone but I'm going to find out what is going on now and report in. I've got to get back to my unit or wherever I'm needed." He tells me with conviction and I'm proud of him for it, especially after his ordeal in the Tower of London.

After thinking for a moment, I give him a proposal. "I hear what you are saying, Josh, and I'm proud that you want to do your duty and get back into the fight. I would've been exactly the same at your age, but will you hold off until I've seen the Colonel again and we know what exactly he wants, what we are dealing with?"

"Okay, I'll agree to that for now, Dad, but I am going back to my unit, sooner or later," he says after a short deliberation.

"I know you are, Champ."

"Stop calling me that, Dad," he tells me, looking around to see if anyone heard it, slightly embarrassed.

"Sorry son, I don't do it on purpose," I say grinning. "Have you spoken to your Mum? we spoke, and I told her I'd get you to call her?" I ask as we start walking again towards the queue for the food.

"Yes, about twenty minutes ago, she was very upset," Josh tells me.

"I expect she is; she will be feeling pretty helpless stranded over there, with what's happened."

"Well she shouldn't even be there; she should be with her daughter," Josh says sternly.

"You're right of course, but she couldn't have known this was going to happen." I try to defend her for some reason.

"Let's not talk about it, Dad," Josh says, probably for the best.

Josh has not forgiven Jessica for leaving and only talks to her through gritted teeth. We have talked about it in the past; on the odd occasion, we have both had a few drinks together when Emily has spent the night with a school friend, or something. One Saturday, not so long ago, Emily had gone to a friend's birthday pyjama party and was having a sleepover, and Josh was home, so we took the chance to go and watch the football at the pub. The game went into extra time and by the end, we were both more than a bit tipsy but we still thought it was a good idea to have a few more 'celebratory' drinks after. By the time we walked home we had both had too much to drink, and on the walk home, Josh got quite emotional, as you do—and his feelings about his Mum came to the surface. He was angry at his Mum, not for leaving me, as he could understand that as I was away a lot on duty; these things happen. And it wasn't because she had moved away from him either, it was because of what she had done to Emily. He couldn't understand how his mother could leave her daughter, especially as Emily was so young. He saw first-hand the effect it had—and still does have—on her and he was finding it hard to forgive her for that, and who could blame him?

The queue for the food isn't too bad and we are soon walking back to our table, me with a plate piled high with bacon, sausage, toast and all the trimmings in one hand and a cup of tea in the other. Josh didn't come away empty-handed either and is eating a bacon sandwich as we walk.

When we get back to the table, I eat my breakfast, which goes down a treat. I debate with myself, going over different possibilities and I listen to the others talking; all the chat revolves around what is going to happen next. Lindsay talks about getting to Oxford again and it sounds like Stan has decided to try and get to some family he has in Bristol.

Stacey is very quiet, and I wonder what I should do with her. Should I get her to her grandparents or keep her with us? I suppose the decision is hers really; she is old enough to decide, but I don't even know what is in store for us?

Dan sounds like he has decided to stay and help out any way he can. He hasn't any family to speak of and knowing him, he would have decided that anyway, family or not.

Catherine hasn't said anything about what she might do; she could go to her mother's; she might be waiting to see what happens with the Colonel before she decides.

As for me, I'm going to do whatever is best for Emily, no matter what the Colonel says and what pressure he applies, I've just got to try and decide what that is.

Are we safest here behind the firepower and defences at Heathrow, or do I get Emily out of London and as far away as possible? If this virus spreads out of the city, will any of the country be safe? So, what is the best thing for Emily? Should I help stop the outbreak here, now? The only other option I can think of is getting to the coast and trying to get over to France or maybe Ireland; surely that would be safest if we could somehow cross over?

A chilling thought crosses my mind, of back when we were flying over the Thames and seeing that Rabids had crossed over the Thames to the Southbank of London. I've no doubt some have been washed out to sea and who knows where they could wash up? Is it possible the virus could spread beyond our shores? From what I've seen, anything is possible; no wonder the authorities are nervous and have closed worldwide airspace!

Chapter 5

My train of thought and my sorry attempts at making a decision are abruptly interrupted as the public address system sounds, surprising everyone in the lounge. The entire group of people in the room stops whatever they are doing, freezing to listen to the address.

"Attention, Attention," a female voice squawks loudly over the PA. "All personnel report to your posts immediately to await further orders; this is not a drill.

"Attention, Attention, all personnel report to your post immediately to await further orders; this is not a drill."

The address repeats five times, but as soon as the first address is complete, the frozen statues all around the room spring back to life. They all rush to leave to wherever they need to be. Last bites of sandwiches are taken, final swigs of drinks gulped down and final goodbyes are said to colleagues and friends. Everyone is back on duty with a job to do and judging by the faces we see leaving, each one has a steely determination to do their duty.

I for one, feel like a lame duck as they all leave, almost embarrassed to be still sitting down watching as these men and women rush towards their unknown fate.

Josh and Alice must be feeling it much worse than me; they both look very fidgety, restless and a bit guilty watching their comrades leave. I am sure they both feel like following them.

Within a few minutes, the room is almost empty with only a few civilians like us remaining, feeling useless and unsure what to do with ourselves. All at once, a quiet descends over us and a tension that wasn't there before seems to surround us.

Emily comes over to me and sits on my lap.

"What's happening, Dad?" she asks nervously.

"I am not sure Em, the soldiers have had to go and do their jobs, I think," I tell her, unsure what to say.

"Are they going to kill the Zombies?" she asks, turning to look at me.

"I think they might be going to try, my love." It then registers what she said. "Where did you hear the word Zombie?"

"Around, everybody is saying it. Zombie is the word for the bad people isn't it?"

"I suppose it is one of them," I reply.

"Well, at least that has got rid of the queue for the food," Dan jokes, trying to break the tension, but I'm not sure it works.

My phone, sitting on the table and plugged into Stacey's charger, starts to ring, making us all jump a little and we all turn to look at it in trepidation.

"It's Colonel Reed." Stacey stutters slightly, looking at the screen before picking up the phone, pulling out her charger lead and handing it to me as I take Emily off my lap and get up.

"Colonel."

"Richards, have you eaten?"

"Yes, Colonel"

"Good, transport is on its way to pick you up from there; it will be with you in a few minutes, so be ready."

"Where am I going, Colonel?"

"They will bring you to me, we have things to discuss."

"What things, Colonel?"

"When you get here, I will tell you, Richards. And bring your man Atkins with you, I'm sure he won't want to miss out." I look over to Dan.

"Okay Colonel, I will ask him."

"Good, see you shortly," he says, and he hangs up.

When the call ends, I hover just away from the group for a moment or two, thinking, trying to figure out what the hell I'm going to do. I can't work it out though. I can't figure out any good options, even favourable ones for that matter. Maybe there just aren't any and I just need to play it by ear and deal with the situation as it happens?

Tucking my phone in my pocket and turning back to the others, I see they are all looking at me, waiting to hear what the Colonel wants.

"The Colonel is sending transport to pick me up for another meeting he asked you to attend too, Dan. You are not obliged, mate; if you want out, now is the time to say and I wouldn't blame you, not one bit," I tell him seriously.

"Let's see what he has to say," Dan replies without having to think.

"Yes, we need to see what the score is."

Sitting back down to wait, Emily jumps back onto my lap and I put my arms around her waist.

"How long will you be, Dad?"

"I'm not sure, not too long I hope; will you be okay waiting here for me?"

"Yes, as long as you're quick," she says looking down at the floor.

"I'll be as quick as I can," I tell her.

"You will be fine staying here with us for a while, won't you Emily?" Catherine says from beside me, "and don't let Reed pressure you, Andy; you don't owe him anything."

"Don't worry, he won't," I tell her, trying to convince myself.

The few remaining people rattling around in the large space are all in small groups like us, and someone from most of these groups has come over to us, introduced themselves and asked us if we know anything about what's going on. One of us tells them what we do know, which isn't much and all of these people seem as ignorant as us, so we learn nothing new of any consequence. All are frustrated, some even angry that they have seemingly been just left here, and once they find out we can't give them any new information, they either move onto the next group or return to theirs.

Ten minutes pass and there is still no sign of the transport to take me and Dan to Colonel Reed, and I must admit the delay is getting me frustrated. We need to know what he wants to discuss, and I am sure I will be able to get some useful intel from the Colonel, which will hopefully help me actually make some decisions. We all turn to look at anybody entering the room to see if it's time, but so far it has just been people returning from using the facilities or just returning from a walk to stretch their legs.

Finally, there is some activity as the door from the stairwell opens and a man and a woman in uniform emerge. They are both holding tablets, but instead of approaching us, they go straight to the nearest group of people to the door from the stairs; they are three men and two women. These two are obviously not here to take me and Dan anywhere, so my guess would be that they have come to take details of who is left here so that arrangements, whatever they are, can be made for them/us.

Suddenly it strikes me that when we get back from this meeting, this place could be empty and everyone moved to another area at Heathrow—or even out of Heathrow, even out of London!

I need to talk to Josh and Catherine quickly and without Emily around to hear.

"Stacey, can you go and see if there is any tea leftover on the food tables, please? I could do with a cup," I ask and wink at her. "Why don't you go with her, Emily, to help?"

"Sure, Andy," Stacey replies and I get a moody 'okay' off Emily; they both get up and make their way over.

"Josh, Catherine; are your phones charged?" I ask as soon as the girls are out of immediate earshot.

Josh says 'yes', and Catherine says she has 'some charge', and they both ask why?

"I'm afraid that when Dan and I are gone, they could move you all and that could be to anywhere. It looks like they are taking details so they can make arrangements to possibly move everyone out of here. Josh, if they give you a new posting or deploy you somewhere else, let me know, keep in contact wherever you are. I don't want to lose you again, okay?"

"Of course, Dad, I will let you know whatever happens."

"Catherine, Josh might have to go, he won't have a choice if he does. Will you stay with the girls until I get back, please?"

Catherine looks at me angrily. "Are you serious! What do you think I'm going to do, let them take the girls off and stand by and wave as they go? You can be an idiot sometimes Andy. I would never let that happen. I am with you, Andy, and that means Emily too. And as long as Stacey is with us, that means her as well." Catherine now looks very offended.

"I'm sorry Catherine; seeing them taking details panicked me a little bit, and I just didn't want to assume. I know I can be thick sometimes."

"Okay then, let's forget it; the girls will be with me."

"Thank you," I tell her. "If they do move you, make sure you stay here at the airport and don't let them take you anywhere else unless absolutely necessary. Phone me if you need to."

"Of course, I will," Catherine says as I give her a hug. "Don't worry; I will look after them," she whispers in my ear.

"Looks like we are on, Boss," Dan says, pointing at a soldier marching towards us from beyond where Emily and Stacey are. He seems to have appeared as if from nowhere.

I shout and wave to Emily and Stacey, and as soon as they see the soldier, they are soon running back to us across the polished floor.

Emily jumps straight into my arms, giving me a face full of blond curls.

"How long will you be, Dad?" she asks.

"Not long, I hope. I'll be as quick as I can," I tell her as I put her down and stay down with her, on my haunches, looking at her seriously. "I want you to listen to Catherine and Josh, while I'm gone, okay?" I put the emphasis on Catherine's name. "You might have to wait for me somewhere else and I've asked Catherine to make sure you are okay, so be good for her, okay?"

"Why would we go somewhere else?" she asks.

"Because they might need this room for something else and need everyone to wait somewhere else. I will come and find you when this meeting is over, so make sure you stay and listen to Catherine."

"Captain Richards?" the soldier—wearing the red beret of the Military Police—asks as he reaches us, but I ignore him for a moment.

"Emily, is that okay?" She has gone quiet but then does answer.

"Yes Dad, just be as quick as you can," Emily says quietly.

"Of course, I will be my love," I tell her, giving her a kiss on the cheek before getting up.

"I'm Richards."

The soldier salutes me and then waits while Dan and I say goodbye to everyone. We tell Stan and Lyndsay good luck in case they do go to join their families before we return. We ask Alice to try and stick around until we're back. We both give Josh and Emily hugs and then finally, I give Catherine a hug, thank her and tell her to phone me when she knows what's going on, or if she needs to at all.

"Lead the way, Lance Corporal," Dan tells the soldier when our goodbyes are done.

Chapter 6

We follow the red beret away from everyone, past the remnants of breakfast that still remain on the tables and past some of the other people left in the Departure Lounge. They look at us quizzically, trying to figure out what is going on, one guy even asking us where we are going. But we don't answer.

We are heading towards a corridor at the end of another row of shuttered-up shops, obviously where this MP had appeared from. As we approach the corridor, I turn and take a few steps backwards to get one last glimpse of my children and Catherine before we disappear into the corridor. Dan doesn't even turn his head and strides straight into the corridor with a look of determination on his face, a determination I am finding hard to grasp inside myself right now.

The corridor is only short and leads to a single heavy door with a keypad by the side of it. The MP pauses at the keypad and punches four digits into it, then turns the handle to open the door.

Beyond the door is a staircase that only leads downwards; the lighting is fairly dim in the stairwell and the stairs seem to go down quite far from what I can see when I look over the side, at least two floors. As we descend farther down into the stairwell, it is eerily quiet and feelings hit me that remind me of descending the stairs into the Tower of London, feelings I try to suppress.

Thankfully, as we go even farther down, the light starts to improve and those feelings fade, it now becoming apparent that the light is natural daylight, not man-made; we must be getting close to the outside of this massive building.

At the bottom of the stairs is a heavy wooden door that has a couple of glass panels in it, with sunlight beaming through them. We reach the bottom of the stairs and the MP punches some more numbers into the keypad by the side of the door.

As we get outside, my mood is lifted by the bright sun that is still low in the sky, but rising in front of us, blue sky is everywhere with no clouds that I can see, and the warmth from the sun recharges my determination.

"You okay, Boss? You seem a bit quiet; we will find them when we get this shit sorted," Dan reassures me.

"Yes, I am good, mate. I went down for a minute back there, but I'm back with it now."

"Good, we are going to need you at full strength," he tells me.

"Don't worry, I am, let's get this done."

The MP gets into the driver's seat of yet another Land Rover Defender that is parked just outside the door, while I get into the back seat behind him and Dan goes around to get into the back beside me.

My watch tells me that it's just coming up to 0730, which I find hard to believe; it feels like it should be at least 1030 or even 1100. The days when I used to 'Yomp' ten or even twenty klicks before brekky are definitely long gone.

The MP drives in a direction both Dan and I recognise; we are going back toward the large hangars and the quarantine building where we touched down yesterday, and soon enough, the swarm of Apache helicopters is in front of us. Approaching them, we can see a large amount of activity buzzing around them, and some rotors are even spinning, whether getting ready for lift-off or if the engines need to be tested, we are not sure.

The MP doesn't turn right towards the quarantine building as I was half expecting, he carries on straight, but slows down taking a narrower path, driving straight through the swarm of Apaches now on both sides of the Defender together with maintenance engineers and crews checking over their helicopter.

Dan and I look at each other, giving knowing looks; the clock that is ticking down is nearing zero!

Eventually, the Defender breaks through the swarm and we go into more open space but by no means clear space. There is still hardware all around, close by, waiting.

"Where are we going?" Dan asks the MP, who's driving.

"Colonel Reed is in the Command Tent," the MP says and points towards a large green camouflaged tent with which Dan and I are very familiar. It is about two hundred meters in front and off to the left on a patch of grass.

"Thank God for that, I thought you were going to say he was in the Air Traffic Control tower for a second," Dan jokes, but I know the Colonel will always be in the thick of the action just where he likes to be, where he can make and influence strategies and give orders.

The Defender pulls up at the side of the tent and all three of us exit the vehicle. It feels good to have the soft grass underfoot, even with my boots on. And I'm sure I get the slightest smell of freshly cut grass, but maybe I'm imagining it?

We walk back down the side of the tent, which is extremely large even by Colonel Reed's standards and the view we get looking back towards the main airport is staggering. A distance away now in front of us is the mass of helicopters which seem to have overtaken the Terminal 4 area of the airport, away to our left.

Further up on our left and in the distance are the cargo hangars where we were taken into quarantine when we arrived. In the far distance, more or less straight ahead is the massive Terminal 5 building where we just left the others. It looks small from this distance and other building obscure all but the left edge of it. On the right of the tent is the South Runway with more terminal buildings beyond it, together with too many military aeroplanes to count, or even see. The North Runway, not visible from here, will be over from them, with the remaining terminals and buildings. Planes are still taking off and landing from both runways, including big heavy cargo planes and small fast jets that all seem to be using the North Runway, which must be the one they allotted for them. I haven't seen any of them over this side of the airport.

The noise from all this machinery reverberates all around us and increases and decreases constantly as activity on the runways varies. The Colonel will definitely feel in the middle of the action here, and something tells me that is exactly why this Command Tent is pitched where it is.

The front of the tent is pointed in the direction of the helicopters and has a large double-flapped opening, which is closed. Guarding the opening is one youngish soldier who will be there to stop unexpected 'guests' from entering the tent, which obviously doesn't include us because the guard and the MP exchange quick salutes and then the MP holds one of the flaps open for us to walk straight in.

The inside of the tent is dimmer than outside, but it is still well lit with two rows of long florescent lighting strips running down the middle of the roof of the large tent. Also, running down the middle of the tent are tables that have been set up in a rectangle shape; their tops are filled with computer monitors, two rows of them facing outwards all the way down the tables; there must be at least twenty monitors, ten each side. There are more tables and monitors around the outside perimeter of the tent, these facing inwards and showing various images—some moving and some static. I see aerial reconnaissance photos of the destruction of London and moving drone footage of the same. Whether this is live or recorded footage, I don't know, and other monitors are showing different maps of London and the wider area, whilst others have text on them that I can't read from this distance.

There is a hive of activity around the tables of military personnel, all of whom are in uniform. Some are sitting in front of their computer monitors, studying whatever it is beaming at them. They look up from the screens on occasion and feed the information they have discovered to one of their colleagues, or they pick up the nearest phone to relay the information. There are personnel walking around the tent too, between the inner and outer tables, talking to the ones sitting down. They are checking and verifying the information before moving on to gain more, desperately trying to quench their thirst for information and to be the one who takes some vital piece of information to their superiors.

But it is at the rear of the tent where all the important information flows to. It is the rear where the decisions and orders emanate from and the rear where the red bereted MP is leading us.

I see Colonel Reed before he sees Dan or me; he is facing the front at the head of a large tactical table, similar to the one back at Orion. But this one is on a different scale; this one is vast. Alongside the colonel, five other high-ranking officers are studying the large screened table; all but one outranks him but it is clear who is taking charge of this operation and of them.

Colonel Reed hasn't been passed over for promotion in his military life, or any other part of his life, for that matter. Way back, when I was still enlisted in the army, there were at least a couple of occasions when the rumour went around that the Colonel had turned down or refused another promotion. He was exactly where he wanted to be in the British Army, still able to be in the thick of the action with his finger on the pulse of operations and a high enough rank to directly influence, decide and direct operations. The Colonel is older than many of the Generals above him; his superiors, in many ways, were in name only, it would be a very brave General who went up against him. A promotion and a seat on some committee in the Ministry of Defence was not for the Colonel.

The MP enters the rear area of the Command Tent and stops just short of the men circled around the tactical table, snapping rigidly to attention and whipping his hand up to salute.

"Excuse me, Sir, I have Captain Richards, Sir," the MP declares forcefully.

Colonel Reed is down leaning onto the tactical table with his hands gripping the side, spread out on each side of his body. He's studying the large map of London displayed on the big screen and raises his short-cut, silver-haired head as he looks sternly at the new invaders of his space.

"You are dismissed, Sergeant," he tells the MP without an ounce of gratitude. The MP swivels a turn and marches back out through the Command Tent.

It is immediately obvious to me that the cordial business relationship the Colonel and I had in my capacity as Head of Operations at Orion has evaporated with the demise of Sir Malcolm and indeed, the demise of Orion Security.

The Colonel lifts himself off the tactical table, rising to his full six-foot-two inches, bringing his arms down to his sides and puffing out his chest. He shows off his broad shoulders and muscular physique that a man half his fifty-four years of age would be proud of.

"Good, Richards, you're here," he says ominously, "and I see you've brought your man with you," he adds, derogatorily, referring to Dan. "Please join us," he finishes, lifting his hand towards the opposite end of the table to indicate where he wants us.

The end of the table is currently taken up by General Wright, but he quickly shuffles around to the side to make way for us. General Wright was once a subordinate of the Colonel, but with well-planned subtlety and deftness, Colonel Reed ensured his rise through the ranks was steady, all the way up to General, so far.

I take up my place at the end of the table, as asked, like a good soldier, playing along to the Colonel's tune for now. Dan does the same, now standing beside me. The Colonel's tune won't last. However, I will play along for now and hear what he has to say and what he actually wants. I will then make my decision and if I have to tell him no, then he will have to swallow it, as nothing he is going to say will override my priority, which is Emily.

Silence ensues around the table for a moment as if everybody is waiting for something to happen, which they are, like some kind of sick challenge to see who will blink first. Well, I, for one, haven't got time for these games and if it is me who has to blink first then so be it; they are all looking in my direction anyway.

"What do you want to discuss, Colonel?" I ask plainly and then everybody's heads turn to see what the Colonel is going to say.

"You know very well what you are here for, Captain," the Colonel says, puffing his chest out even further, revelling in his power.

I decide to test him, to see if I can prick his inflated ego a bit. "No, Colonel, I don't know why you called us here, so if you have something you want to discuss, I suggest you get on with it," I tell him.

This doesn't go down very well with him, unsurprisingly, and I can feel his men gathered around the table cowering slightly, waiting for his response.

"You know damn well why you're here, man!" he starts angrily, "I got you out of a very dark hole yesterday, on your word that you would give me Sir Malcolm's computer and his safe. You provided me with one, but then proceeded to try and make a fool of me! The Home Secretary took a very dim view of the events and even then, I cleared you to land here in your stolen Lynx helicopter. I expect you to get me that fucking safe, Richards!"

The Colonel isn't irate, but he is not far off, as some of the blood has definitely left his chest and gone to his face, which is a shade of dark red now. Maybe it is time to try and calm the situation.

"As I have explained to you, Colonel, we couldn't shift the safe; if we could have, we would have but our time ran out and I didn't try to make a fool of you by commandeering the Lynx. I had no choice. The safe is still there and I am sure you have enough capable men to get it if you think it is that important."

"Major Reese, explain to this buffoon why that safe is important." I would say that I was offended by the Colonel's slight, but I've been called much worse.

The only officer who doesn't outrank the Colonel around the table, an average-sized man, who doesn't look like he has seen much—if any— 'action', starts to speak.

"Captain Richards, I was in charge of the facility where this virus escaped from, and I was tasked with moving out of the facility and shutting it down. Unfortunately, a terrible accident happened, the virus was released and a large fire broke out which destroyed the building. To add to this unfortunate incident, all the records related to the particular virus we think has caused this outbreak were destroyed in the fire... genetic sequences, details of possible anti-viruses all destroyed. Now it is my understanding that Sir Malcolm once oversaw the facility where the accident happened and may have kept files related to this type of virus. Don't ask me how, but apparently, he kept them to try and force the MOD to destroy the viruses. This never happened and according to the Colonel, the records could be in his safe and could prove vital in stopping this virus or at least dramatically cut the time it takes us to stop it." The Major finishes his appeal.

Major Rees's speech is honest and passionate, but it doesn't give any reason why getting the safe requires Dan or me. We could easily brief another team, tell them what to expect and the terrain of where the safe is in the Orion building. A team much younger, fresher and not as rusty as me and Dan.

"Thank you, Major," the Colonel says. "So, Captain, tell me what you need to go and get the safe?"

"I understand what Major Rees is saying, Colonel, but as you know, I am not a Captain any longer and I haven't been for over five years, I'm prepared to brief a team and oversee an operation to retrieve the safe, but I cannot go on the mission; my daughter needs me, I am afraid," I tell him in all sincerity.

"You have forced my hand then, Richards." The Colonel says, filling me with dread at what he will do to get his way. "Your daughter is safe here behind our protection, but what about your son, he is still a serving member of this

Army isn't he? And your actions will have a great bearing on where he is posted."

"What is that supposed to mean, Colonel?" I ask in trepidation.

"You will have gathered, Richards, 'Operation Denial' to take back the city is due to get underway in a very short amount of time, at 1000 hours in fact, and the infantry are gearing up now to move out. Your son will be joining them as we speak and he will be in the first wave to re-enter the city. We are expecting heavy losses with that first wave. Operation Denial will not stop, however, until the city is secure and every one of these Zombies is dead; we mean to exterminate them completely, at any cost!

"Now, if you were to lead this mission as you said you would, yesterday, I would, of course, let you assemble your own team. Handpick each man if you like, and I will defer to your judgement as you know the terrain and what you will need to complete your task better than me.

"The initial action plan, drawn up to complete this mission, is for the team to chopper in after Operation Denial is well underway, to retake the city and—using it as a diversion—to slip in, complete the mission and be back here quick-time.

"So, Captain do you want to rethink your position?"

Images, of Josh marching into London flash through my mind and my stomach drops to the floor. Both Josh and I know full well what will be waiting for the poor souls that try to re-enter the city. The Colonel is right about one thing at least, to expect heavy losses; God only knows how many Rabids there are in the city now, in London, with its population of eight million plus. I wouldn't like to guess.

My mind races, trying to outmanoeuvre the Colonel. The thought of leaving Emily behind again frightens me and her reaction will be awful. This time, it will be me and Josh leaving her. The Colonel has made it clear the only way for Josh to not be in that 'first wave', is if I have him reassigned to my team.

I can feel the tension around the table as the anticipation rises; they wait for my reaction. Dan, beside me, keeps quiet for a moment. He knows me well enough to give me time to think without trying to give me his thoughts and distracting me at a time like this. I value Dan's input above all others in this type of situation and he knows it. He will give me his take when the time is right and plans will change and adapt with his input—or the plan could be scrapped completely and we'll go with his, which wouldn't be the first time.

After what seems like an hour but is no more than a couple of minutes, I come to my conclusion.

"Colonel, I'll accept the mission on the conditions that I have control. And that when it's complete, we, including my son, are free to leave… and that my daughter is kept securely here with Catherine Hamilton and Stacey Jones, who arrived with my daughter—until I get back. Oh, and I will need to see them before we get underway."

A satisfied look crossed Colonel Reed's face. He knew he had a winning hand before this charade even started. I had no other option but to accept, since no matter how easy the Colonel tried to make the mission sound, it was either that or allow my son to march to a fate worse than death, and he knew it.

Josh would kill me himself if he knew I was making deals to get him off the front line, that is for certain, but so be it. Josh is a proud soldier, but I am his father and he will always be under my protection.

"And what about you, Atkins?" The Colonel turns to Dan.

"I'm in," Dan says without hesitation.

"There was no way out of that one, Boss, he had you by the testicles." Dan turns, talking quietly into my ear.

"Agreed," Colonel Reed says, triumphantly.

The Colonel makes the mission to retrieve the safe sound so easy, but he, as well as I, know that any mission, even the ones that look so simple on paper, can go sideways at any moment.

My time in the Special Forces taught me all too well that no matter how good the mission plan is or how many backup plans there are, how much preparation you make and how many times the mission is rehearsed, it can all go to shit before the first boot even hits the ground. Mission intelligence is wrong, the weather changes, engines fail, weapons jam or somebody just fucks up; there are too many variables to predict with any certainty how a mission will play out. Even the most meticulously prepared mission plan can go seriously wrong at any moment and then if you are too far in to pull out, you just have to go in as hard and as fast as you can and trust in your training, your team and the luck they bring.

Lieutenant Winters, who took me to the briefing with the Colonel earlier this morning, appears out of nowhere at Colonel Reed's side but slightly back, and waits patiently as if he knows he is about to be called upon by the Colonel at any moment.

Colonel Reed's face changes; he knows he has won this little battle with me and has already moved on, feeling no compulsion to gloat. The look of satisfaction he had when he had won has been replaced by his game face. I expect he has also seen a change in my face, my initial look of anger and frustration at losing, replaced by a look of concentration and determination. There is absolutely no point in dwelling on this loss, as my training and experience have taught me that, and it is gone, I've already picked myself up and moved on too; my concentration now is on winning the next battle.

Chapter 7

Lieutenant Winters continues to stand back from Colonel Reed, as if he is apprehensive of approaching the inner circle of the officers gathered around the tactical table. I am not even sure that the Colonel knows that Winters is there.

"Winters," the Colonel says abruptly without looking behind himself. I should have known that Colonel Reed had Lieutenant Winters exactly where he wanted him, too.

"Yes Sir," the Lieutenant replies without hesitation.

"Captain Richards has a mission he needs to prepare for. See that he gets everything he needs, then report back to me with the mission details," the Colonel orders, still without looking around.

"Yes, Sir." Lieutenant Winters responds, whilst standing to attention.

"Captain Richards," the Colonel says to me. "That safe needs to be back here A-SAP, the mission will be ready to go by 1500 hours at the latest, understood? Oh and no fucking about this time, Captain; you won't be cleared to land again here without the safe, am I clear?"

"Crystal clear, Colonel," I reply, knowing he isn't bluffing.

Lieutenant Winters turns sharply, still at attention towards the exit at the front of the tent and then he starts to walk with conviction out of the rear of the tent and back into the buzz of the front area with its numerous staff and humming computers.

"Please follow me, Captain," he says on his way out.

Dan and I fall into formation behind Lieutenant Winters as he leaves, our spot at the table immediately filled by one officer or another keen to be in the Colonel's direct line of sight. They all move onto the next order of business, almost as if we were never there, although I am sure that at least some of their deliberations involve me and Dan, and our imminent mission.

Exiting the tent, we all squint momentarily from the bright sunshine, the sun now climbing higher in the sky, its warmth now building into what looks like is going to be a hot day ahead.

Parked just in front of the tent is yet another Land Rover Defender. This one isn't a standard-issue army Defender, however, it is a relatively new one and probably one of the last to come off the production line before Land Rover discontinued manufacturing them. The Defender is painted gloss black with dark tinted windows, and my guess would be this is the vehicle in which the Colonel is ferried around by Lieutenant Winters who heads straight for the driver's door.

"Please, get in," the Lieutenant says and so Dan and I do. I get into the front passenger seat and Dan gets in behind the Lieutenant.

When we are all in the Defender, Lieutenant Winters pauses before starting the engine.

"Colonel Reed has arranged a small hangar just over there," the Lieutenant says pointing to a group of buildings near to the mass of helicopters. "You will be able to use it as your base for planning and executing the mission, it has all the equipment you should need but if anything is missing, let me know and I will get it for you."

The Lieutenant then reaches for the ignition but pauses just before he is about to start the engine, as I ask him a question.

"What time is the mission to retake the city due to commence?"

"The first waves moves out at 1000 hours," he tells me.

I glance at my watch, which tells me it is 0815, so it is not long, not long at all until they move out. I don't envy any of the poor souls tasked with being the first to re-enter the city. I wish I could think of an argument against that course of action and offer a better plan, but I can't; as horrific as it sounds, that is the only plan that has any chance of stopping this virus here and now. To hold off, to try to contain the virus and wait for some kind of cure of which there is no sign, would be to risk the infected breaking out of the quarantined area of the city and the virus spreading. That would risk the whole country succumbing to the virus and that cannot be allowed to happen, at any cost!

So, how can I intervene to stop my son marching into the city side by side with his comrades? They will all be somebody's sons and daughters, but I know it is the only course of action to possibly save the country. I guess I will have to struggle with that thought, but I just can't stand by and let Josh go in that first wave when I can stop it. Wouldn't every parent do the same, if they had the chance? And Josh was probably only assigned to the first wave because of me, so Josh will continue to play his part in this nightmare ordeal, just by my side, where I will do everything to protect him.

"Lieutenant, make arrangements for my son, Joshua Richards, to join my team immediately," I order.

"Yes, Sir, of course," the Lieutenant replies with no qualms.

"Also arrange for Second Lieutenant Alice Ward to join us."

"Boss, I—" Dan starts to say something, but I quickly shoot him a look that shuts him up. He is probably worried that she won't be up to the task, and with Josh on the team too, the risk of having two younger, inexperienced personnel on the mission could be risky, but I am confident we can find them both a task that won't raise the odds of the mission being a success.

Lieutenant Winters is slightly confused by the second name I request but nevertheless complies.

"Okay, let's have a look at what we got in this hangar," I say.

Now Lieutenant Winters does start the engine and we move off across the grass until with a slight bump, we get back onto the smooth asphalt and we pick up speed towards the buildings the Lieutenant pointed out.

"So how long have you been under Reed's command?" Dan asks the Lieutenant as he drives.

"Three and a half years now and about two years working for him directly," he responds.

"And how has that worked out for you?" Dan presses.

"I think it's safe to say it has been interesting at times," Lieutenant Winters says without giving much away.

"I respect your loyalty, but come on Winters, give us some juicy bits?" Dan presses further with a big smile on his face.

"There really isn't much more I can say," the Lieutenant says, not rising to Dan's baiting.

Dan is just about to have another stab at the Lieutenant when I intervene.

"Alright, that's enough Dan. Brief them on the mission plan to take back the city, Lieutenant," I say, half expecting him to be tight-lipped about that too, but instead he is quite the opposite.

"The first wave moves out at 1000 hours as I said and they will be moved into position by transport. Surveillance is showing that the infected have slowed their spread slightly, they seem to be taking their time as they reach each new area of the city, as they move outwards. So, they are still far enough inside the original cordoned off area within the boundary of the North Circular Road and the first troops will be dropped at eight insertion points in the West and North West of the city.

"Once in position, those troops will start to fan out on foot and in hardware, clearing the streets as they go, building to building where necessary. They will have massive air cover as you will have seen and we expect to push the infected back and into the open, hopefully in numbers, where they will be eliminated from the air where possible. As the troops push the infected back, we expect them to move out into the open and move East towards the Eastern part of the city, which has been fortified to eliminate them as they reach those areas." The Lieutenant finishes his briefing just before we pull up the buildings.

"How many troops are going in the first wave?" I ask him.

"There will be approximately forty-five thousand troops going in."

"That doesn't sound enough," I hear myself say, almost to myself.

"There are another thirty-five thousand that will be moved into position immediately after the first wave, to do

64

any clearing up and to bolster the first wave, and there are a further twenty-five thousand on standby… these figures don't include the air support," the Lieutenant informs me.

"Okay, thank you, Lieutenant, only time will tell I suppose, but it sounds a bit dicey to me," I tell him, without offering anything constructive. Lieutenant Winters applies the hand brake to the Defender and we all get out.

The noise of helicopter engines and rotor blades slicing through the air reverberates around us, coming at us from all the engines being tested, which are not far from us now and the noise hits the buildings we have just pulled up by and bounces back to hit us for a second time. Without saying anything, Lieutenant Winters walks off in the direction of the building, leading the way to the hangar that will be our base for the duration of our mission.

He opens a door into the building that has a large roller shutter next to it, and goes straight in with me and Dan following close behind.

As we enter, the majority of the noise from outside is cut off and we find ourselves in a big but not massive aircraft hangar, which at some point must have housed one or, at the most, two light aircraft. The hangar is now mostly empty, with a few old oil drums, tools, various other items and rubbish scattered around the perimeter walls. The central area, however, is mostly clear. That is apart from the equipment, on trollies that have been brought in, as the Lieutenant had said, along with tables and chairs.

The tables have comms equipment and two computers on them, complete with computer towers, mice, keyboards and monitors; one of the monitors is turned off, but the other is on, showing a view over London. Seated in front of it, not looking at the monitor but looking at me, is Josh.

"Joshy boy, you sneaky little bugger," Dan says as Josh gets up and comes over to us. "How long have you been here?"

"Twenty minutes or so after you left, they came to get me and Alice. I'm not sure where they took Alice but they took me to get fresh kit and then brought me here and told me to wait for you to arrive," Josh says, just before I pull him in for a hug.

Josh does look smart in what is definitely a brand-new combat uniform, boots and all. For a second I wonder if Colonel Reed was bluffing the whole time about sending Josh in with the first wave, but then I realise if I weren't here, that is exactly where Josh would be now.

"Don't worry, son, Alice will be joining us shortly too. Isn't that right, Lieutenant?" I say turning to him.

"I will get onto that, Captain, but you are going to need more boots than we have here to complete your mission and time is not on our side so I suggest we look at options?" he says quite bluntly.

"Agreed, Lieutenant; what Special Forces teams are available? I presume you had one or two lined up in the event I didn't take the mission?"

"You are correct, Captain; give me a minute to check which teams are still available and haven't already been deployed," the Lieutenant says, getting his phone out of his pocket and walking away from us to make his calls.

"What mission, Captain?" Josh asks.

It feels strange him calling me Captain but I understand he won't want to be calling me Dad, especially if he is going to be surrounded by the almost mythical Special Forces operators.

"You know I was supposed to bring Sir Malcolm's safe from the Orion building yesterday? Well, we have been tasked with retrieving it today and the mission needs to underway by 1500 hours," I tell Josh.

"I am surprised you have agreed to take on that mission; what about Emily, have you told her yet?" Josh says looking a bit confused.

"Let's just say Colonel Reed made me an offer I couldn't refuse, and no I haven't told Emily yet, but as soon as preparations are underway here, I will go and see her."

"What offer? Must have been something important for you to agree and leave Emily again. She is not going to be happy; she was upset when they came to get me." Josh is looking even more confused now, and who can blame him?

"I don't want to go into the ins and outs now Josh; we need to concentrate on the mission ahead of us, so let me worry about Emily, okay?"

"But," Josh starts.

"Josh, leave it now," I interrupt him. "I want you to check the inventory on that equipment, make sure it is all present and correct." I can see it in Josh's face that he is about to protest and try and delve further. "Now, soldier!" I tell him before he does.

"Yes Sir," he replies and goes to do exactly that.

Of course, I can understand Josh is confused and has legitimate questions as to why I would agree to take on this mission and leave Emily again, and he is wondering what leverage the Colonel has over me to get me to agree. I can only hope it won't play on his mind for long because there is no way I am going to tell him that the Colonel used him as the bargaining chip to get me to agree; at least, I won't tell him now, maybe when this is over. I need Josh's attention on the mission, we can't afford for him to be feeling guilty and torn because of what transpired between Colonel Reed and me, that could be fatal for the whole mission.

Josh is making a start at going through the equipment and Dan has gone over to him and is probably consoling him a bit, but knowing Dan, he is trying to take Josh's mind off our conversation and moving it onto the mission where his mind needs to be.

"Captain," Lieutenant Winters says from behind me and I turn to see that he has finished his calls and is coming back towards me.

"Yes, Lieutenant?"

"I have arranged for Second Lieutenant Ward to be transferred to your team; she will be transported here shortly."

"Very good, thank you, Lieutenant," I reply.

"Two Special Forces patrols are also inbound; they will be here in about thirty minutes, I'm afraid I can't give you any more information on the patrols, at this time."

"Do you know if they are both SAS?" I ask him.

"I don't, Captain, all I know is that command is sending two patrols."

A patrol of UK Special Forces consists of four men, meaning there will be eight joining my team. Each member of a patrol will have a specialist skill, along with their basic Special Forces training, like demolition or medic for example, but all will be highly skilled in combat procedures. The two main fighting branches of UK Special Forces are the SAS, (Special Air Services) and the SBS (Special Boat Services), both of which are among the elite of any combat forces in the world. I don't say that out of any bias because I was UK Special Forces, believe me. I have seen action around the world with Special Forces from other countries and very few compare.

Whilst I will be confident of the men's abilities if the patrols are from either branch of the Special Forces, it may be easier if they were both from the SAS. This is only because I was SAS and there is a deep-seated rivalry between the SAS and SBS and while I doubt there would be much of an issue if one or even both patrols were SBS. Especially in these times, I don't want misguided rivalries affecting how we work as a team on the mission.

Another issue, if they are SBS, is that I was a Royal Marine who decided to join the SAS instead of the SBS. This can be seen as treachery by some in the SBS because the Royal Marines are sea-based and the vast majority of Royal Marines who join the Special Forces go for the SBS as a natural progression. Some SBS operators also have a tendency to look down on Royal Marines, and they see them as somehow inferior, as some SAS do with the Parachute Regiment. This could be an issue for Dan; he was a bloody fine Royal Marine Commando but never felt the calling to try for Special Forces. I personally never had any time for these rivalries. SAS, SBS, Marine or Para—as far as I was concerned, we were all part of the same fighting force and as long as you did your job that was good enough for me.

"Do you know where my daughter is now?" I ask the Lieutenant.

"Yes Captain, she has been moved to the family area, close to the food area where she was when you left."

"Okay, good, I think now will be the best time to go and see her, before the patrols arrive, don't you?" I ask him and the Lieutenant agrees.

Before we leave to see Emily, which I know is going to be difficult, I go and see Dan and Josh. Josh seems to have put his questions to one side, at least for now, and his mind seems to be on the task at hand. He is getting through taking an inventory of the equipment, with some help from Dan. I explain where I am going and ask for them both to hold down the fort here while I am gone, which they agree to with no problems. I do warn them, however, that the Special Forces patrols may arrive before I get back and I ask Dan to get them to double-check their equipment and wait for my return when I will brief them on the mission.

"I'll handle them, Boss, no worries," Dan says with confidence.

Special Forces operators can be cantankerous and a law unto themselves at times, something I was guilty of when I was still active. This wasn't, at least for me arrogance, it was because I was always at peak physical fitness, I trained as hard as possible, drilled over and over. I was to some extent a tightly wound spring. The last thing I or my colleagues needed was some 'Herbert' trying to tell us how to do our job; we knew how to do it better than anyone, and we were always prepared for action. We craved it!

The downtime was the worst, both on and off base, it was wasted time between operations and training, hence my relationships on the outside suffered greatly. Looking back, I must have seemed so distant to my ex-wife Jessica, even when I was on leave and we were together; to be honest, I didn't want to be there, and I longed for my phone to ring, to be recalled back to base or to some high-risk operation in the UK or overseas. Action was all I was interested in. It was like a drug and most of the time there wasn't enough to go around.

Army command understood this and left us to our own devices most of the time. We were like caged animals and the cage door was only opened when the shit hit the fan and our particular skill set was required.

So, while I appreciate Dan's confidence in handling the patrols when they arrive, I know how they think and they might not take kindly to an ex-Royal Marine in civilian clothes and a young squaddie telling them to check their equipment and wait. There isn't any other option though, I need to see Emily, Catherine and Stacey and getting that done now so that my full concentration can be aimed at the mission is the best course of action.

I check Dan's sizes so I can pick him up a fresh combat uniform while I'm gone, but the Lieutenant tells me he will get that arranged for both of us; he takes our sizes and he assures us that the uniforms will be here when we get back. The Lieutenant and I then make our way out of the hangar and to the Defender.

Chapter 8

The engine starts on the Defender and we leave the hangar behind, driving back through the swarm of Apache helicopters, towards the departure lounge from earlier.

Crews, engineers, air force personnel and other airport staff are absolutely everywhere, loading ordnance, fuelling and checking; this doesn't surprise me, as it's only an hour and twenty minutes until Operation Denial, to take back London is due to get underway. There are personnel all around, and we have to drive slowly through the melee and have to brake sharply once as an American pilot walks straight out in front of us, not expecting cars to be driving through. He slams his hand down on the bonnet of the Defender, shouting and gesticulating as only an American can, before carrying on his journey.

"What role is the U.S playing in today's operation?" I ask Lieutenant Winters.

"Initially, they are supplying air support at our request; we just haven't got enough helicopters to provide the amount of air support and cover we need. No other support has been requested as of yet. We shouldn't need it, although if the mission goes badly, command may have to change their position."

Some might think that this is very generous of the Americans, helping the UK out in its time of need and they would be right, it is good of them. Make no bones about it, however, the Americans have a vested interest in seeing the UK overcome this outbreak.

You hear on the news about the British-American special relationship and your eyes probably start to glaze over, but when you have served in the military, you actually see that relationship in action. The Americans have by far the larger Armed Forces, but even they need Allies and the UK is their closest military ally. We speak the same language, we, on the whole hold the same values and the UK military is formidable, so invariably if there is trouble in the world, the UK and U.S are in the dirt together, side by side.

That's not to mention our entwined economies; the international markets have already been hit hard by this outbreak in the UK, and if the UK's economy were to fail it, would have serious ramifications around the world. Not just in America, although they would be hit particularly hard and I suspect the Americans like the world economy just the way it is.

Even with all that aside, why wouldn't the most powerful Armed Forces the world has ever seen want to get in on the action, Allies or not? An Army is only as good as its last battle and if that Army doesn't feed off the battlefield, it has a tendency to become rusty and complacent. There is a reason UK forces suddenly pop up somewhere around the world where trouble has broken out, where you think we have no cause to be; there is no better training than the real thing and it's the same for the U.S. military.

The U.S has so far committed air support, which is relatively low risk and good PR for the current U.S administration. The camera shots will look great on the news and win votes for sure, but you can bet your bottom dollar U.S Special Forces are chomping at the bit to get on the ground and see some real action, as I would have been when I was active SAS and I wouldn't be at all surprised if they are going in, in some capacity, secretly.

"Let's hope command doesn't have to change their position, but the infected are so fast and strong, I just hope that the first troops going in know what they are going to be up against and are briefed fully," I tell the Lieutenant.

"Believe me, Captain, they have been, none of them will be under any illusion of what they are going to be up against."

"I bloody hope they have," I say.

The cabin of the Defender goes quiet as the journey nears its conclusion, both of us, I suspect, contemplating what is in store for those troops as 1000 hours approaches.

We pull up and Lieutenant Winters applies the hand brake, turns off the engine still in silence and we both get out and go over to the same door we exited from earlier, that leads back up the stairs and into the departure lounge.

"Is there any chance of getting my M4 back, the one I had when I arrived yesterday before we went into quarantine?" I ask the Lieutenant as we climb the stairs.

"I'll have to see on that one, Captain, I am not sure what happened to weapons that were brought in. The equipment in the hangar includes M4s?" he says looking a bit bemused.

"See what you can do, as I doubt if anyone else arrived with an M4 Carbine and I'm quite attached to mine."

"I'll make some enquiries," he volunteers and I thank him.

Having reached the top of the stairs, we walk across the departure lounge and the Lieutenant leads me to the stairwell that we could have used instead of climbing down the escalator earlier this morning. We go up one floor and come out at the same level as the top of the escalator, but instead of going down the same corridor that leads to the conference room area, we go left down another corridor and not far along, I start to hear voices.

An over-elaborate, ostentatious sign tells me that our destination is the First-Class lounge, which I suppose makes sense. The people in there will feel comfortable, with the facilities they need, while not feeling they are been held—effectively under house arrest—but if they did try to leave the two uniformed guards, one either side of the entrance would have something to say about it.

As we approach, one of the guards reaches for the door handle and pulls the door open for us, not saying a word as we go into the lounge.

With the fair amount of overseas travelling I did for Orion Securities, I am well used to these lounges; they are all much the same, although I'm not sure I have been in this one before. It has the same large windows, comfortable sofas, tea and coffee facilities, food counter and bar area as the rest of them. In here, however, all the large television screens are blank, switched off, so as not to upset or excite the 'inmates'.

I see Emily, Catherine, Stacey and Stan immediately, but there is no sign of Lindsay, so maybe she is in the toilet or somewhere?

Catherine gives me one of her stunning smiles when she sees me and Emily who was sitting down gets up and comes over to me as I walk towards them.

"Finally, Dad," Emily says as she gets near to me, "it's boring in here, can we go now?"

"I missed you too," I joke to her as I lean down and pick her up into my arms.

"Well can we?" she persists.

"I'm afraid not, I've got some more meetings and work to do." There really is no point in me telling Emily the real reason we can't leave, getting her upset and worried; it would be too much for her to process. I am going to totally play it down to her, tell her that I am just helping out with planning and other boring stuff. Emily protests more and asks more questions but I stick to my guns, play it down and tell her she will have to stay with Catherine and Stacey, for the time being. Eventually, Emily calms down and accepts that we can't leave yet.

Lieutenant Winters has taken himself off into another part of the lounge with his phone stuck to his ear, hopefully making enquiries about my M4, although he may have more important matters to deal with.

"Where is Lindsay?" I ask as I put Emily down.

"She left about ten minutes ago; her mum is coming to get her," Catherine tells me.

"That's good news," I say, "how about you Stan, did you have any luck with your family in Bristol?"

"Yea, I'm due to leave, soon, I hope. I'm getting the train to Bristol."

"At least the trains are still running," I joke, badly.

"Have you seen Josh?" Catherine asks me.

"I've just left him, he is busy working. In fact, we are going to be working together, so at least I can keep my eye on him," I say, mostly for Emily's benefit. "How are you holding up, Stacey?" She has been very quiet since I arrived back.

"I don't really know, Andy, I feel a bit numb about everything, I suppose it will take time to process."

Stacey sounds tired and looks pretty down. She can't know what to think; are her parents dead, infected or still holed up and hiding somewhere? The poor girl must be in turmoil, trying to figure out what has happened to her parents and to make matters worse, she is stuck in here with nothing else to do but think about it. It must be constantly going around in her head.

"I wish there was something I could do, Stacey," I say, feeling very helpless and sorry for her.

"I know you do, Andy."

"Catherine, can we talk for a minute?" I ask, indicating with my head for her to come with me.

She uncurls her legs and gets up from the sofa to follow me the short distance to one of the empty sofas, and she sits next to me, taking my hand in hers.

"This is a very strange courtship isn't it?" Catherine says to me, smiling.

"I know, I'm sorry," I'm suddenly worried that she has had enough of this situation, of me and my baggage already. "I wish things were different, normal."

Catherine must have seen the worry cross my face, and her hand grips mine tighter and she looks deep into my eyes.

"That was a joke, Andy. You must admit it is strange though, and that's not your fault; if it wasn't for you, I'd probably be stuck at Orion with everybody else who was there, and heaven only knows what would have happened. Anyway, if things were still normal, I'd still be waiting for you to make a move, if you ever did, and you should know me well enough by now to know I don't do normal," Catherine says and I feel myself blush slightly.

"That's lucky then because I don't think things are going to be normal for a while yet," I tell her.

"I can see you've got something on your mind; what does colonel Reed want from you now?" she asks.

"He wants Sir Malcolm's safe and I've got to get it for him."

Catherine's whole face changes to confusion and anger, "He wants the safe, well why doesn't he go and get it himself? Why on earth would you agree to go back to Orion? That place will be overrun by now. It's too risky, tell him you've changed your mind and you're not going back!"

"That's exactly what I did tell him, Catherine, but he used Josh to force my hand."

"What does that mean?" she asks looking even angrier.

"If I didn't agree, he was going to send Josh in on the front line of the battle to take back the city, which moves out at ten o'clock this morning. I couldn't let that happen."

"That slime ball used your own son to bribe you? Wait until I see him!" Catherine looks livid now, and I wouldn't like to be in Colonel Reed's shoes if she does catch up with him.

"He didn't give me a choice; he knew I couldn't refuse," I tell her.

"So, what are you going to do?"

"I'm assembling a team to get the safe; that's where Josh and Dan are now, starting to prepare."

"Andy, it's too dangerous. Let's get them both and get the hell out of here."

"We probably could, but not Josh. Josh is still enlisted, they would not let him leave and then you can bet the Colonel would carry out his threat. I've got to go through with it, I've just come back to tell you what's happening and to see if you will wait for me until I get back. I don't like asking you again."

"It's not about waiting for you; of course, I will. I've told you I'm with you, but it's about you going back to that building. I don't want to lose you now and I'm thinking of Emily." Catherine looks like she was about to get upset for a moment, but she quickly pulls herself together, I squeeze her hand.

"It is risky, but I'm getting two Special Forces teams to go in with. We will fly in, get the safe and get out, and if all goes to plan, we should only be there a very short time. Colonel Reed's operation is going to be huge and will act as a diversion. With any luck, it will have drawn most of the Rabids away and out of the building," I tell her, sounding as confident as I can.

"That's too many shoulds, if's and lucks for my liking, Andy."

"You're right, but if I think it looks too bad when we get there, I'll turn us around and abort."

"Yea, like that's going to happen," she says sarcastically.

"We've got to move out by three at the latest so I estimate we will be back by four and the Colonel has given me his word that we can all leave here then. I haven't much of a choice, but I'll get it done, you're not going to lose me."

"We had better not, Andy, so don't try to do anything foolish."

"I won't. I'd better get back to it, I've just told Emily that I have meetings and work to do around here, there is no point worrying her."

"No there isn't, and don't you worry about her, she will be with me, so do what you've got to do and get back to us in one piece, okay?"

"I will," I just manage to say as Catherine leans in, giving me a long forceful kiss on my lips and for a moment, I forget about the mission and all the other shit, losing myself in her soft luscious lips. My feelings are growing for her by the second and I promise to myself that I will get back to her as soon as I possibly can!

Mine and Catherine's spell is broken too soon, however, by the sound of more sniggering coming from a certain young lady sitting nearby. Suddenly, I feel like a schoolboy again, kissing my very first girlfriend while our friends snigger in the background and as Catherine and I pull away from each other, I am sure I'm blushing a bit.

Emily is still sniggering behind her hand as I get up from the sofa; this is definitely the first time she has seen me kiss any woman apart from her mother and I am not surprised by her reaction. She could have reacted totally differently, badly even; it feels awkward for me so why shouldn't it for her? I know she likes Catherine and I'm sure she will get used to us.

I pick Emily up just as she calms down, and hug her tightly into me, saying "I've got to get back to work now, I'll be as quick as I can, so be a good girl for Catherine and Stacey, okay?"

"Yes Dad, try not to be too long."

"I'll try," I put Emily down and tell her I love her, and she seems fine and I'm glad she doesn't know what is really going on.

"Are you going to be alright here for a while longer, Stacey?"

"Yes, I'm alright thanks, Andy," she tells me, attempting a smile.

"Stan, good luck with your trip, I hope everything works out in Bristol, mate."

"Thanks, Andy," he says as he gets up and gives me a vigorous handshake. "It will be cool I'm sure, and if not, at least I'm at a seaport so I'll get on the first boat back to Jamaica," he says, laughing deeply.

"Right I'm off, see you, girls, later."

Before I leave, I can't help but give Emily one last kiss on the cheek.

"Don't forget me," Catherine says, and I don't.

Lieutenant Winters is standing over by the exit, checking his watch and looking eager to get on with things as I approach him.

"Right, Lieutenant, let's get on with this."

"Yes, Sir," he says as he turns to get the door.

As we leave, I take one last look back at the girls before they disappear from view. I now have to try to put them to the back of my mind, knowing the best thing for a successful mission is concentrating on the mission with no distractions, and that is what will give us the best odds of getting us back together as soon as possible, all in one piece.

Chapter 9

Lieutenant Winters and I have made our way back through the Departure Lounge without much said, and are climbing back into the Defender.

He quickly starts the engine and before I know it, he is turning the vehicle into a sharp 180-degree arc and we are aiming in the direction of the new Forward Operating Base for the mission, at the hangar where Josh and Dan are.

As we drive toward the FOB and the Apache helicopters, we are met by an obstacle and I can only hope that this is the worst one we will come across today, wishful thinking maybe.

The path through the centre of the Apaches that we came upon on our way, is now cordoned off with bollards and a man in a high-vis jacket. He is directing us to go right and down the side of the long hangar that goes all the way down to the quarantine area. My first thought is that the American pilot we startled on the way and who slammed his hand on the bonnet has put a complaint in and so the through path has been closed.

"Bloody hell," Lieutenant Winters exclaims. "I'll get this idiot to move the bollards and let us through!"

He is about to pull up and stop. However, the sound of one of the Apache motors starts accelerating up to full power, the noise whining through our doors' open windows.

We can't see which one of the Apaches it is though, in the mass of helicopters before us. Lieutenant Winters pulls up short of the bollards just in time for us to watch as an Apache Attack helicopter on the far side from us, starts to lift off, raising above over the rest of the helicopters still on the ground. The powerful motor of the helicopter has it lifted into the air in no time and as it lifts, it starts to fly forward, its body and rotors silhouetted by the sun in front of us as it goes. Then another less obvious whining noise starts as another Apache starts its take-off, and it too is soon in the air and following the first. Within two or three minutes, four more Apaches are in the air and they all follow in the direction of the first, towards London.

There is a lull in the action following the lift-off of the sixth Apaches, it seems that these are only the initial sorties, probably providing air cover for an offshoot of the main mission, due to move out in only another forty minutes or so.

The Defender springs back to life almost as soon as the lull begins and Lieutenant Winters drives straight for the bollards and the high-vis jacketed man, coming to a sudden stop in front of him.

"Let us through," the Lieutenant shouts as he pokes his head out of his window.

The man in the high-vis who is clearly a civilian, more than likely an airport worker, is having none of it. "Sorry mate, the road is closed; you'll have to go down that way," he says, pointing again down to our right and the long hangar.

"For fuck's sake, man, we've got urgent business, now move those bollards!" Lieutenant Winters' sudden outburst takes me by surprise; he struck me as a man who would not lose his cool so easily.

"Sorry mate, more than my job's worth, this road is closed," the man says, not intimidated at all by the outburst. He doesn't move and smiles at us, his bushy moustache raising, following his lips.

"Fucking jobsworth," the Lieutenant says under his breath as he pulls his head in, getting even more irate.

He slams his foot on the accelerator and just as I think he is going to plough through the bollards or even through the man, he swerves the Defender to the left in the opposite direction of the one the man told him. The man moves, suddenly thinking the same as me, and he jumps to the side, falling over himself and knocking over some of the bollards. He ends up in a heap on the ground in amongst the bollards.

The Lieutenant motors down, accelerating as we go parallel to the helicopters; he only slows a little as we go up a small verge and onto the wide grass area that runs between the helicopters and one of the airport's runways. Immediately turning right, he picks up speed again, travelling in the direction of the FOB and I have to hand it to him, this is a much quicker route than our friend in the high-vis jacket pointed him to—even if the grass does throw up quite a few bumps.

No other Apaches take off as we travel past them on our right side, while on our left are ten Chinook helicopters, lined up in two rows of five, lengthways on as we pass them. Their double rotors hanging low give the impression our roof might hit them. Not that that slows down Lieutenant Winters who is almost giving chase to a USAF C10 Galaxy transport plane that has just come into land on the runway, away to our left.

With the Apaches coming to an end and then behind us, the Defender veers slightly right. We almost jump into the air as the Defender hits a larger grass verge and we hit the tarmac again. Thankfully, the FOB is now in sight and this seems to calm the Lieutenant a bit because he eases the speed slightly and his hands relax on the steering wheel.

"It looks like your team has arrived," the Lieutenant says just as I'm thinking. Two military vehicles are parked up outside the roller shutter of our hangar FOB.

"Yes, it looks that way, now the fun will really start. Have you any further information on who has been assigned?" I ask.

"I'm afraid not, I just sent the request up the chain, I did stipulate a demolitions expert, for the safe though."

"Good, he will be needed, I'm a bit rusty," I tell him.

"I'm not surprised, Captain, it's been a few years."

"It certainly has, I never thought I'd be putting a uniform on again, but that is one of the least surprising things lately."

"You can say that again."

"Are you assigned to us until the mission is complete, Lieutenant?"

"Those are my orders."

"The Colonel likes to keep a close eye on his assets, doesn't he?"

"You know him well," the Lieutenant says sarcastically, with a hint of bitterness.

"I certainly do. What's your first name, Lieutenant?"

"Robert, Sir."

We park up next to the two new vehicles outside the roller shutter and I thank the Lieutenant for an interesting journey.

I have to admit to myself that I am actually quite nervous, now that I actually think about the job as I enter the hangar. I was in charge and gave out orders at Orion Securities the whole time I was employed there, and it came naturally to me. It was, in fact, easy compared to the military. The whole dynamic at Orion was different. I was dealing and responsible for employees and Orion only employed the best professionals in every aspect of the business, people who took pride in their work and were rewarded for it. The orders were, therefore, in effect, instructions and it was very, very rare that there was a threat to life in the instructions I gave. Now, I have to revert back because I am going to be dealing with hardened Special Forces operatives who know their shit and don't take any. They can smell weakness a mile off and I have been out of the mix for a long time, so something tells me it is going to be very testing earning their respect in such a small amount of time.

Lieutenant Winters may see my trepidation because he takes the lead, opens the door and heads straight into the hangar.

"Right, form up!" the Lieutenant says loudly and forcibly almost as soon as we get into the hangar.

There are three separate groups of people milling around inside the hangar. I am pleased to see Alice is with Josh and Dan over by the tables with the computers and comms equipment on; Josh and Alice are seated in chairs and Dan stands by them in his new combat uniform with his arms crossed across his chest.

The other two groups stand in small separate circles talking, and immediately I see that one of the groups all have the sand colour beret of the SAS whilst the others have the green berets of the SBS. This should be interesting, I think to myself; this is not the dynamic I would have chosen, all SAS or SBS would have been preferred but you can only play with the toys you are given so we had all better make the best of it!

Josh and Alice immediately get up from their chairs to come and form up, and the eight Special Forces men thankfully all break from their small circles and form a line in front of the Lieutenant and me. The green berets on the left, the sand berets in the middle and Josh and Alice on the right, Dan comes over and takes a position behind me, on my right shoulder.

When everyone is formed up and stood to attention, Lieutenant Winters addresses them. "This is Captain Richards and he will be leading today's mission on the direct orders of Colonel Reed." The Lieutenant then takes a step back, leaving the floor to me, and I'm suddenly a bit self-conscious that I am the only one in here not in uniform.

"Thank you, Lieutenant. At ease, men," I start. "You don't need me to tell you about the horrific events that have unfolded over the last couple of days. Today could determine certainly the fate of London and possibly the whole country. I know some of us at least have had contact with these infected Zombies, or Rabids as we will call them, but everyone needs to listen up to what I am about to say.

"The Rabids are quicker, stronger and fiercer than you will expect. You must anticipate them, as they have no fear and they are vicious. You can shoot them or even blow them up but there is only one thing that will stop them, and that is by taking their brains out, so that means headshots or if you can't make a headshot, take their legs out, and that will slow them down. Is that clear?"

"Yes, Sir," all of them say in unison.

"I have two more observations from my contacts with the Rabids. The first is that they are not trying to kill you. They are trying to turn you into one of them; they may feed on you for a while, but believe me, their aim is to turn you. That is bad enough when there is one of them but from what I have seen, they like to hunt as a pack and they work as one too, so don't be fooled into thinking they are just brain-dead creatures. Because that is not what I've seen, in fact, I think there is a hierarchy between them, so be aware, okay?"

Another, "Yes Sir," sounds off.

"I will brief you on the mission in due course, but right now, I want to know who we have here. Who are the team leaders?" I ask.

Two men, one from the SBS and one from the SAS patrols stand forward, snapping to attention again. The SBS man is on the far left of me at the end of the line and the SAS man is on the left of his men too, in the middle of the line.

I approach the SBS team leader first, moving in front of him. He is a tall muscled man of about six-foot-two inches, and he has a hardened face enhanced by a long scar that moves diagonally down the side of his right cheek. I would put his age as early thirties.

"Name and rank?" I ask the burly operator.

"Sergeant Dixon, Sir."

"Speciality?"

"Demolitions, Sir."

"And your team?"

"Corporal Downey, Medic, Lance Corporal Kim, Signals, and Trooper Collins, Sir." Each man stands to attention when his name is called before reverting back to ease.

"Thank you, Sergeant, fall in," I tell him and he immediately steps back, falling back in line.

The SAS team leader is slightly smaller than the SBS leader but is still quite a unit of at least six foot. He is also slightly younger and doesn't have the hardened look of Sergeant Dixon but is rugged nevertheless.

"Name, rank and troop?"

"Corporal Simms, Air Troop, Sir."

"Speciality?"

"Linguist, Sir."

"And your team?"

"Lance Corporal Watts, Demolitions, Trooper O'Brian, Signals, and Trooper Thomas medic, Sir."

Again, each man lets me know who they are by standing to attention when their name is announced, and Corporal Simms falls back in when I'm finished with him.

"Okay, men, fall out, and get your kit out of the vehicles, get it checked and await further instructions." They obviously arrived just before the Lieutenant and me because none of their kit is in the hangar yet. "Sergeant Dixon, join me when you're finished."

"Yes, Sir," he replies.

My watch tells me it's 0947, only thirteen minutes remaining until Operation Denial starts.

"Lieutenant Winters, can we get a feed of Operation Denial on those monitors?" I ask, pointing towards the tables.

"Yes Captain, I will be able to link us into the feed, I'll get on it immediately."

"Good, and while you're doing that, I'll get changed."

"Your gear is over here Boss," Dan tells me, "I got changed in that small office at the back."

"Okay, thanks mate," I tell him. "How are you doing, Alice?" I ask on my way over to collect my gear.

"I'm good thanks, Andy, I was a bit confused when they plucked me out of my new unit. We were gearing up to move out, back into London," she says.

"Sorry if I ruined your plans, Alice."

"Oh, don't worry, I was in no rush to get back into that rodeo, our whole Platoon looks nervous as shit, including me. Dan and Josh have filled me in as to why I'm here and it's a much better bet. Thanks, Andy."

"No thanks needed, and I do hope it is the better bet; this isn't going to be the main event but it's still high risk," I tell her seriously.

"Yes, it is, but I'd rather be doing my part with this team than the nervous-looking bunch of freshmen I've just left."

"You may be a Yank but you're one of us now," Dan interjects.

"Who you calling a Yank?" Alice asks Dan, smiling.

"How did Em take your news, Dad? Josh asks, then looks around looking sheepish, in the hope that none of the Special Forces were in earshot of him calling me Dad.

"Well, I was a bit sparing with the truth. I told her I had work and meetings around here and didn't mention what we really are doing, so she was fine. She had a grump because she is bored, but that was all."

"Definitely for the best," Josh says in agreement.

"Right I had better get changed," I say as the new men start to bring their gear in and Lieutenant Winters gets the computer screens on. "Would you like to join me, Dan?"

"How could I refuse such a tempting offer, Boss?"

"Keep calm mate, I just want your take on the new arrivals."

"How disappointing, but come on then," Dan jokes as he starts towards the small office, he got changed in.

The office is small, with one desk squeezed at the far end that leaves just enough space on one side to get around to the chair. Dan goes around the side of the desk sideways on, to get to the chair and he sits heavily down into it, then swivels to the side and looks out of the one window that looks out into the hangar. I close the door and stand behind it to get changed which gives me at least some privacy, putting the holdall with my gear in onto the floor.

I bend down to unzip the dark green holdall and inside, I immediately see the sand-coloured beret synonymous with the SAS, with its famous winged dagger insignia and the motto 'Who Dares Wins' running across the dagger, placed on top. Bittersweet feelings run through me when I see my new beret, having given so much to 'The Regiment'. I could never have imagined I would ever contemplate wearing the beret again, but contemplate I do. Is there any need for me to wear the beret, and do I even want to? Technically I'm not even in the SAS and will it rub the four SBS members of our team up the wrong way? I pick up the beret and look at it for a moment before reaching over to the desk and putting it down until I decide.

"Bet you never thought you'd be putting that on again?" Dan says with a hint of concern.

Dan knows all too well what effect being in the SAS has had on my life, it has come up several times when the two of us have been drinking and putting the 'world to rights'. He shares many of the same issues from his time serving as a Royal Marine Commando, the waste and horror of the battlefield, friends and comrades lost and the effect it all has on you and your loved ones back home.

"You're not wrong there, it's a bit of a head fuck mate, to say the least," I tell him.

"They just keep coming lately and something tells me we're not finished yet. Look on the bright side; at least you won't have to write up a report after this mission," Dan jokes.

"Are you sure about that?"

"Err, no," Dan says and we both laugh.

While I put on my new combat uniform, Dan and I discuss our upcoming mission. Our discussion firstly centres on Colonel Reed's initial plan that he mentioned back in the command tent. To fly in when Operation Denial is advancing, using it as a diversion, fast-roping onto the roof of the Orion Building, re-entering the building through the hole we blasted into the roof to retrieve the safe, then we fall back to the roof to be picked up by the waiting helicopters. This mission plan, on the face of it, does seem like a favourable option and neither Dan nor I have thought of a better plan in the time we have had to think about it since the command tent.

We both agree that any other option would involve substantially more troops to execute. If we were to try and make the Orion building safe and clear of Rabids, for example, air support and troops would be needed to firstly secure the grounds of the building and form a perimeter, and then more troops would be needed to clear the building. Such a plan would require troops in the hundreds to be on the ground in addition to aircover. Even if we had that number of troops at our disposal, it would take extensive planning, timing and air transport to fly the troops in. And even then, the risks would be colossal and unpredictable. Colonel Reed and his cronies must have discounted this type of plan as quickly as we have.

We both agree that the mission will be based on and planned around the one touted by the Colonel and we start to delve deeper into it.

Now kitted out in my new combat uniform, including body armour, I feel more like I belong in the team, never mind commanding it. I don't use the new boots that were in the holdall though, I stick with my worn-in and comfortable hiking boots. I have used the new hip gun holster that was in there, even though my old shoulder holster is also in place with my Sig inserted, as I intend to take one of the Glocks that I saw with the equipment in the hangar with me, as well as the Sig.

As Dan and I are delving further into our plan for the mission, there is a knock at the door. I assume it is Sergeant

Dixon reporting to me as ordered, but the door opens and Josh sticks his head in.

"It looks like Denial is underway, the Apaches are all starting to take off," Josh tells us.

Both Dan and I check our watches which tell us it's 1010 hours.

"I've got to see this," Dan says excitedly as he gets up from his chair and bashes his way out from behind the desk.

"You and me both," I tell him as I quickly head for the door Josh has already vacated.

As Dan and I exit the small office, I realise I have inadvertently picked up the sand-coloured SAS beret that I had put onto the desk, whether this was a force of habit or something else, I can't say. Deciding I am overthinking it, I lift the beret and fit it to the top of my head, and mould it around my head with my hands until it is snugly in place and pointing down the right side of my head.

Everybody else from the hangar is already standing in a group on the sun-drenched tarmac outside, looking at the awesome sight in front of us. I go and stand with them next to Josh, to watch as one after another, legions of Apache Attack helicopters lift off and take to the air.

There must be twenty Apaches or so in the air already by the time I have joined the others, but these don't fly off into the distance; they move forward slowly, allowing others to take off behind them and join the expanding formation. The noise is deafening from our relatively close distance and only gets louder as more take to the air. There is a definite strong breeze, buffering us from the downdrafts of the accumulated rotors.

Away to our left, ground crew choreograph this flying dance, making the pilots of the Apaches due to take off next wait until the ones they have just released have flown off to a predetermined safe distance. When the next ones are released, the ground crew duck down, in some futile attempt to escape the serious buffering they must still receive from the rising helicopters.

I look around at my newly assembled team and they are all looking up and taking in the fascinating sight. Even the hardened Special Forces members of the team can't take their eyes off the sight and they talk to each other with their heads still lifted, moving to the side slightly when they have something to say. The different Regiments are also talking together, which is a very good sign. I definitely haven't seen such a large swarm of helicopters in the sky at one time, and I doubt if any of us have. And by the time all of the helicopters are in the air, I would doubt if anybody else ever has.

"Incredible isn't it?" I say nudging Josh at my side.

"You can say that again, I've never seen anything on this scale, have you?" Josh almost shouts in reply.

"No, this is the most I have seen in the sky at any one time, there must be forty or fifty, up there."

I assume the reason none of the Apaches is flying off is that command has decided they all need to arrive at the same time at an agreed point as the troops on the ground. This will allow for the troops to get into position before the noise of the helicopters starts to 'wake up' the Rabids and they get into a frenzied state; the value of the element of surprise cannot be overstated on the battlefield.

We really need to get back into the hangar to carry on with preparations for our mission, I think to myself, but it is hard to pull my eyes away from the sky. The time is 1025 hours and just as I decide to give myself another ten minutes, Josh nudges me to bring my attention to where he is pointing to, at the front of the swarm.

The lead Apaches have tilted forward and are now moving off at greater speed. And as they do, the ones behind them follow suit, tilting and picking up speed, to follow. The ripple flows down the waiting Apaches as the ones in front of them move off, so they tilt forward to pursue. The view could almost be a scene from Apocalypse Now, the swarm of helicopters flying off into the sun, but it would have been impossible for the budget of that film to produce anything like the scene we are witnessing now. It is on a totally different scale.

I count the Apaches as they go. Eleven lines of five have moved off and then the ones now in the air and still here revert to the holding pattern as previously. As I suspected, the Apaches are moving off in different squadrons so they can give air cover to the troops on the ground at their different insertion points into the city. The ones that have left and flown off were heading due North East, and that tells me they are heading towards the North of London, I expect the next squadron will go further East, more towards North West London, a shorter distance. This pattern will carry on until all the Apache squadrons are on their way to their designated rendezvous and I expect them all to arrive there at the same time, to coincide with the ground troops.

Deciding the ten minutes are up when the first squadron of Apaches is disappearing in the sky, I pull my eyes from the next squadron preparing to go.

"Okay people, let's get moving; we have a mission to prepare for in less than five hours!" I shout over the din.

Everybody averts their eyes too and moves off to carry on with their tasks at hand, while the Special Forces men go to their vehicles to grab more of their kit. I, Dan, Josh and Alice head back towards the hangar, and it's only then I notice Lieutenant Winters isn't out here.

We find the Lieutenant sitting in front of a computer monitor inside the hangar, typing away at the computer's keyboard and clicking its mouse. He seems to have several different tabs open on the screen but it doesn't look like he has a feed of the unfolding mission up yet.

"Any luck?" I ask him.

"Not yet, the IT guys were supposed to have set these up ready, but as usual, they have done half a job, I'm just downloading a couple of programmes to get us on; give me ten minutes please, Captain," the Lieutenant says, frustrated.

"No problem, you seem to know what you're doing so I'll leave you to it," I say, teasing him.

"Thank you, Captain," he replies, not rising to me in the slightest.

Behind the tables and the Lieutenant, leaning against the wall is a flip chart easel with a big A1-sized paper pad attached to the front of it. The Lieutenant seems to have thought of everything we are going to need for our mission.

"Josh, get the pad off that will you?" I ask, pointing.

Leaving the Lieutenant to play with his computer, I move down to the other end of the two long tables, where conveniently there is a new box of black markers sitting.

"You ready, Dan?" I ask.

"Always ready for some drawing and mission planning, Boss."

While we wait for the feed to come through on the Lieutenant's screen, Dan and I pick up from where we left off in the office. Under normal circumstances, a mission like the one we are about to carry out could take days or weeks to prepare for, if time allowed.

Firstly, every scrap of intelligence available would be studied over and over, which could include, maps, aerial reconnaissance, relevant reports and statements and interviews with anybody who might have intel, anything that might give us insight into the objective or an advantage.

Different options and methods to carry out the mission would be studied, before the final overall plan to successfully execute the mission objective was decided on. That plan would then be dissected piece by piece until every possible detail and scenario was understood and planned for, and every risk was identified and mitigated against. When that was done, we would do it again from the start, and again, until we were satisfied, we hadn't missed anything, and all eventualities were accounted for.

A detailed plan then had to be drawn up for the mission, one everybody could clearly understand. This plan gives minute-by-minute, step-by-step detail of every aspect of what is required from every team member to carry out the mission. If the objective was in a building, for example, floor plans would be printed off or drawn up by hand, aerial pictures are blown up, timings listed, and so it went on and on.

This was all before rehearsals started. Again, if the objective was in a building, a life-sized model has been known to be constructed to practise and rehearse in, and if there wasn't the time, then pallets and containers could be laid out to approximate the building's floor plan. The team would then rehearse over and over, as many times as possible, the plan changed and honed whenever problems were identified, until every member of the team knew exactly what their task was, where and when they had to be at any given moment and what risks and threats might arise.

All this planning and rehearsing meant that when the mission was being executed, it was almost second nature to the team and that raises the prospect of a successful mission considerably.

Most of that planning has gone out of the window for this mission, as we haven't got the resources or the time, so Dan and I concentrate on compiling a more basic plan, but still as detailed as possible. We need to know as soon as possible any equipment we need that isn't here already so we can get it here in the tight time frame, and that's going to include at least two helicopters. We also need to brief the team sooner rather than later so that they can process the plan and understand their tasks.

As Dan and I work, Josh and Alice look on but at a distance, not wanting to distract us or break our concentration. They are there if we need them and occasionally, we do ask them for help, to get us some information or equipment like the large map of central London that is now spread out on the table.

We are so engrossed in our task that we don't see Sergeant Dixon approach us.

"Reporting as ordered, Sir," he says, standing to attention.

"Thank you, Sergeant, at ease. Our mission's objective is to retrieve a safe from a building in the Paddington area of London."

"From Orion Securities, Sir?" he asks, taking me a bit by surprise, which he sees. "Excuse me Sir, but I Googled you when I heard we were being assigned to you."

"Fair enough Sergeant. Anyway, the safe we are retrieving is secured to the floor of the building by thick welded brackets. Its size is about 750mm wide by 500mm high," I tell him, holding my hands apart to show him the approximate size, "and it's probably 400 deep. As a demolition's expert, what do you suggest, to break it free from the floor?"

"That's quite a big safe, Sir, it's going to be very heavy. I would suggest leave the safe and take the contents. I assume it's an electronic one, Sir."

"Yes, it needs a thumbprint and code, it's not going to be easy to open," I tell him.

"Do you know the make and model, Sir?"

"No, I don't," I confess.

"It had a logo on that said 'SecLock'," Dan interjects.

"That's the make and it's manufactured in the UK," the Sergeant tells us. "With the right equipment, I should be able to crack it but it could take time. The easiest way could be if somebody with some clout got in touch with SecLock and got them to tell us how to open it; the least they can tell us is the model, they will have a record of the sale to Orion, no doubt."

"Very good Sergeant, Lieutenant Winters will be able to help with that."

"I have the feed up," Lieutenant Winters announces, interrupting Sergeant Dixon's and my discussion about the safe.

"Get what you need to get that safe open," I tell the Sergeant as I turn towards the Lieutenant.

"Yes, Sir," he says as I move towards the end of the table showing the feed. Dixon follows me, and he, in turn, is followed by Dan, Josh and Alice.

In moments, the whole team is gathered around the table, the Lieutenant remains seated and I stand next to him, not taking the spare chair on the other side of him but wanting to be on my feet to see this.

The view on the monitor is very clear and it shows a view from high above a road with two lines of vehicles moving along. The images must be being transmitted from a drone flying overhead, because from the left of the screen we see Apaches moving slowly towards the lines of vehicles.

"Where is this?" I ask the Lieutenant.

"This is the North Circular Road, between Ealing and Acton," he tells me.

The vehicles look like a mix of military transport trucks and normal civilian coaches to the right of the road, and on the left, moving in the same direction is a line of Assault vehicles. At least some of them are Challenger Tanks, although it is hard to be sure from the height we are looking down from. I suppose it makes sense that coaches are being used when you consider how many troops are being moved into position, all at once.

Then it starts to happen; the vehicle, which is a truck, stops at the back of the line and troops that look like ants from this distance start spreading out from the back of the truck. After a short pause, the truck starts moving again before stopping to let more troops disembark. As the line of vehicles stretches out, more of them come to a stop and more troops hit the ground, and I am sure this is being repeated all along the North Circular Road. Each time troops disembark, one of the Assault vehicles also stops until the troop carrier is out of the way. It then turns East into the nearest main road that leads deeper into the city and the troops move East too, following it. The Apaches then fly forward, taking up a position in front of the tank that's leading the troops; they will be relaying reconnaissance intel to their unit on the ground and will be able to respond first if any targets present themselves.

Chapter 10

Only a very short time ago, Private Jason Robbins had made the mistake of thinking that he had landed a cushy number in Terminal 4 of Heathrow Airport. He had been posted, virtually straight off the train from Scotland, to a conference area in the terminal where he had mainly been tasked with escorting VIP's and top brass around the terminal and making sure they arrived at their desired destination without getting lost in the large terminal. He had done a good job, he thought, he had very quickly memorised the layout of the terminal and hadn't led any of the dignitaries astray. He had been polite, courteous, efficient and hadn't spent that much time in the food hall, but that seems like a distant memory now.

All too quickly, the VIP's that needed an escort had thinned out, until they virtually dried up completely and it was then inevitable that he, along with the other five members of his squad that were posted with him were reassigned back to his Brigade of the Royal Regiment of Scotland. They had all arrived back just in time to hear the briefing for the Operation, Operation Denial that they were to rapidly take part in.

Before Jason had time to properly register what was happening, he found himself climbing into the back of the transport truck he now found himself in, squeezed between and bumping shoulders with his mate Den on his left side and an unfamiliar squaddie on his right.

The Major who had briefed them earlier told them that they would be entering London from the West and then moving East into the city. Each squad was to exit the transport when ordered, go past the troops and barriers that were already stationed all along the North Circular Road and follow their armoured escort into the city. Their task was to eliminate all hostiles they had contact with and clear their area street by street and house by house if necessary and keep moving East. The briefing included a description of the area of London they were entering, a place called Acton, and squad leaders were given maps of London but there weren't enough maps to go around the rest of the troops.

Jason finds his head is spinning as he sways around in the back of the claustrophobic truck, squashed in against the other members of his squad. There is no air, he thinks to himself, finding it hard to breathe; there are too many people in here for the oxygen and the heat is almost overpowering, sweat running down his back. At least three people have been sick on the floor that he has heard, and he is starting to feel nauseous. The smell of the vomit wafting from all around isn't helping. Trying desperately to take his mind off the rising feeling that he is also going to be sick at any moment, determined to not suffer that embarrassment in front of his comrades, Jason tries to take his mind off it and think of something else.

Jason turns to look at Den, whose face is covered in sweat and is looking as green as Jason is feeling; his eyes look like they are almost glazed over too. Deciding that Den is at least as nauseous as him, Jason decides to try and take Den's mind off his stomach at the same time.

"What time have you got, Den? Jason says loudly, above the noise of the truck, but Den doesn't seem to register Jason's voice. "Den, what time you got?" Jason this time almost shouts at him, whilst nudging him as best he can, already pushed up tight against him.

This time, some life returns to his mate's face and eyes and Den pulls his arm up, which has been squashed down against the man next to him.

"I got ten thirty-five," Den eventually says after struggling to focus on his watch.

"We should have been at our drop-off point by now. They said ten-thirty at the latest in the briefing?" I question Den, partly to try and keep him lucid.

"I dunno mate, but if we don't get out of the back of this truck soon, I'm going to spew!" he tells me, without an ounce of humour in his voice.

"You're not the only one mate, it can't be much longer, try and hold it together," I encourage him.

"I am, believe me!"

Jason suddenly has images flash through his mind of those war films that show men in the boats on their way to the beaches of Normandy being sick on the floor, or into their helmets. He never really considered what effect this would have on their ability to function properly, never mind go into battle and fight when they actually landed on the beaches. He understands now because all he wants is his bed and maybe a bowl to throw up in!

The truck comes to an abrupt halt and everybody jerks towards the truck's cabin, squashing them together even more. Light hits Jason's face followed by fresh air as the curtain at the back of the track is whipped open, but this comes as only a tempered relief because it means they are about to exit and go into battle.

"Squad A7, move, move, move!" the Sergeant at the back of the truck shouts as the hinged rear barrier swings down and crashes against the back of the truck.

The light entering the confined space increases, as men start to jump down from the rear of the truck and

Jason's squeezed body starts to feel some relief until suddenly, he is looking at empty floor space with bright light beyond.

Jason's jelly-like legs move him forward as quickly as they can. He pauses at the back of the truck's ledge trying to compose himself, giving his legs a chance to prepare for the jump.

"Move it, Soldier," rings in his ears as he jumps off into the air, concentrating hard in a desperate attempt to control his landing and not land on any of his squad that have not controlled their own landing and are splayed out on the road, their legs letting them down, still not recovered enough to make the simple jump they all have done many times before.

Jason staggers but manages to stay upright, sharp pains travelling up his legs as if he has broken the bones in his feet; his brain tells him that it's because his feet were asleep, though. Beside him, Den lands, but his legs look like they aren't going to hold. Jason grabs his arm, steadying him and pulling him forward at the same time, to get him out of the way of others that are jumping.

"Thanks, mate, I was going over then," Den says.

Their squad looks a shambles right now, as the truck's engine revs behind them, pulling it forward to its next drop off, a short distance up. Five or six of the team are still off their feet on the road, some trying to get up but others looking like they won't achieve it, moaning and holding their ankles, while others are bent over retching.

"Form up, on me. Form up, on me," Squad leader Corporal Ford shouts from the side of the road, adjacent to where a barrier is being moved from across a road that leads into the city, into the quarantine zone.

The men that can't stand to move and form up are dragged from the path of the tracked Warrior assault vehicle that is turning to lead the way into the city, its cannon pointing the way.

Jason's head is clearing as he breathes in the fresh air and his stomach is settling, a large gulp of water from his canteen helping. He checks on Den, who is looking a better colour and is alert, so he quickly checks his equipment ready for the off and Den follows his lead.

As the Warrior moves past the thirty members of A7 squad and past the barrier, crossing the threshold into the quarantine zone, Corporal Ford follows it in and his men fall in behind him, their senses heightened. Overhead, an Apache helicopter flies, tracking the Warrior on the ground, staying ahead of it. Its role is to scan the area below, find targets and attract the targets to it, getting them out into the open so that they can be engaged either by it or the ground troops, or both.

Jason finds himself on the left flank, his SA80 rifle gripped in both hands across his body as the Squad move down, spread across the road, following the Warrior. Almost immediately, he sees curtains twitching in the houses by the side of the road, as the poor residents who are trapped in the quarantine zone look to see what this new intrusion into their community is. Jason can't imagine how these people must be feeling, trapped in their homes, unable to escape the pending doom on their doorstep—especially the people in the houses here, so close to the cordon, yet so far from safety. He knows they have been told by the authorities to stay in their homes and barricade themselves in as best they can, but it must take some courage to do that and not try and flee past the cordon. It must be even harder for the parents with their children trapped with them.

They have no choice but to stay put though; if they try to cross the cordon, they will be shot, the authorities have made that very clear and although it hasn't been shown on any TV station, Jason has heard rumours that more than a few people have met that fate trying to cross. So, they have to stay indoors, there is nowhere else for them to go; to go outside would be too great a risk, as nobody knows where the Zombies are, and they could be just down their street or next door!

"What's going on!" a voice shouts away to Jason's left.

As Jason swivels around, he raises his rifle all in one swift motion, to see a frail-looking elderly gentleman in his dressing gown and slippers standing in his doorway. The man now has at least ten rifles pointed at him, but that doesn't seem to faze him in the slightest.

"Please go back inside and lock your door, Sir, this is a military operation," Den shouts back at him.

"Fuck that, Sonny Jim," the man replies, "what the fuck is going on?"

"Sir, we are here to make the city safe, so please go back inside and let us get on with our jobs." Den tries again.

"How long is that going to take, son?"

"I don't know, Sir," Den tells him.

"For fuck's sake," the elderly man says before turning around, going back inside and closing his door.

"You should become a politician," Jason teases Den.

"Piss off!" is the only reply he gets back, as they move forward again.

Corporal Ford soon calls 'Halt', though, checking his map. He then tasks three men to break off from the group to recce Station Street, a smaller road, leading off this main road. He shows them exactly how much of Station Street is in their assigned area, how far they need to go before returning to the main Squad.

The three troops head off on their recce of Station Street and the main Squad move forward again. Only a short distance is travelled until another road junction is met and three more men are despatched down it. This is repeated as the squad moves along. The main Squad will not fall below six men, and when there are only six left, no others will be sent on recces until others return. When a road is reached with only six men remaining, the Squad will wait until others return. All Squad members have comms but everyone is under strict instructions to only use the comms when needed, since there isn't enough bandwidth for anything more, with the amounts of troops that will be on the ground in London today.

Just as Jason is starting to think the mission is going well, his stomach turns again but this time it's because he hears the crack of gunfire in the distance. He immediately lowers to one knee as do the rest of the Squad, their heads darting from side to side, trying to determine where the sound is coming from. There were only a couple of shots fired, but is it coming from one of the streets that their Squad is in, do they need back-up? The Warrior in front of them stops when the Squad does, at least giving some protection from that direction; every member of the squad would like to be sitting inside that vehicle right now and craves the safety it offers.

"Where do you reckon that gunfire is coming from?" Jason asks Den, nervously.

"Not sure mate, but it sounds far off, wouldn't you say?

"Could be, it's hard to tell with all these buildings around, could be coming from a couple of streets over?" Jason answers.

Den swiftly and suddenly raises his rifle back up the road they have just travelled down and Jason follows his lead ready to fire, his heart racing.

"Hold your fire!" Corporal Ford shouts from behind them, "they're ours."

Jason's finger moves away from his SA80's trigger, as he too sees that it's three of their Squad running down the road, returning from their recce. *Bloody hell*, he thinks to himself, *I nearly opened fire on them, I got to pull myself together!*

"All clear down Station Street Sir, but we heard gunfire, thought you may be in trouble," the young squaddie named Pete announces quite calmly as the three get close.

"Okay, Private. Take covering positions, while I see if our eye in the sky knows where it's coming from," Corporal Ford orders and then presses his comms button to talk the Apache flying around some distance in front of them.

The Squad cover their positions behind their rifles, while the Corporal talks into his radio, Jason covering up the road. He sees more movement and this time, leaves his finger off his trigger, seeing quickly that it is three more of their Squad returning. That leaves only six men still out on recces. Jason will be glad and feel more secure when everyone is back; he has a feeling that something is about to happen, but maybe it's just the tension getting to him.

Gunfire at different volumes is now sounding off at a regular rate, but none of it seems any closer to the first shots they heard, Jason thinks; it is definitely increasing in rate though. The more shots he hears, the more it seems to increase the fear he is feeling. He quickly looks around at the rest of the Squad, all of their eyes wide, searching for any threats. And most look pretty nervous and scared too, which somehow comforts Jason slightly, knowing he isn't the only one bricking it.

"The other Squads shooting might be farther into the city than us; how far d'you think we have come?" Den asks Jason.

"I'd say about a 'klick', maybe a bit more," Jason estimates.

"Na, it's more like two klicks", somebody says.

"Listen up," Corporal Ford says, "From what they can see up there, the action is more North of our position, so we carry on. On your feet."

As the whole Squad gets up onto their feet, they see three more men coming back from their recce to re-join the main group, and they ask what is happening.

"Tight formation," Corporal Ford orders as he signals the Warrior to continue.

Now the Squad, instead of spreading across the road, form up behind the Warrior, using it for cover. They all scan their areas avidly, their rifles at the ready, knowing for sure that this is no training exercise if they were in any doubt before.

All too quickly, they come to a halt at yet another road that will need three men to leave the Squad and recce, all of them hoping that they aren't the ones tasked with it. There is safety in numbers and that number is being cut to only three, for those who get the job, isn't very appealing. They all have the same sinking feeling that the enemy is close, and the appeal drops even further when it also means leaving the 'comfort blanket' of the Warrior behind too.

"Jason, Den and Tyrone, you're up."

Even before the Corporal calls his name, Jason all but knows he will be going. He thought he had been lucky to have missed the last ones, but he would take one of those recces now, over this one.

"Yes Sir," Jason says for the three of them.

The Corporal, who already has his map out as the three of them gather around him for instructions, looks up at Jason.

"Right Jason, you are Team Leader, understood?" the Corporal tells him.

"Yes Sir," he replies.

"This is Barnard Road," the Corporal says, pointing at the map that he is showing to Jason. "It goes all the way down to this road, which is—" The Corporal pauses, looking, "...Swan Road, Swan Road is in Squad A6's area but your team needs to recce Barnard Road, all the way down to Swan Road, including this school, here, Wilmot School. There are also three roads off Barnard. Two are cul-de-sacs and this road that goes down and around until it meets Swan Road; recce the two cul-de-sacs and that road down to Swan Road and then return, understood?"

"Yes Sir, understood," Jason replies.

"Okay get moving, on the double!"

Jason, Den and Tyrone break off from the main Squad's right flank and run across the main road and into Barnard Road, Jason taking the lead.

Curtains move as they enter the road and shadows can be seen moving behind the windows of the houses, as residents look out to see what is going on. Sometimes, they see worried or even frightened faces appear behind the glass. A few of the residents come out of their front doors, maybe in hope that it's over and the danger has passed, or they shout to the three men to see what is happening. The three soldiers don't slow their pace or stop to talk to them; the best that they can do is to shout back for them to go back inside and lock their doors.

As the entrance to Wilmot school approaches, they slow their pace considerably until they come to a stop at the sign for the school, which tells them that the school is a Primary school for younger children. Besides the sign is a small roadway that leads down into the school grounds and the school building that can be seen, to the right behind some trees.

"We might as well check this place out first," Jason says, panting slightly from the run.

"I dunno, mate" Den replies, "I don't like the look of it down there, it looks really spooky. They can't be in there, look, the gate is locked, isn't it?" he says referring to the steel red gate blocking their entrance to the road down.

"We have our orders, Den," Jason tells him.

"Yeah, let's get it over and done with, it does look fucking creepy, though," Tyrone says.

"Right, you first, Tyrone. I'll cover while you two get over the gate," Jason orders.

"Yes Sir, Mr Team Leader," Tyrone jokes as he goes for the gate.

The gate behind them, the three soldiers make use of their training as they descend the slightly sloped road that leads into the school, covering each other as they move.

Reaching the small car park situated in front of the main building of the school, they pause. They can see the school is quite dated, probably built in the 1980s, even though it has been refurbished by the looks of it.

"Come on mate, that'll do won't it, it's all locked up. Let's get out of here," Den says, looking at the dark deserted building, sounding very nervous.

"We'll just check the perimeter," Jason says and starts moving around to the right of the building.

"Bloody hell, mate, do we have to?" But Den has no choice but to follow Jason and Tyrone as they move, their rifles raised. A cloud crosses the sun, casting a shadow over the whole area, making it feel even more sinister. Den picks up his pace immediately to catch up with the other two.

"You alright there, Den, feeling a bit creeped out?" Tyrone teases Den as he comes up behind him.

"Schools creep me out, especially primary ones, all those small chairs and tables are just weird and don't even get me started on the little toilets, they give me shivers," Den replies.

Tyrone chuckles to himself at Den's confession as they come to the end of the building's front and start to move around the side, after checking it is clear.

The right of the building only has a narrow alleyway leading down the side of it, with overgrown hedges from the property next door overhanging across the top. Together with the sun going in, it makes it very gloomy, spooky even, and this quietens Tyrone's chuckles as he starts to go off the idea of going down there. Jason feels it too, but he presses on; he doesn't want to show his nervousness to the other two, never mind their orders.

The alleyway is eerily quiet as they go into it, even the sound of gunfire they could clearly hear before is all but silenced by the walls all around and the overgrowth above them.

"I got a bad feeling about this!" Dan half whispers, bringing up the rear as they move down slowly.

Jason, bunched up behind his rifle, leads the way, his hands clammy on the rifle's steel but still ready to fire. He turns his head to the side slightly, towards Den and Tyrone. "We got an open door here." He pauses just short of it, contemplating what to do.

"Just shut it, Jay," Den suggests.

"Shh, I think I can hear something," Jason says, and they all go silent, listening.

"I can't hear anything, so shut the door and let's get the hell out of here," Den again suggests.

They listen again and then they do hear something, a distinct ominous scraping, coming from somewhere inside the school. It only lasts a couple of seconds before it's gone. Fear roots all three of the men to the spot, all of them unsure what to do; they are almost frozen and then the scraping starts again.

"What the fuck is that?" Tyrone whispers.

Jason manages to inch forward, forcing himself to try and hear the sound more clearly. The scraping sounds close, but how close inside the school is hard to tell—and then it stops again.

"Who's there, show yourself!" Jason shouts at the doorway.

As soon as his shout ends, the scraping increases in volume and it's definitely moving now, moving towards the open door. Jason's fear rises to a new level as the sound gets nearer, and he feels himself shaking and his arms go slightly numb with adrenaline. He doesn't really register Den almost shouting at him to 'shut the fucking door'. Jason is steeling himself ready to fire, his finger poised on his rifle's trigger.

The scraping stops, just as something comes low and fast out of the doorway; it takes Jason a second to register what it is, but his body has tightened from the adrenaline. His finger inadvertently squeezes the trigger of his SA80 rifle and the bullet it fires instantaneously hits the open door.

The bullet hits about thirty centimetres above the Fox's head that is itself now frozen, its eyes locked on Jason, stunned from the loud shot of the rifle. Neither of them moves for a second, both looking at each other, then the Fox comes back to life, bares its teeth at Jason, snarls, before it turns and runs off down the alley, towards the light.

"It's a Fox," Den says, stating the obvious, "I nearly shit myself; I hate foxes!"

"Fuck me, Den, there isn't much you do like, is there?" Tyrone says.

Jason's composure slowly returns, and he lowers his rifle, saying, "I didn't mean to shoot! It could have been kids messing about in there, I could have shot one."

"Well, it wasn't it was a fox and your bullet missed it. Don't sweat it, mate," Tyrone says in some twisted way to comfort Jason as lads do. "Right," he continues, "I need a piss, it's got to be clear of Zombies in there, else that Fox wouldn't be in there. Come on, Den, let's find the little toilets."

"Hilarious, you are," Den replies to Tyrone's 'piss' take.

"Hold up," Jason says, "we don't know for sure it's clear, so let's be careful."

But Tyrone is already past Jason and going into the doorway that leads into the school; at least he has his rifle raised, Jason thinks to himself. Jason follows him in, as does Den, reluctantly.

"That's what the scraping noise was; the fox must have had its nose in this!" Tyrone says as he kicks an empty can of beans down the hall that has bright but messy paintings stuck to the walls on either side. The can skids along noisily.

"If the Zombies didn't know we were here before, they do now. Keep the noise down!" Jason says.

Tyrone and Den, who looked a bit sheepish, go off to find the toilets while Jason waits for them near the doorway to the alley.

After a couple of minutes waiting, Jason wanders into the nearest classroom. Walking through the open door and seeing the miniature tables and chairs takes him back in time and the walls, covered in more bright paintings only increases his reminiscing. He goes over to the large windows, their panes of glass stretching virtually the whole length of the room to look out over the tarmaced playing area outside with a grassed sports field beyond it. As he arrives at the windows, he stands, reminiscing some more and then the sun comes out again, making him squint.

Suddenly, the almighty sound of gunfire seems to envelop him, and he immediately assumes that Den and Tyrone are in some kind of trouble and they are having to use their weapons somewhere in another part of the school. The adrenaline, kicks in again, flooding his body and he is just about to turn to rush to find them when he realises the noise is coming from outside. His head moves closer to the window in front of him and looks up to the left and he sees where at least part of the noise is coming from.

The Apache—that must be the one that was assigned to their Squad—is hovering not far away to the left and Jason can clearly see from the tracer bullets coming from beneath the Apache's belly that it is firing heavily at the ground below it. If the Apache is firing that much, it is almost certain that the Warrior and his Squad are firing too, meaning they have contact and are under attack.

Jason's brain works hard to figure out what they should do; surely, they need to return to the Squad as quickly as possible to back them up. There is no point in carrying on with this recce now, the Squad has found the enemy. As Jason decides on that course of action, he sees the Apache firing missiles down at the ground, closely followed by a dulled explosion and then smoke mushrooms rising up from the ground. There must be one hell of a fight going on, and they need to get moving; their Squad is in trouble, but just as Jason is about to go, something catches his eye.

Somebody is running across the grass of the sports field, but the sun in his eyes makes it difficult to properly see who it is. Is it a Squad member who has somehow got detached from the main Squad or a civilian spooked by the noise of the gunfire and trying to get away?

All too slowly, it dawns on Jason what is running directly at him across the tarmac. He has seen them on television, and the fear rises in him to a new height as the realisation sinks in, and for a moment he is paralysed with that fear.

Jason has a split second to decide to fight or run from the Zombie that is almost at the window…the window Jason is now involuntarily backing away from. Deciding that the creature is still outside, Jason goes to run, but his decision is too late. He knows that as soon as he sees the Zombie launch itself at the window.

The Zombie hits the window directly in line with Jason who hasn't moved more than a couple of metres back from it. Instinct takes over and he dives to his right as the Zombie smashes through the plate glass window, which shatters into shards and scatters all over the classroom and all over Jason.

He tries to roll as far away as he can from the creature which has landed in the middle of the classroom, crashing into the small tables and chairs, sending them tumbling across the room. Jason's roll has gone as far as it can as he hits the wall underneath the classroom's blackboard, coming to a sudden stop. His mind is a blur of fear and desperation, so whether his military training takes over his body or if it's acting survival reflex, he doesn't know. All he knows is that his head is raising from the floor at the same time his hands and arms are bringing his rifle to bear.

Jason's eyes meet the black pools of the creature's eyes as it looks at him, and it doesn't take its eyes off Jason as it slips and slides on the broken glass against the hard floor, trying to get up from where it landed. The male Zombie is almost up onto its haunches, its arms outstretched in front of it as it prepares to jump again, to jump at Jason, its grey translucent skinned face with a large fresh gash down the side which oozes dark red, almost black, blood, that drips onto the floor below. As the creature goes to jump, its grotesque mouth opens to reveal its black gums and yellow teeth, its lips all but disappearing as the mouth opens wider.

Jason is transfixed in fear, his body pushing back against the unmoveable wall, recoiling as far as he possibly can from the horrendous creature in front of him. Jason's finger is on the trigger of his rifle and somewhere in his mind, he knows he has to pull it, but his finger doesn't seem to understand or register the fear confusing his body's functions.

The Zombie has no such confusion. Like a starving animal out hunting, it only has one thought, to catch its prey. And it jumps.

As the Zombie jumps at him, Jason somehow resets his body's functions just enough and he pulls the rifle's trigger. The shot blasts out of the rifle and the bullet hits the flying Zombie's body. It tears right through its body and then carries on its trajectory into the wall on the opposite side of the classroom. The Zombie's body recoils from the bullet's force but not enough. It is going to land right on top of Jason!

If only the rifle had been switched to automatic.

In reflex, Jason's arms raise to protect him from the impact of the flying creature, bringing the rifle up with them. The Zombie lands on Jason and out of sheer luck, it's neck lands across the body of the rifle with a force that stuns it for a moment, but then it tries to press home its advantage and goes for Jason again.

The Zombie pushes forward, its face and teeth only centimetres away from Jason's face. It growls and gnashes its teeth, desperately trying to close the gap and to bite its prey's face. Jason, resists, his body now using all its strength to push back against the rifle, to push that mouth away from him. He doesn't even register the black blood and drool that are dripping down onto his face and neck, his only thought is to push and keep the creature off.

His arms are failing him though, he can feel it, the strength gradually sapping away from them. *Push, push,* he desperately thinks, but the Zombie is winning, drawing its mouth closer a millimetre at a time, its strength overpowering his arms. Jason looks into the creature's deadly eyes; is that going to be the last image he sees before the end?

Multiple gunshots erupt from Jason's left as Tyrone opens up his SA80 rifle into the creature that is attacking his comrade. Tyrone's shots are good, measured, targeted to the Zombie's body to ensure he doesn't hit Jason, but they don't seem to have much effect. The creature is still alive and still attacking. Thinking quickly, Tyrone flicks the rifle out of automatic, aims and takes a single shot to the Zombie's head.

The Zombie's body immediately drops and goes limp, only its head staying up, held up by Jason. Tyrone steps forward and raises his foot, pushing it against the creature's body which slowly rolls over until it flops off Jason and lands on the floor next to him.

Jason seems frozen, his arms still raised, holding his rifle in mid-air as if he is still holding off the Zombie. Tyrone lowers himself down to Jason, whose eyes are wide. Still and in shock, his face is a mess, the left side and his lower chin and neck covered in a red/black substance.

"Jason, it's dead, you're okay," Tyrone tells him, "talk to me mate, can you hear me?"

Slowly, Jason starts to come around, his eyes start to blink and close a bit to a more normal size and his arms slowly relax and lower the rifle.

"Is it dead?" Jason eventually says.

"Yes mate, it is, but we need to go, more might be coming."

The thought of more coming seems to spring Jason back to life and he starts to get up; he tries too quickly though. His head goes dizzy, so he has to stop on one knee to give time for oxygen to replace whatever chemicals his brain was flooded with, to keep going in the creature's attack.

He knows he is in shock; his limbs are cold and shaking and he feels very queasy, but he can't try to recover here. *Tyrone is right, more are probably coming, especially following all the noise that has just happened.*

The dizziness eases off, so Jason tries again to get to his feet and with the help of Tyrone, he manages it.

"Where is Den?" Jason asks.

"He went off to find the staff toilets; he wouldn't use the children's ones we came across, funny bugger."

"He has his moments, but we need to find him and get back to our Squad, I think they are under attack," Jason tells Tyrone. "Are the back playing fields clear?

Tyrone eases over towards the back of the classroom, the glass from the smashed back window crunching under his feet into even smaller shards as he goes, stepping slowly towards it, his rifle up, at the ready.

"It looks clear. I think you were unlucky and got a stray one," he says.

"Unlucky is one way to describe it, I can't believe how fast and strong that thing was, I thought I'd had it! You killed it just in time. Thanks, I owe you one," Jason tells him seriously.

"No need to thank me, bro, we got each other's backs," Tyrone says as he comes back across the room.

"No doubt, but thanks."

"Come on, let's go and find Denny boy," Tyrone says, slaps Jason on the back and they leave the carnage of the classroom behind.

Chapter 11

"Any idea where the staff toilets are?" Jason asks.

"No, but I guess they will be by the main entrance to the school, so this way," Tyrone replies, taking the lead.

The two men make their way through the dim corridors of the school, moving as quickly as they can, but deliberately, covering each other and checking their corners, taking no chances after what has just happened.

As they approach the main entrance to the school, the light increases somewhat, the sun coming through the large windows of the square open area adjacent to the main doors. There is a reception desk at the side to greet visitors that come through the main doors, and various offices around the perimeter, but they can't see any toilets.

"Where the fuck is, he?" Tyrone asks.

"That's got to be the Assembly Hall through those doors," Jason says pointing to a set of double doors opposite the main doors. "The staff toilets must be down that corridor there," Jason's arm moves to point down a corridor opposite them on the other side of the square.

"Cover me," Tyrone tells Jason and he steps out from the corridor to cross the square; he's crouched down, his rifle aimed in front of him, and it swings from side to side as he crosses, checking blind spots. He reaches the other side and he immediately backs up against the opposite wall and points his rifle back towards Jason to cover him as he crosses.

Jason crosses the square and enters the new corridor straight away, hoping the staff toilets are near; they are, just inside the corridor, on the left.

"Here they are," Jason informs Tyrone, who backs up towards him, keeping his rifle trained on their rear.

"Go and get him, I'll cover us from out here," Tyrone says.

Jason lets his rifle down, its strap holding it against the front of his body and he pops the holster on his hip open and takes out his Glock sidearm, which is far more suitable for confined spaces. Holding the pistol up but close to him in his right hand, he pushes the door of the Gents' toilet open with his left and enters.

A second door is just in front of him and he pushes this one only slightly open and peers into the toilets through the crack.

"Den, you in here?" he says quietly, but no answer comes.

Surely Den hasn't decided to use the Ladies', Jason thinks to himself, *Den can be a strange one sometimes and I wouldn't put it past him… There is only one way to find out.* He pushes the door open wider and goes in.

Jason sees the feet first, sticking out of the end cubicle, along the floor and he immediately feels his body tighten. Something is horribly wrong. He goes in further towards the cubical and as he does, he hears a squelching sound. Fear is now coursing through his body again and he fights the urge to retreat back into the corridor, to tell Tyrone and get him to come back with him; his mate needs help and there isn't a second to lose. Jason takes three quick steps forward and turns swiftly into the open cubicle, his Glock out in front of him at arm's length now, his finger on the trigger.

Den's face stares at Jason, his head pointing to the right and propped up against the base of the toilet. Den's eyelids quiver a small amount, but all the colour has disappeared from the skin of his blood-splattered face. And he must see Jason's arrival because his mouth opens slightly in a futile attempt to try and say something to him.

Jason's fear is partly replaced by rage, rage at the creature that is on top of Den, its head buried into the side of Den's neck, the top of the head moving as it eats. Jason himself had been so close to this fate only minutes ago, but Tyrone had found him just in time. He only wishes he could have been there for Den.

The shot rings out around the close confines of the toilets as Jason shoots the Zombie in the back of the head if only that gave him any satisfaction, it doesn't, all he feels is disappointment and sorrow that he wasn't in time to save his friend.

Quickly holstering his weapon, Jason drags the creature off Den, his anger giving him the strength to pull it out of the cubicle before he slams the limp body against the nearest wall. He then goes back into the cubicle to try and help his friend, even though Jason knows it is too late, the mission briefing making it very clear what happened if you were bitten. Den is not moving at all now, even his eyes are still, the quivering ceased. There is no sign of life at all, and there doesn't even seem to be any blood coming out of his horrific neck wound.

Jason barely hears Tyrone come into the toilets and stand behind him at the cubicle's opening.

"Bloody hell, man, how did that get in here? Err fuck, sorry Jay, this is bad," Tyrone says, stumbling over his words before gathering himself. "Jay, we gotta go, sorry about Den, but we gotta go. They could be anywhere, that shot was loud!"

"Okay, just give me a second to think!" Jason barks.

"We gotta go, man," Tyrone says, getting panicked.

"I can't leave him like this." Just as Jason says it, Den's body starts to convulse.

Jason backs away from Den quickly, taken by surprise and not knowing what to expect next. The convulsing stops as quickly as it started though, and Den's body goes limp again. Jason takes his Glock back out of its holster and aims it at Den's forehead.

"Whoa, what you doing?" Tyrone exclaims.

"He's going to turn; I'm not going to let that happen to him."

Jason refocuses his aim and goes to shoot, but can't seem to pull the trigger. He tries to block out Den's face, but it's still there, looking at him. He tries to shoot again, his face grimacing, but he fails. He is just about to give up when Den starts convulsing, badly this time, and he doesn't stop. Jason steels himself, aims, and shoots his friend in the head. Den's body goes limp.

"Let's go," Jason tells Tyrone as he pushes past him.

They both have to put these recent appalling events out of their minds, and they both know that without it being said, they need to be fully focused if they are going to get out of this building and back to their Squad—if their Squad is even still alive?

Jason takes the lead as they exit the toilets and he quickly takes the decision not to go back the way they came. The Zombie that got Den must have wandered in through the open alleyway door into the building, and that means there could be more in that direction, so Jason takes them left out of the toilets.

Moving slowly, Jason's rifle aims forward up the new corridor while Tyrone's rifle aims backwards, covering their rear. At the first door on the left, they come to a stop. Jason is planning to go into the first room on the left of the corridor they find, open the window and get out of it, and that will place them at the front of the building and closer to the road leading out of the school, up to the red gate.

He tries the door handle, but the door is locked, and Tyrone gives him a pissed-off look when the door doesn't open. There is one more door on the left side further down the corridor; they both hope for better luck there and move on.

The two men breathe a sigh of relief as the door starts to open. Jason takes it slowly though, his rifle aiming into the gap and moving with the door as he swings it open to reveal an empty classroom. As he is about to step into the unfamiliar classroom, there is a definite echoing noise from somewhere inside the school, from the direction of the alleyway door. Swiftly, they both go into the classroom and quietly shut the door behind them.

"I'll check the windows, see what you can put up against that door to wedge it," Jason instructs Tyrone.

As Jason approaches the windows, he does so slowly, studying the carpark and grounds outside them; he's not sure he could handle another Zombie smashing through the glass again. It all looks clear, so he goes over to the only one of the windows that opens, praying that it does open and isn't locked. With another sigh of relief, the white handle pulls up and the window cracks open, letting a breeze that smells of smoke hit Jason's face and increasing the sound of gunfire.

"We're in business," Jason tells Tyrone in a loud whisper.

"Let's get outta here then, before we have visitors," he responds as he finishes putting one of the small tables under the door handle.

Jason, pushes the window wide open, climbs up onto the cupboard in front of the window, stoops and jumps down the short distance onto a small grass verge that is between the building and the tarmac. Tyrone is covering him as he goes. As soon as he lands, he moves to the side and crouches down, his back against the building, his rifle up and scanning to cover Tyrone's jump.

With them both out, Tyrone pushes the window closed before they move right towards the small road, staying close to the building and using it as cover. At the end of the building, Jason peers around the corner, down towards the playing fields. When he is sure it's clear, he signals to Tyrone, who immediately runs, staying low across the small carpark to the flowerbed and trees beyond. Tyrone then nestles into the greenery, his camouflaged uniform doing its job and he covers Jason's run. They repeat this well-trained method, one covering the other like clockwork as they move up the road towards the red gate.

Jason is now one move away from the red gate, covering Tyrone from the side of the road, when he sees it; a Zombie comes out from behind the far side of the school building and onto the road. *Shit, it's too late to stop Tyrone!* He's already moving towards Jason's position, and Jason holds his breath waiting to see if it sees Tyrone.

For a moment, Jason thinks the Zombie isn't going to see him, and it looks like it's looking elsewhere. Jason is wrong; the Zombie does see Tyrone moving and immediately it takes off, sprinting unbelievably fast at him and as it does, it lets off a ferociously loud scream.

Tyrone stumbles as he hears the scream, as if the scream physically jolts him and he nearly goes down, he manages to correct the stumble brilliantly though and he keeps going, not daring to look around. Tyrone races past Jason and is getting near to the gate, but the Zombie is catching him fast. Jason is quite sure that the Zombie hasn't seen him in the undergrowth, so he waits, surprising himself by how calm he feels, as this female creature tears up the short road, nearing his position. When the Zombie gets within ten feet of Jason, he opens fire on it, shooting a short burst into its legs, which are ripped from beneath it and it goes down hard, its face smashing into the road. Jason immediately breaks cover, stands and shoots the withering creature through the head, he then turns and makes a break for the gate, reaching it in seconds, he jumps, placing one hand on top of the gate to help him glide over the top of it. Tyrone, is already over, with his rifle aimed over the gate to cover Jason's retreat.

"That was bloody well done, thanks mate, they are so fast, aren't they?" Tyrone says still aiming over the gate to check no more Zombies are coming. When he is satisfied there aren't, he ducks down behind the gate to join Jason who has taken a low position against the adjacent wall to cover the Barnard Road and to get his breath back.

"It would be amazing how fast they are if it wasn't so frightening mate," Jason replies to Tyrone.

They both go quiet for a moment, taking stock of their situation, which isn't very inviting. Gunfire and explosions are constantly sounding, it seems from all directions; some of it is far off, but that noise is overpowered by the closer sounds of battle, the majority of which seems to be coming from the direction of the main road where they last saw their squad. Neither of them would have imagined that when they had left their Squad only a short time ago and they saw the poor people stuck in their houses, that they would be now jealous of those people and the relative security those buildings are affording them. The temptation to knock on the nearest door and take shelter is very tempting, especially from their exposed current position. Who knows, they may even be offered a cup of tea and a biscuit?

"Are you ready?" Jason asks Tyrone, drowning any thoughts of them bugging out.

"No time like the present, my good friend."

So, they move, leaving even the small bit of cover offered by the corner of the gate and wall behind. As soon as they turn right onto Barnard Road, they can see the junction with the main road. Somehow, they both remembered it being farther when they ran down from it to the school. Thankfully, it still looks relatively quiet on Barnard Road. They don't take any chances though and move from one covering position to the next, working their way up to the junction, which they are both dreading reaching. Neither of them sees any people peering out of their windows as they go; the residents have retreated to take refuge wherever they feel safest in their homes, and who can blame them, with a battle against the Undead taking place one street over!

Before they know it, Jason and Tyrone have reached the junction, stopping only about two meters away from it to assess what is actually happening, taking shelter in the opening to a path that leads up to a front door. Their vantage point is useless, however; all they can see is the junction and some of the main road that leads out of the city, which all looks the same as when they left apart from the smoke haze now hanging over the junction. The smoke is drifting up from where the battle is and from the noise alone, it is obvious they need to move position to get a look down the road towards the city.

"Cover me, I'm going to have a look around the corner," Jason tells Tyrone and starts to inch out of the opening and around to the right, following the low wall that traverses around the corner of the road. Passing the Barnard Road sign, he gets closer to getting a view, his head darting from one side to the other constantly looking for threats that might spring out of nowhere. Gunfire cracks and explosions are now loud and close; he gets down onto his belly, his rifle gripped in both hands out in front and he crawls the last meter or so. His legs and feet help push him forward and gradually the battle scene reveals itself to Jason's unwanting eyes.

At first, Jason's shock is subdued by his confusion, and he struggles to make sense of the scene being acted out around 100 meters down the road. Trying to get his head around it, he is hampered further by all the smoke that blurs the view. His first impression is of a riot; there are agitated figures moving all over the wide road, and they seem to be concentrated around a mound in the middle. Then he sees it, his brain contorting as the realisation sinks in and suddenly, the shock hits him.

Machine-gun fire is erupting from the mound; it's the Warrior, the Warrior is buried under a mound of Zombies, hundreds, if not thousands of them covering it completely, apart from the opening where the machine gun is firing.

Someone is firing that machine gun, so the crew or at least one of them must still be alive inside the Warrior, but where is the rest of their Squad? Jason searches the mob, but he can't see any Squad members. Have they retreated, are they dead or worse?

Jason concentrates, looking closer, and eventually makes out one of the figures that looks like it is wearing camouflage but he isn't fighting; he is climbing up the mound, ignored by all around, and he is going to the side of the small opening where the machine gun is firing. The figure, who is definitely in camouflage, stands and starts strangely clawing at its front. The figure then falls to the side straight in front of the machine gun opening, and as it does, the figure explodes into a ball of flames and smoke. As the smoke slowly clears, there is one thing missing; the sound of the machine gun has been silenced.

"It sounds like World War Three! What is going on, how are the lads getting on?" Tyrone says from behind Jason, his legs bent and his back pinned to the low wall, his rifle aimed outwards.

Jason doesn't know how to answer Tyrone's question, as he can't find the words.

"Jay?"

"It's terrible, have a look for yourself," Jason eventually says, rolling onto his side to look at Tyrone.

Both men's concentration drops for a moment as they prepare to swap positions and they don't see it until it's almost upon them—and by then, it is too late to react. A tall long-haired male Zombie runs down the centre of the main road, its long black coat raised into the air, flowing behind it from the speed it is travelling at. Jason, panicking, tries to bring his rifle into some kind of firing position but he is too slow.

The creature doesn't slow or move in their direction; it stares straight at them though, and then, as it draws level with the two of them, its mouth opens and it lets out a ferocious ear-piercing scream in their direction, its grey, vile dead face and black eyes crawling with evil malice.

Inexplicably, the creature doesn't attack, but it runs right past them, runs towards the battle ahead of it, seeming to pick up even more speed, almost floating above the road.

Jason finally has his rifle in a position to shoot. He is too stunned to shoot, however, and too late, the creature is gone. The two men watch it go until they see it jump far into the air, flying into the centre of the melee.

"What the fuck," Tyrone manages to say eventually. Jason is still too stunned to speak. "It ran right past us, why didn't it attack us, Jay?"

I don't know," Jason manages to say eventually, "I think there is more going on here than meets the eye... these Zombies aren't just mindless animals, there is at least some remanence of intelligence left. I saw one in a combat uniform claw away at his front and then explode; he must have been pulling the pins on his grenades, so he knew they were there and what they did?"

"What we gonna do now Jay, our Squad is gone? What we supposed to do now and where is the aircover?"

"I don't know, maybe it had to refuel or it ran out of ammo?" Jason replies.

"Come on man, you're the Team Leader, what we gonna do now?"

"We're too exposed out here, we got to get off the street, regroup and see if we can raise somebody on comms," Jason says, his wits returning.

"Let's try comms now," Tyrone suggests.

"No, we got to get off the street and find cover first!"

Jason gets to his feet and joins Tyrone low against the wall, and he starts looking for possible shelter they can make use of. Nothing presents itself; he won't go knocking on any doors, asking the residents to help them, he won't put them at risk any more than they already are, so he is looking for an empty property.

"Let's try going back down Barnard Road, look for an empty house or something," Jason tells Tyrone. He doesn't want to go back down there, but the alternatives are worse.

The two men only catch a glimpse of the Fast Jet as it flies at a tremendous speed overhead of them, down the main road towards the battle and the Warrior, the roar of the jet as it passes confirming to them that they didn't imagine it.

"Take cover!" Jason manages to shout seconds before the immense explosion hits.   Both men drop, hitting the pavement, their arms going over their heads to try and protect themselves from the explosion. A bright flash of light pierces through their feeble defences immediately, very closely followed by the sound of the deafening explosion and the shockwave that shakes the very ground beneath them. The resulting gale-force wind assaults them as the atmosphere around the area is forced away from the impact faster than the speed of sound.

The wind dies down and Jason turns his head slightly, daring to look at the impact from beneath his arms. He cannot see the impact though; all he can see is smoke and dust that rises into the air in the shape of a mushroom.

"Are you okay?" Jason asks Tyrone.

"Yeah man, I think so," he says into the ground.

"Stay down, the flying debris hasn't hit yet," Jason orders.

Even from their distance, the debris comes down, chunks of rubble and metal raining down onto them; thankfully, they seem to be far enough away to be out of range of the big chunks and it quickly subsides to be replaced by dust and ash.

Jason moves as soon as he feels it is safe; they have definitely got to retreat now, and if any of the of Zombies survived the explosion, there is no telling in which direction they will be going.

"Let's go," he tells Tyrone urgently as he gets to his feet.

Both men are up on their feet ready to evacuate the area. They struggle to move, however, they just stand there on the corner of the junction, looking at the devastation spread out before them.

Thick smoke and dust hang in the air where the bomb hit like a death shroud hanging over it, blurring their view. The two men stand there like tourists on a beach waiting for the sun to set as they wait for the smoke to dissipate. They can see the damage the bomb has caused all the way up the road from the epicentre, and all but a few of the windows in the houses they can see are shattered, blown inwards and debris covering the road, pavements and front gardens, up to and far past their position. And dust rains down all around.

Their attention is drawn back to ground zero as the smoke does eventually start to thin somewhat and the devastation there is almost total. A crater sinks deep into the ground where the Warrior was; it has been vaporised completely and the area around the crater is scorched completely from the searing heat, almost completely burnt to black.

It is the houses on either side of the road in the immediate vicinity that shake them to their core. The front facades of at least five or six of the houses on both sides of the road are absolutely demolished and the damage continues inside to the inner or even back walls of these houses. Any residents hiding and taking shelter in those houses were doomed. The damage to the houses continues up the road, diminishing the farther away from ground zero they are, but their damage is still extensive. Black smoke rises from them as fires burn in the remnants of the buildings.

"There had to be people in those houses," Tyrone says, "families, children! How could they bomb it?"

"Collateral damage, I'm afraid," Jason replies, solemnly.

"Look!" Tyrone says, pointing, "are those survivors?"

Jason's eyes flick back to the epicentre and through the smoke, there are figures appearing slowly from the devastation. There are survivors and more getting up from the ground constantly; these survivors are not human though. Even from their distance away, it is obvious. Unbelievably, even around the area close to the crater that is burnt to black, the ground moves like black tar, as slowly the creatures attempt to raise themselves, their burnt skin indistinguishable from the singed black ground.

Bodies raise up closer to them too, the shockwave having blasted them all the way up the road. Jason and Tyrone can see these clearly, can see the injuries they have sustained that, if they were human, would be incapacitating or terminal. Bodies are broken and arms are missing. Even the creatures missing lower limbs are coming back to life and moving any way they can, the horrible injuries not stopping these creatures.

A close one lets out a blood-curdling screech and both men know it is directed at them, as well as to tell its kin that fresh prey is close!

"Retreat?" Tyrone asks urgently.

"Definitely," Jason replies.

Chapter 12

From what I've seen on the screens, Military Command's and Colonel Reed's Operation Denial isn't going to plan. *It's going to shit and quickly*, Andy thinks to himself. Granted, that was only one Squad in a small area of the city, but they were swamped and overrun before they had travelled even two klicks into the city, the poor buggers.

The Apache ran out of ammo, became a lame duck and had to return to base. It hardly made a dent in the enemy, there were simply too many Rabids and they stayed spread out, not giving the Apache a decent target to get its teeth into. But as soon as the Apache flew off, the Rabids massed, attacking the Warrior, throwing themselves into its tracks and swarming all over it until it stopped moving and was disabled, the whole sorry episode just going desperately downhill from there.

Andy has the monitors turned off, the team needs to prepare now, without distraction, for their mission—and with less than three hours to go, there is a lot that needs to be done.

Lieutenant Winters is proving invaluable in aiding their preparations, his organisational skills astounding. Problems arise and he fixes them. He seems to know who to contact, where to go and how to overcome almost any situation or issue that arises and when they hit a wall, he will traverse that wall or offer an effective alternative.

The safe issue, for example... Sergeant Dixon briefed him, and he immediately contacted the SecLock head office, his phone call coming out of the blue at the company. Within around five minutes, he had talked his way up to be speaking to the Commercial Director of the company and demanded that they provide the information Sergeant Dixon needed for the safe as a matter of national security. Here he hit a wall; the Commercial Director point-blank refused to furnish him with the information. The Lieutenant didn't lose his temper or make any threats, he simply thanked the gentleman and put the phone down. He then got his mobile phone out, looked through his contacts put the phone to his ear, and he was then, we found out after the call, speaking to the Deputy Director General of MI5, the second-in-command of the Security Service. Within a few minutes of that call ending, the Commercial Director of SecLock had phoned him back, apologised profusely and emailed over all the information the company had for Sir Malcolm's safe, the information that Sergeant Dixon is now poring over.

We frankly stood watching the Lieutenant in awe as he did his work and when it was done, Lieutenant Winters didn't grandstand or look for plaudits, he simply moved onto the next task at hand. None of us was left in any doubt why Colonel Reed kept him as his assistant and we're grateful he has been loaned to us for this mission.

"Okay, Boss, what's next?" Dan asks.

"What's the time now?"

"1135 hours," he tells me.

"Okay, that's twenty-five minutes until the helicopters are due to land here; how's the equipment coming?" I ask him.

"All but ready to load. It'll be done by the time they get here," Dan tells me as we both look over to Josh and Alice, who are doing the last-minute prep on it.

"Well, I think this mission plan is as good as it's going to get," I say, standing up from the table. "The first thing we will do when the helicopters arrive is get the pilots in here so we can brief everybody on the plan before we load up. I am going to talk to Josh and Alice now, and I don't want any protests or distractions while the briefing is underway."

"Agreed, I'll get them into the office. It's tight but we should all fit in, just about," Dan says.

"Okay, let me get seated first."

"Of course, Boss, go and get yourself comfy," he says, smiling, and I roll my eyes.

Things are moving on, I think to myself as I go to the office, the two Lynx helicopters that Lieutenant Winter has arranged and that we will fly in on will be here in no time, and then the countdown will really start to wind up.

I squeeze around the desk and sit down into the chair, and as soon as I do, I see Dan approach with Josh and Alice.

The two younger members of the Team stand to attention at the not so far end of the room and Dan stands to the side of the desk with his back to me, looking at them, waiting for me to start.

"At ease," I tell them before I start and they both relax, their hands going behind their backs; their faces do give away their nerves, however. "Dan and I have completed the mission plan and I wanted to talk to you two before the main briefing so you are clear what you will be doing to help the mission to a successful conclusion, okay?"

"Yes Sir," they both reply.

"Each of you will be assigned to one of the Lynx and your tasks will be to provide air cover while the rest of the team are on the ground, is that clear?" I tell them.

"Yes Sir," they both say, less enthusiastically.

"We don't know what we are going find when we get down, so your job is going to be vital to the mission. You are going to have our backs and I know you are both up to the task; any questions?"

"If I may, Sir?" Josh says.

"Carry on, Josh."

"Wouldn't we be more useful on the ground with the team? Like you said, we don't know what we are going to find and surely as many boots on the ground as possible would be an advantage... and I know the terrain?" Josh says, with his chin up.

"We don't have any more men, Josh, and the team is set. I know you want to get into the action, but we need air cover and you two have that task; I can't afford to lose any of the other men off the ground, and besides, this is what they train for," I tell him.

"What about..."

"No Josh, you have your orders, is that understood?"

"Yes," he pauses, but I wait, "Sir."

"Alice, have you anything to say?"

"No Sir, only that you can count on me, Sir."

"Thank you, Alice."

"Dan, anything to add?"

"I don't think so, I know these two are up to it. They will have the best seats for the show," he says.

"Thank you for the insight, Dan. Okay, let's get ready for the Lynx to arrive. Dismissed."

Josh and Alice briefly stand to attention, turn and leave the office.

"Well?" I ask Dan.

"Didn't go too bad, Josh was bound to want to go in with you. He'll be okay, I'll have a chat with him."

Lieutenant Winters knocks on the window to get our attention; he is holding up the telephone.

"What's this?" I say, getting a bad feeling.

I take the phone off the Lieutenant who is looking serious, and he mouths to me that it is Colonel Reed; this isn't going to be good.

"Colonel?"

"Richards, how is your preparation coming along?"

"We will be ready to go on time," I tell him.

"We have had to move that time forward. Richards, I need you in the air by 1345 hours, I have spoken to Winters and he says that is achievable, agreed?"

"That would be a rush, Colonel, and is not preferable for the mission; what is the reason?" I question.

"Operation Denial is having very mixed results," the Colonel tells me, unsurprisingly. "It could go either way and the Prime Minister wants contingencies and wants them now. Major Reese believes that if Sir Malcolm did keep the records and details of this strain of virus, then they could be vital in formulating a way to halt its spread or even cure it. The PM has been briefed with that theory so you can imagine the pressure he is applying; he wants the contents of that safe at Porton Down in the quickest possible time frame. He has ordered the mission be brought forward, apart from which the weather forecast is deteriorating and storms are likely from 1600 hours, which is terribly bad luck all round!"

"I see; he does know that there's no guarantee these files are in the safe?"

"Of course, he bloody does, man, but we won't know either way until we have looked, will we?" the Colonel barks.

"Understood, Colonel, I will pull the mission forward."

"Put me back on to Winters," the Colonel orders without any sign of an acknowledgement.

"God wants you," I tell the Lieutenant sarcastically and hand him back the phone,

"Heads up!" I shout across the hangar and everyone looks in my direction. "The mission is pulled forward; we take off at 1345 hours."

Josh and Alice look at each other warily while the Special Forces guys just nod and go back to their preparations. It's par for the course for them, as they are well used to mission timings changing at the drop of a hat.

"What's Reed saying now?" Dan asks me.

"Nothing new really, only that the PM is pinning his hopes on this safe by the sounds of it and therefore the whole country is… he wants the mission done A-SAP and so has ordered it pulled forward."

"No pressure then?" Dan jokes.

"He did tell me that the weather is going to get worse, possible storms at 1600 hours."

"That could be bad news, so I'll see if I can get any more detail on that," Dan says seriously.

With about ten minutes until the two Lynx are due to arrive, I go over to see how Sergeant Dixon is getting on with planning the safe crack. He has set up a table and is leaning over it, looking at the information and schematics SecLock emailed over to us. With him are Corporal Simms, the SAS Team Leader, and Lance Corporal Watts, the demolitions expert from the SAS troop. I am hoping they have identified a method to open the safe because if they haven't, we will have to revert to good old-fashioned brute force.

The men don't get up or stand to attention when I arrive, and I didn't expect them to; these are Special Forces Operatives. They do greet me with a few 'Sirs', but don't stop their discussions or planning, nor would I want them to. I do need to know what they have discovered, however.

"Report," I say.

"Sir," Dixon says, as he does stand up to address me directly. "The details of the safe sent over are extensive, but the bad news is that there is no way to override the electronic lock without disassembling the input facility, the keypad, Sir. The good news is that with the right equipment the good Lieutenant is arranging for us, we can take the input facility apart and should be able to override the locking mechanisms electronics and open it. That's the good news, Sir, but it will take a bit of time."

"Specifically, how much time, Sergeant?"

"Without a test run, I can't say for sure, Sir?"

"Best estimate then Sergeant?"

"Ten to fifteen minutes, Sir, maybe twenty."

"Are you certain this method will work?" I ask.

"Eighty percent, Sir; we are confident that we will be able to open the safe with a high-voltage portable plasma cutter; the Lieutenant is arranging for one as a back-up, Sir."

"Why don't we just cut it open then?"

"Cutting it open would take longer, approximately thirty minutes, possibly more—and it runs the risk of damaging the contents, Sir."

"Is there another back-up plan, Sergeant? We won't be cutting it open; we cannot risk damaging the contents," I tell him.

The Sergeant pauses for a moment, "back to plan A Sir, break it free from the floor and take the whole thing with us. From what you described, we can use the plasma cutter to cut it free, rather than using explosives, Sir."

"Very good, Sergeant, that is the back-up plan in case the electronics thing doesn't work. I want your full attention and concentration on cracking the electronics, so study the schematics, draw it up on paper and imagine the steps in your head, whatever it takes to get it printed into your brain, understood?"

"Yes Sir," he says vigorously.

"Lance Corporal Watts," I call.

"Yes, Sir."

"Have you used a plasma cutter before?"

"Yes, Sir."

"Good, are you familiar with the one you will be using?"

"I don't know until it arrives, Sir."

"Well, when it gets here, I want you to familiarise yourself with it. You are tasked with cutting the safe free if needed. I want you to ensure it is working, so practice with it, find something to test it on; cut the axles through on one of the vehicles outside if you need to, just make sure it works, as we can't afford any surprises, understood?"

"Yes, Sir," Watts says over-enthusiastically.

"Carry on," I tell them and leave them to their work.

The other Special Forces men are double-checking their kit and getting what they need over by the roller shutter door, ready to load onto the Lynx. There isn't that much kit to load, most of it staying in piles on the floor of the hangar. We are flying in on a short mission so it is mainly only combat equipment, firearms basically, and there is no need for provisions or sleeping gear, etc.

Josh and Alice have finished checking the equipment that was here when we arrived at the hangar. They have identified what equipment we will need and what is surplus to requirements, also. I go over to check how they have done.

"Good job you two, there is enough firepower here to start a small war," I say looking around the equipment.

"It's not far off," Josh says. "How are you feeling about this mission, Dad?"

I notice Josh call me Dad; he could be looking for some fatherly reassurance, and I guess he and Alice both are. They are both young and quite green, and the action they went through yesterday was their first real experience of battle. It takes time to sink in and come to terms with. I know that very well.

"I'm confident; we have an achievable goal, a top-notch team and Dan." My joke has the desired effect by lifting the mood slightly. "Are you two okay with your mission roles?"

"I am, Andy," Alice says, "the mission comes first, and you need your best people on the ground. I understand that we will cover your backs, won't we Josh?"

"Yes Dad, I'm good with it. You have got to concentrate on the mission and I would be a distraction down there for you. Alice is right, you can count on us," Josh says and then taking me by surprise, he comes and gives me a man hug. "You've got this, Dad," he tells me into my ear, and I squeeze him tighter.

"Thanks, Champ," I tell him as we release. "I wasn't expecting that," I say pointing to the new men with my eyes.

"They know you're my Dad, I was speaking to them earlier and they were asking about you, so I told them. They ribbed me a bit, but only banter, they seem good lads."

"Yes, they do," I agree. "Right, the transport will be landing anytime now, so let's get the roller shutter open."

"Boss, can I have a word?" Dan says, he is sitting with Lieutenant Winters.

"I'll do the roller shutter," Josh volunteers.

I tell him thanks as I go over to Dan and the Lieutenant.

"What's up?"

"The weather the Colonel mentioned, it looks like it's going to be bad and I mean really bad. The forecast says thunder and lightning and storm-force winds for the London area," Dan tells me with a stern look on his face, knowing the implications for the mission.

"Time?"

"Still estimated for 1600 hours, but that's an estimate, it could come in earlier?"

"Bloody hellfire!" I curse our luck and turn away from the two men to think.

I hear the motor of the roller shutter start up; it freewheels for a second until the slack is taken up and the lifting starts; it knocks constantly then as each separate slat starts to lift, and it then whines all the way up until it comes to a juddering halt at the top.

A weather forecast as bad as this has serious ramifications for any mission, and many I have been involved in have been bumped to the next day or cancelled completely because of such a forecast. To make matters worse, we are flying in and that can't be changed; there is no option to adapt and drive in instead for obvious reasons, and this mission cannot be cancelled, so I don't need the Colonel to tell me that. Suddenly, Josh and Alice staying on the helicopters isn't looking so secure. Fucking Hell!

"Okay, we are still a go," I tell the two men, urgently. "We will go as soon as we are ready. We can still get in and out before the weather comes in, agreed?"

"Yes, Boss, agreed, it's tight but do-able."

"What's the ETA on the Lynx?" I ask the Lieutenant.

"Inbound, Captain, two or three minutes."

"Okay, good," I say trying to sound positive. "And the other equipment we need?"

"All the equipment is loaded onto the Lynx," the Lieutenant informs me.

"Very good. Dan, inform the men please, no mistakes, but we need to go as soon as we are ready, briefing as soon as the pilots arrive." Dan gets up and heads off to inform the men.

"Anything else we need to know?" I ask the Lieutenant.

"I have set up communications, Captain, I will oversee the mission from here, I have secured our own channel so we are set at my end, and I have nothing else to report."

"Thank you, Lieutenant."

Josh and Alice are over by the roller shutter, basking in the fickle sun, watching for the helicopters approach. I walk over to them.

"Everything okay?" Josh asks.

"Storms are forecast at 1600 hours. We are pulling the mission forward again, and we go as soon as we are ready," I tell both Josh and Alice.

"You Brits and your weather, can't you sort it out?" Alice jokes.

"I wish we could," I tell the American.

"This looks like our transport," Josh says, his hand above his eyes to shield them from the sun as he points into the air.

"Transport inbound!" I shout into the hangar as I see the two helicopters approaching, so that everyone is aware things are about to speed up.

Dan and a few of the other lads come over to see, but Sergeant Dixon and the two other men stay inside to concentrate on the mission goal.

As the first Lynx homes in on our position, Corporal Downey steps out onto the concrete expanse outside the hangar, heading to the right past the vehicles that are parked up, and he starts to signal to the helicopter's pilot. He is directing the first Lynx to land to its left-hand side of the hangar and sure enough, the pilot starts his descent following the Corporal's direction.

As the Lynx closes in on its landing spot, we start to feel the downdraft and the decibels start to rise from its rotors and engine. The pilot brings the helicopter in swiftly, lifting the nose as he angles in, almost as if he knows the urgency of the turnaround we need to achieve. Corporal Downey is directing him all the way. The wind gets severe as the pilot descends the last few meters to the ground and I can imagine Sergeant Dixon behind me holding his paper plans down, so they aren't blown and scatter everywhere. He's cursing.

The first Lynx touches down with a bump and immediately, the pilot kills its engines, this gives us small respite though, because the second is already making its approach and coming in just as swiftly as the first. Corporal Dixon has run over to the left of us so that he can aid the second pilot with his descent and before we know it, the two Lynx helicopters that will transport us on our mission are parked up in front of us!

"Well done, Corporal," I congratulate as the noise of the second engine winds down.

The first pilot is already climbing down from his ride and the second one is opening his door to get out. I walk out to greet the first pilot as he hits the ground. To my relief, the first pilot isn't a youngster like the one we managed to overpower so easily yesterday, on top of the Orion building. This one is more mature and judging from his descent, is a very capable pilot.

"Captain Richards," I say as I reach him, extending my hand.

"Wing Commander Buck," he says, shaking my hand firmly. "This is your mission isn't it, Captain?"

"Yes, and I assume you know the weather forecast?" I reply as we walk to meet the other pilot.

"I'm afraid we do; it is looking particularly bad. This is Flight Lieutenant Alders," the Wing Commander says as he introduces me to the other pilot, who is younger than him but still in his late twenties, I would estimate.

"Captain Richards." I introduce myself and shake his hand. "We are pulling the mission forward to as soon as we are ready to try and miss this weather, but my team need to familiarise themselves with the equipment you should have on board," I tell them both as we all walk back toward the hangar.

"All the equipment is on board my Lynx, Captain."

"Thank you, Wing Commander, I will get it unloaded," I say.

"Please call me Buck, Captain."

"Okay, thanks, Buck."

We enter the hangar and I ask Dan to get everyone together for the briefing.

"Oh, I nearly forgot," Buck says as he unslings a rifle from his shoulder. It was hanging on his back and I hadn't noticed. He hands me the rifle, an M4 Carbine, *my* M4 Carbine! "I was asked to make sure you got this," he tells me.

"Brilliant, thanks," I say as I look down at my M4 and then check it over. "Lieutenant Winters," I shout across the hangar, holding up the gun. "Thanks," I tell him when he looks up, he gives me a smile and little flick of a salute in acknowledgement. The M4 is as I left it, but I will check it over properly after the briefing; for now, I go over and put it on the table.

With my team now fully assembled, it's time to get the briefing done, so I turn from the table, crossing my arms across my chest ready, and wait for them all to gather from around the hangar.

"Gather 'round, gather 'round," Dan says as he arrives at my side and everyone quickly does. Josh and Alice are at the front right, the two pilots on the left, with the helicopters outside behind them through the open roller shutter, and the Special forces lads are mixed up in the middle and I am pleased to see them that way.

"Okay, firstly, thank you for your attention," I start. "You all know why we are here and how important this mission could prove to be; this virus has got to be stopped at all costs, for the sake of London and possibly the whole country, beyond even. I expect everybody to bring their A-game to this mission, full commitment and no excuses! We know the goal and we cannot fail, is that understood?"

"Yes Sir!" everybody says in unison.

"The pilots who have just arrived are Wing Commander Buck and Flight Lieutenant Alders, make yourself known to them. Wing Commander Buck will carry myself, the SBS Troop and Josh, while Dan, the SAS Troop and Alice will go with Flight Lieutenant Alders. That way, each Lynx will have one of the options for sorting the safe onboard. Lieutenant Winters will oversee the mission and comms from here, understood?"

"Yes, Sir."

"The bad news is that the weather is going to be shit at approximately 1600 hours, so we need to get underway as soon as we are all ready. I am particularly referring to Sergeant Dixon and Lance Corporal Watts; your equipment is here, so as soon as you are satisfied that you are set, we will get underway, so be as meticulous and as quick as you can. I know that is a contradiction, but that's the way it is, understood?"

"Yes Sir," both Dixon and Watts reply.

"Our plan is a simple one in theory, but it heavily depends on what we find when we get to the target as the aerial pictures will only tell us so much. We fly to the target, which is an estimated ten-minute flight time, and we'll recce the target area and eliminate any x-rays in the target area that may cause a threat, and then fast-rope onto the roof of the building. Josh and Alice will stay onboard the Lynx to provide air cover, so you two work with the two pilots to familiarise yourselves with the door guns, in case you need to use them.

"Once we are on the roof, the first thing is to make sure it is secure, Dan will brief you on the building layout and team areas in a minute.

"The following will stay on the roof to provide cover for the insertion team: Dan, Collins, O'Brien, Downey and Thomas, and again, Dan will give you your positions. That leaves the following as the insertion team to secure the safe: Dixon, Simms, Watts, Kim and me, understood?

"Yes, Sir,"

"Good, as soon as we have secured the contents of the safe, we get out and return to base. If you think this mission sounds easy, you are mistaken; we are going deep behind the enemy's lines, the enemy is fearless and ferocious, and it will go to any lengths to get its prey and that prey will be us. There will be no backup, we only have a small window of time and this mission cannot fail.

I have full confidence in this team and I'm confident the mission will be a success, so let's watch each other's backs and get this done!"

"Yes, Sir!" the whole team replies with determination.

"Dan will now go through the building's layout, team tasks and positions. All yours, Dan," I finish.

Dan turns to the flip chart easel standing next to him, with a hand-drawn plan of the building drawn in black marker pinned to the front. He starts to brief the team on the building's layout, including the roof and inner layout, paying particular attention to the layout of floor seven that the safe is on and Sir Malcolm's office. He points out on the drawing and explains to each member of the team their required positions both on and in the building in detail, and their tasks. He goes through it again and again; any questions are answered until everyone is certain where they need to be and what they need to be doing.

Dan wraps up his part of the briefing with some words of encouragement before handing back over to me.

"Thanks, Dan. Right, everybody knows where they need to be and what they need to be doing and if all goes to plan, we could be in and out in less than thirty minutes. We all have to be prepared for the unexpected, however; cracking the safe is a major potential bottleneck. If we have to go to plan B and cut the safe out, it is going to extend our time on the ground considerably, but we have to hold our positions until it is done. One way or the other, that safe is coming back with us, understood?" I tell them all.

"Yes, Sir."

"Okay, let's get moving, I want to be in the air A-SAP."

The briefing quickly breaks up and everybody moves onto their next task with purpose. The first thing to do is to get the new equipment off the helicopters and the team gets to it, while they introduce themselves to the two pilots as they go.

The first thing I see coming off Buck's Lynx is an oversized black hard plastic briefcase that I assume has the equipment Sergeant Dixon needs to override the safe's electronic lock. He brings the case straight into the hangar and places it on top of his table before flicking the latches free and opening it up.

Corporal Watts is next to come away from the Lynx carrying a brand-new boxed plasma cutter, while Lance Corporal Kim brings up his rear carrying a gas bottle, that I take it the plasma cutter requires. They both come inside with their kit and they go over to the far side of the hangar to set it up, out of everybody's way.

I have a sudden frightful thought when I see the plasma cutter come out of the box and they go to plug it into the wall; does the Orion building have power? It had lost power yesterday, before our retreat.

"Lieutenant," I say urgently as I rush over to him.

"Yes, Captain?"

"Can we confirm if the Orion building has power, there was a power cut yesterday, because that plasma cutter is going to be a useless dead weight without it?"

"I hadn't considered that; I'll see what I can find out, straight away," the Lieutenant replies, concerned.

"We can't afford any delays, Boss, the forecast is saying the storm is getting worse by the minute!" Dan tells me from his seat in front of one of the monitors that has the MOD weather forecast on it.

"Is there any good news?" I ask, joking in frustration.

"Looks like it's going to be fine tomorrow afternoon," Dan jokes back.

"That'll be right," I reply.

While Lieutenant Winters makes some calls to try and get an answer on the state of Orion's electricity, I ask Dan if we have any drones flying in the area that might give us some insight?

"Let me see," he says as his hand reaches for the computer mouse. "I don't know what it would show us; it is broad daylight, so we won't be able to see if there are any lights on?"

"We need a drone in the area anyway to get a fresh look at the target area before we go," I tell him.

"I'm on it, Boss," he tells me.

Turning away from the table to let the men do their jobs, I try to think if there is anything else we might have overlooked. This is always the trouble when a mission is planned for 'off the hip'; important aspects get overlooked and information that is vital gets missed completely and then the mission invariably can go South very quickly.

My mind is too flustered and cluttered to think properly, and I need to concentrate, I need to play the mission through in my mind.

"I'll be back in five minutes," I tell Dan, turning back to him.

"Okay, Boss, going anywhere nice?" he asks.

"I'm afraid not, mate, just want to think the mission through, see if I can think of anything else we have missed, I'll be outside."

"Okay, no worries, I'll be here, Boss."

Walking off, I head straight to the sunshine, outside, to leave the bustle of the preparations behind, for a short time. The men take no notice of me as I go, they are busy either testing their equipment or getting the equipment that is ready to go onto the helicopters.

I catch a glimpse of Alice with Flight Lieutenant Alders out by his Lynx and Josh is with Buck. Josh is seated behind the rotary barrel of that Lynx's minigun, Buck pointing as he takes Josh through how to operate it. Josh looks like he is eager to let it rip. I hope it doesn't come to that.

Going right out of the hangar, I carry on walking and look for a quiet spot that will give me some peace and quiet to think, if that is even possible at this busy airport.

Not far past the hangar, the building comes to an end and before the next one starts, there is a small alcove which is out of sight of the hangar but still close enough that if anyone shouts for me, I will still hear them. Beggars can't be choosers so this spot will have to do, and I go just around the corner and sit down on the tarmac. My back leans against the whitewashed wall and my knees bend up for my arms to rest on, then finally, I put my head back against the wall, the sun feeling good on my face as I let out a sigh.

My thoughts are not immediately centred on the mission, as my mind wanders to Emily, where she is now and what she is doing, hoping she is still okay. Then, I allow myself to think of Catherine for a moment; I am taken back to yesterday when she met us out of the lift at the Orion building. I can't help but think of how gorgeous and vibrant she looked in the red dress she had on, how it clung to her body as she walked in front of me and the long black zip that went all the way down the back. Will I ever be lucky enough to find out what that long zip was hiding? God, I hope so.

Forcing my mind back to reality, I have to leave those fleeting thoughts behind and get my head back in the game. I clear my mind and start to play out the mission in my head. I try to visualise the whole mission from when we take off to when we land back at Heathrow. Every part is thought out, and I try to envisage each step that has to be taken to carry out the mission, much like a sprinter does just before the starting gun is fired. There is so much more to visualise for this than a sprinter must for their ten-second sprint.

I open my eyes after several minutes and look down, staring at the tarmac, feeling as though I have accomplished nothing. There are just too many variables to consider and too many things I can imagine going wrong; there are threats at every stage of this mission. I knew before that it was going to take a large slice of luck to accomplish this mission, and this process has brought that home to a sharp point and made me feel more dejected about it.

My phone buzzes in my pocket, so I lean to one side to enable me to pull it out of the tight space. There is a message from Catherine; did her subconscious tell her I was thinking about her or is it pure coincidence?

'Hi Andy, I just wanted to let you know that Emily and Stacey are fine, we are still stuck in the same room and it is pretty boring, to be honest. Suppose it could be worse. Good luck with the mission, I'm thinking of you, how much longer until you go? Luv C.'

Perhaps it wasn't a coincidence, perhaps it was the Universe pulling us together. Whatever it is, it is great timing, because Catherine's message has picked me up out of the doldrums somewhat.

I click reply. 'Hey, how did you know I was just thinking about you? Thanks for letting me know about the girls, and I can't wait to see you all again. We go in about half an hour, so this will probably be the last message for a while. Try not to worry too much, love Andy.'

After I click send, I get up from my stoop, slip my phone back in my pocket and stride back towards the hangar, my son and my team. We have one option and that is to succeed, there is no way I am not going to see those three girls again, no matter the odds!

On the way back, Josh sees me approaching and comes running over.

"You okay, Dad?"

"Yes, Champ," I tell him and give him a confident smile. "Just needed a bit of time to go over the mission in my head away from all the noise. Nothing to worry about."

"I see, did you get them straight?" he asks.

"I just wanted to make sure we hadn't missed anything obvious and couldn't think of anything, so all good," I tell him and put my arm around his neck, pulling him into me playfully. "I just heard off Catherine, she says they are all fine; bored, but fine."

"Good, won't be long until we get back to them," Josh says, pulling away from me as we get near to the hangar.

"Nope, not long," I agree as my phone buzzes against my hip again; it's another message from Catherine. 'Come back safe to us. XX', it reads, and I quickly type, 'You can count on it! Xx'.

Chapter 13

"What have we got, gentlemen?" I ask Dan and Lieutenant Winters.

The Lieutenant answers first. "There was a power outage in the Paddington Basin area yesterday, which would have affected Orion. I have spoken to London Utilities and they informed me the power has been restored to that area. They could give no guarantees for the Orion building, however."

"Dan, do we have drone footage?"

"Not yet, but a drone has been tasked and we should be online within five minutes," he tells me.

"We are going to have to assume the Orion building has no power, so what are our options?" I ask.

"We will have to take a generator with us. There are portable ones," Josh suggests from beside me.

"I'll get one arranged," the Lieutenant says without having to be asked.

"Josh, get Corporal Watts over here, please," I ask.

Josh, runs across the hangar to where the Corporal, currently shrouded in bright blue light from plasma, is testing it, sparks flying off whatever piece of metal he has found to cut up to test it on.

The Corporal looks up to Josh through his blacked-out safety goggles, before he pulls them up off his head. He follows Josh back across the hangar to us.

"Corporal, the building might not have power, so we are getting a generator to take with us; do you know of any problems with using one with the plasma?"

"No, Sir, there should be no problem," he tells me.

"As soon as it arrives, get it tested, as I don't have the greatest faith in generators,"

"Yes, Sir," he says, looking slightly confused.

He wouldn't look confused if I told him about the generators failing at the Orion building yesterday and the resulting fate of many friends and colleagues one floor below me.

"Thank you, Corporal, carry on," I tell him.

"The drone is approaching the target," Dan says from behind me.

The Corporal and I spin around at the same time as he goes back to his plasma and I spin to look at the drone's approach to the Orion building.

"Ten minutes until the generator arrives," the Lieutenant says as I start to focus on the video footage from the drone.

Even from high above the ground, the picture quality coming in from the drone is excellent, and it still surprises me how far technology has come in such a short time. When I was serving, for the most part, we were lucky if we had a few blurry aerial photos taken from miles above the target area to study before a mission. You literally had to use a magnifying glass to look at them, more often than not. Now we are getting live footage of the target area, and if somebody told me it was full High Definition, I would believe them.

"What are we looking at?" I ask.

Dan checks the grid reference on the screen of where the drone is. "The Orion building should be in view any second now."

And then, there it is, we are looking down at the distinctive triangular-shaped building sitting next to the Paddington Basin canal. The drone is too high for us to see much detail, but I can just about make out the hole in the roof that we escaped from yesterday and that is probably only because I know it is there.

"Tell the pilot to take the drone as low as he can," I tell Dan.

Dan picks up the headphones that are sitting on the table, puts them on and then pulls down the microphone. It swivels on Dan's right earphone until it is in front of Dan's mouth. It takes a minute or so for Dan to speak to the pilot, but the drone is soon descending as it circles around the Orion building. The view of the building improves constantly.

"That's as low as he can get without risking crashing," Dan says as he lifts his left headphone off his ear and onto the side of his head so he can hear both of us and the pilot.

We study the improved view for a few minutes, although there is still a lot of smoke in the area that clouds the picture. As the drone circles, one of us will lean in occasionally if we see something that might be of interest, closer to the screen, trying to get a better look.

"Rabids are still all over the front grounds, inside the perimeter fence," I point out. "There aren't as many as yesterday, but I was hoping they would have all but gone by now."

"They aren't really moving, they look almost asleep like they were when we got to the Tower of London yesterday. That'll soon change when we arrive," Dan reveals.

"Yes, do you think there are enough of them to build up to the broken windows again?" I ask.

"Doubtful, Boss, there would need to be a lot more of them; we will attract more when we arrive but I don't think we will be there long enough from them to pose a threat," Dan surmises.

"Agreed," I say, "let's concentrate on the building then. Can anybody see any signs of the power being on in there?"

"Is that a light," Josh says, pointing, "or is it the Sun reflecting on a window?"

We all look but none of us can say for sure, in fact, we can't see anything that would confirm the building has power.

"The roof is still clear, which is a good sign. Tell the pilot to switch to infrared, and let's see if the Rabids show up and we can see how many and where they are in the building," I tell Dan, who starts to speak into the microphone to the pilot.

"I doubt they will show up, they are cold-blooded," Lieutenant Winters informs us. "That is the report I have seen, from the specimens we have," he tells me as I look at him, quizzically.

"I'm not going to ask," I reply.

The picture on the monitor flicks off, then almost instantaneously comes back on again and is showing the footage in infrared. We learn nothing from the infrared camera; it seems the Lieutenant is right about the Rabids, and they are as dead as the building they are occupying. It shows no heat sources, so I get the drone's camera switched back.

"Tell the pilot to fly over the hole in the roof and to concentrate the camera on it. Let's see if we can get a look inside Sir Malcolm's office," I tell Dan, who relays the order.

Almost immediately, the drone adjusts its course, coming around to get in line for its flypast of the hole in the roof of the Orion building. At the same time, the drone's camera motors turn the camera, so it is pointing directly at the hole; it zooms in and the motors work to adjust the camera's direction, to compensate if the drone sways offline. The camera is now fixed on the hole, moving as the drone approaches its target. It points straight down into the hole when the drone is directly overhead, and still moves, fixed on the hole as the drone flies past.

Even with the pilot slowing the drone's speed as much as possible, the footage is fleeting, but I think I do get a look inside at the large red and gold patterned Turkish rug that adorns the floor of Sir Malcolm's office. Or is my mind playing tricks on me?

"Did anybody see anything?" I enquire, but nobody is sure. "Can you play it back in slow motion, Dan?"

"Hold on, let me rewind it."

Dan rewinds the footage and plays it back slowly, and he even freezes it, with the clearest view inside the building he can find; it is stuck on the screen for us to study. It was Sir Malcolm's rug that I saw and the only other thing we can make out in his office, apart from the edges of his furniture on the periphery of the hole, is some rubble on the floor, tarnishing his beloved rug. We can't even see the sideboard containing the safe from the angle we have, but we know it is there. More importantly, there is no sign of any Rabids in the office, which gives us all a bit more confidence for the mission ahead.

"Okay," I say, "there is one more view I want to try and get. Tell the pilot to make a flypast of the long side of the building; he is going to have to get lower, as I want to see if we can see inside through the top floor windows, of floor seven."

"Boss, the pilot said he was as low as he could go?" Dan reiterates.

"Tell him, Dan. It's worth the risk, and we've finished with the drone anyway if it crashes." Dan gives me a very sceptical look but starts talking to the pilot.

A couple of minutes pass, and Dan goes quiet, waiting.

"No dice, Boss, he says he can't do it; his Squadron Leader won't give him permission," Dan finally says.

"Put me through to the Squadron Leader," I tell Dan.

Again, a couple of minutes pass, and this time Dan is talking, nearly arguing constantly.

"Here they are," Dan tells me, takes off the earphones and gives them to me.

"Squadron Leader?" I ask.

"Yes, this is the Squadron Leader," a female voice replies.

"I'm Captain Richards, carrying out a critical mission under the direct orders of Colonel Reed. This flypast is vital to our mission under the Colonel's orders. I order you to sanction the flypast, my team is about to enter that building. If there is a chance to see inside, we will take it, understood?"

"I will speak to my superior," she tells me.

"Colonel Reed is your superior today, Squadron Leader. We are moving out imminently, with no delays, so authorise the flypast now. That is an order."

The Squadron Leader is silent for a moment before she tells me, "you have your flypast, Captain."

"Thank you,"

"Good luck with your mission," she tells me and is then gone.

My eyes revert to the monitor as I pull off the earphones and hand them back to Dan.

We all watch in silence as we see the drone start course corrections again through its camera, the ground below getting closer and closer and seemingly speeding up. The camera then turns upwards so that it is pointing out to the side of the drone and we start to get fast-moving views of buildings shooting past. They are almost a blur and it is impossible to identify any of them.

Dan is talking to the pilot, who is giving him a running commentary on his approach; Dan relays some of it to us. 'One minute', he tells us, 'thirty seconds', 'approaching the target, here we go'.

A bright blue flash that lasts no more than a couple of seconds, if that, crosses the screen. There is no mistaking the mirrored blue glass of the Orion building as the drone surges past, close to them, and I suddenly have strong doubts whether we will find any usable footage from that brief flash.

Almost as soon as the flash of blue has fleetingly passed from the screen, the footage comes to an abrupt end, black, grey and white static filling the monitor's screen and we look at Dan to see what's happened.

"Yep, it's crashed into the next building," he tells us. "That's definitely coming out of your wages, Boss, only ten million quid or so."

We all burst out laughing, which draws looks from the other members of the team around the hangar. They are probably wondering what on earth we could be laughing at. They understand, however, that even in the tensest of situations, humour is very often what helps get us humans through, relieves the stress, and sometimes even helps stops the mind cracking.

"No chance; this is the Colonel's show, that is going on his tab," I retort, eventually. "Rewind," I tell Dan, forcing myself to stop laughing, although I hold no hope that we will see anything.

Dan, rewinds, plays and freezes the footage frame by frame several times, until we have to admit that the footage is useless, and Dan turns off the monitor. The mirrored glass of the building did its job, kept prying eyes out, even though no one could ever have imagined the beneficiaries would be a Zombie horde holed up in the building.

Sergeant Dixon hasn't moved from his area with the table he set up, as he and Corporal Simms have pored over the equipment; it looks to me like a briefcase computer, with various cables protruding from it and its instructions that arrived on the Lynx. Finally, he gets up from the table, leaves it and approaches me, with Simms close behind him.

I have given the Sergeant space and time to familiarise himself with the equipment, without having me asking how it's going or how long it's going to take, which would not have helped. I had to trust he was working as fast as he could.

"Are you happy?" I ask the Sergeant as he gets to me.

"I think that would be overstating it, Sir. The equipment is 'state of the art' though. I have familiarised myself with this model now and have prepped all that I can ready for it to be used on the safe when we get there. That is going by the plans SecLock supplied, Sir."

"Was the Corporal much help?"

"Yes Sir, very much, I've shown him everything as a backup, just in case," he tells me, his scared face not showing one ounce of trepidation. This man is ice cool.

"Excellent, Sergeant, are you ready to load it up?" I question.

"Yes Sir, we are good to go."

"Thank you, Sergeant. Corporal, carry on," I tell them.

With that, they salute before spinning around and go to load up. That only leaves the generator holding us up and that should be here any minute. I check my watch, and it tells me it's 1340 hours; so much for getting underway earlier, at this rate, we will miss Colonel Reed's new mission time of 1345.

Looking out of the open roller shutter, I can see no sign of any vehicles approaching that may be bringing the generator. Lieutenant Winters must feel my eagerness to get going because as I turn to ask him where the generator is, he is already picking up the phone and tells me he is 'on it'.

Instead of just waiting in frustration, I decide to give the team its final brief before the off. All of the team is outside milling around, our equipment loaded onto the two Lynx. Everything is in place apart from the bloody generator. Some of the team are alone, walking around, psyching themselves up for the now imminent mission, trying to suppress their nerves and fear while others are in small groups chatting and joking, trying to take their minds off the same nerves and fears. Everyone has their own mechanism to deal with fear, to stop them turning and running away as quickly and as far as possible. The ones who tell you they aren't scared shitless are either lying or have lost their mind!

My stomach is churning like a volcano about to erupt and occasionally it feels like it might explode. I fixate on the mission; that's my mechanism, constantly thinking, looking for any advantage, any weakness in the enemy. The fear is always there though, threatening to overwhelm me, but I control it and use it to concentrate my mind. I even nurture some of it, as fear heightens the senses, gives you an edge.

"Gather 'round!" I shout as I reach the entrance to the hangar, under the rolled-up shutter high above.

Josh, nudges Dan, who is talking to his pilot, Flight Lieutenant Alder, to get his attention to my call; the people chatting break up and come quickly over, as do the members of the team who were having a moment to themselves.

Dan joins me at my side, while Lieutenant Winters comes up behind me from inside the hangar, his phone call finished and tells me that 'the generator will be here any minute'.

My hands clasp behind my back and I stand up straight, trying to look commanding as I prepare to address the team, hoping they see my confidence in them and not the fear burning through me.

"We are going into the heart of the enemy's territory, an unfamiliar enemy, an inhuman enemy that doesn't hold a gun or wear a uniform, but they can be killed nevertheless. We are going on a mission that could save our way of life as we know it, we go because we must and because it is our duty to try.

"We have the equipment we need, and I know we have the team we need to get our task done. Let's get in and out safely and as quickly as possible; we will have each other's backs and remember, if you can't be sure of a headshot, go for their legs, do you understand?"

"Yes, Sir!" The team roars.

"Okay, get your gear and comms on and load up, let's do this!"

"We got this, Boss!" Dan slaps my back as he moves out.

"Alice," I shout, just before she goes.

"How are you feeling?" I ask as she comes over to me.

"Shitting bricks, Sir," she replies, and she does look extremely nervous.

"That's okay, it's only natural. I've got full confidence in you, so just try to stay calm and not dwell on anything; there will be time to get things straight in your head when it's over, okay?" I try to calm her.

"Yes, Sir," she says looking slightly better.

"Good, I'll see you back on the ground."

"You will, Sir," she salutes and then she is off to load up.

A vehicle is coming our way that must have the generator and that is my cue to rush back into the hangar to put my last bit of kit on. My pre-prepared body armour is lying on the table, the heavy armour laden with kit, including comms transceiver, grenades and as many magazines as it is possible to cram into it. I have to throw the bulging armour over my head and Lieutenant Winters assists me in doing it up at the sides. He also helps by plugging my comms headset into the transceiver before I put the headset on, over the top of my head. Lieutenant Winters gives me another quick radio check before I fit the helmet that Josh and Alice have put out for me. My new Glock is also waiting for me, and I pick it up, check the magazine before I pull back the action and put the piston into my hip holster.

Finally, I lift my trusted M4 Carbine Assault Rifle up, give it one last check over and then lift its harness over my head, adjusting the harness straps so the rifle sits in my favoured position at my front.

"Are you ready, Captain?" The Lieutenant asks and suddenly I feel like a nervous schoolboy ready for my first day at big school.

"As I'll ever be."

"Good luck, Captain," the Lieutenant says, offering his hand.

"Thanks, keep me apprised on the storm," I say, as I shake his hand.

This is it, I think as I hear the engines on one of the Lynx start up, closely followed by the second one behind me and my stomach does another somersault. I release the Lieutenant's hand and take a hold of my M4's pistol grip with my left hand, the tactical fingerless glove moulding around the grip as my hand contracts around it to keep the gun steady at my front.

As I leave, I see Dan standing on the tarmac by the side of the Lynx on the left, the rotors buffeting him, waiting for me to come out. He sees me coming and gives me a friendly salute which I return, and he turns to climb aboard his transport. I break into a slow jog, aiming right to the other Lynx, grabbing the dark ballistic glasses hanging on the outside of my body armour as I go and slip them on. Have I put them on to protect my eyes from the sun or to hide the fear in my eyes from Josh and the other members of the team? I put the thought out of my head and duck slightly as I go under the helicopter's spinning rotors.

Josh is on board, waiting for me by the hold door when I arrive. He offers me his hand and I take it, then I place one foot onto the step and my legs push off. As they do, Josh pulls me up and into the Lynx's hold.

With everyone and all the equipment on board, there is no excuse to delay any further. Our comms are synched to the Lynx's so I can talk to Buck straight through my headset.

"Let's get underway, Wing Commander."

"Roger," Buck's voice sounds clearly through my headset.

"Shall I close the hold door?" Josh asks.

"No, leave it open, let's see what is out there," I tell him.

Josh and I sit down into the seats behind us, pull over the lap belts and push them home with a click. Neither of us wants to fall out of the hold door before we have even started.

Wing Commander Buck powers the engines of the Lynx to full throttle, the downdraft created by the rotors above us counteracts the weight of the loaded helicopter and it starts to lift off the ground. Buck eases us up and back, away from the hangar, the Lynx tipping back as its nose raises, flying us back. When he is satisfied that he is at a safe distance, he levels off and starts to turn to the right, away from the hangar. As he turns, we get a view of the hangar below us. Lieutenant Winters is standing in the sun on the tarmac just outside the hangar, watching us leave. The second Lynx has just started its take-off, its rotors a blur of speed and power.

The view is fleeting as we rapidly turn and I can only hope and pray that we will see it again, if and when we return from the mission. Our view of the hangar is overtaken by the expanse of Heathrow's terminal buildings, its massive hangars and beyond them, the very outskirts of the Greater London suburbs with the green of the open countryside beyond again.

Wing Commander Buck completes his turn and waits, hovering, stationary in the air, waiting for Flight Lieutenant Alders to complete his take-off. As soon as he gets confirmation it is complete, the Wing Commander dips the Lynx's nose and accelerates forward, forward towards central London and the Orion building.

Chapter 14

There are six seats in the hold of the Lynx, back to back and they run down the middle of the hold, looking outward towards the doors. Three of the SBS troop have their backs to us, seated on the other seats. Josh is next to me in the middle seat on our side and Sergeant Dixon is seated next to him at the tail end, the big black briefcase nestled between his feet, under his protection.

The Lynx virtually retraces the course we came in on last night as we leave Heathrow, steering clear of the runways, under the direction of Air Traffic Control. As we quickly approach the airport's perimeter, I am amazed at how far the construction of the new perimeter wall has progressed in the relatively short amount of time. Lorries laden with concrete blocks and other construction materials are lined up in several areas along the perimeter, waiting for their materials to be unloaded and added to the wall. JCB's and construction teams are busy all around, constantly building the wall higher and longer. The east side of the wall looks complete and is now the military's domain, machine-gun posts and missile batteries pointing outwards, sitting on top of hastily constructed scaffolding towers that protrude up the back of the wall.

Tapping Josh on the knee to get his attention, I pull my headphone off my right ear and he does the same with his left headphone so that we can talk privately.

"How are you feeling?" I talk loudly into his ear so that he can hear me over the din of the Lynx's engines.

"The nerves are going big time, how about you?" he says into my ear while he shows me his left hand, which shakes slightly.

"My nerves are going too; that's to be expected, you'll be okay in here," I tell him.

"Yes, I know, I'm worried about you down there though," Josh says, looking concerned.

"I'm confident, so don't worry too much, and just concentrate on your task. It will help."

"I'll try."

"Use your rifle to cover us; it's more accurate, so only use the minigun if you have to," I tell him.

"Yes, that's what I am going to do," he says.

"Good lad, we'll get through this!" I tell him and slap his knee.

We both put our earphones back into place and lose ourselves in the sound of the background static that is the only sound coming through the earphones. We are all quiet for the start of the flight, the whole team contemplating the mission ahead.

As Heathrow fades behind us, the Lynx flies over the suburbs of London, the greenery intertwined with roads, broken up by housing estates and industrial estates, but the greenery wins out. It is only when you get high up that you realise how many trees and green parks there are in London. Many people think of London as a sprawling concrete metropolis, the evidence below us proving that is not the case.

We cross overhead the six lanes of the M4 motorway and then the Lynx turns slightly and starts to follow it for a while. The traffic using the motorway is mostly going East into the city and all of that traffic is military. There are vehicles going in the opposite direction, probably people who can still leave the city having decided that their decision yesterday to try and ride it in out in their homes was the wrong decision.

Every moment that passes takes us deeper into the city, the M4 motorway behind us and the roads and buildings beneath us getting more concentrated. There is definitely a tinge of smoke in the air and this builds as we get close to our target. We can't see it but we can definitely smell it in the air that blows through the open hold doors and it emphasizes why we are all here.

I unbuckle my seat strap and being careful to hold the handrail, I get up and step over towards the cockpit and duck my head into it. I almost wish I hadn't decided to have a look forward out of the cockpit windows because the feeling of dread in my stomach tightens from the view I get.

London is almost entirely shrouded in smoke, thick black smoke, rising up from the burning city below. The smoke is densest in Central London and that definitely includes the Paddington Basin where the Orion building sits. Plumes reach up high above the city, too many plumes to count and the wind has also spread the smoke across the city, especially across North London. Smoke envelops wide areas of the North and the smoke then tapers away as far as the eye can see, thinning to an acrid mist as it travels.

"Shocking, isn't it?" Wing Commander Buck says from the pilot's seat.

"Very," I tell him, "I was expecting it, I saw it yesterday, but the smoke's much worse today, much worse."

"It looks like London in the 1950s and the smog it used to suffer, apart from the tall buildings that is," Buck points out.

"I almost wish it was the 1950s," I say.

"You and me both, Captain."

"What's our ETA," I ask, as we fly deeper into the smog.

"Seven minutes to the Orion building," he tells me.

"Okay, keep me updated on our arrival time, please."

"Of course, Captain."

I duck out of the cockpit, swing around, plonk back into my seat next to Josh and check my watch; it's 1357 hours, so we will arrive at Orion at 1404.

"You heard the Wing Commander, seven minutes until target area," I say to everyone. "Check your gear and get ready to descend."

Josh picks up the pack of thick heat-resistant gloves that the team will need for the fast rope descent onto the roof of Orion, and he hands me a pair and then a pair to the rest of the team, starting with Sergeant Dixon. I push mine under the side of my body armour to hold them while I check my gear. They are too thick to wear for anything but the descent, but they are vital to stop your hands from friction burning on the rope.

Sergeant Dixon is going to have the trickiest descent because he will be taking down the equipment in the plastic briefcase, and I see him getting the straps ready to secure it to his body. Me and the rest of the team only have our weapons to carry down. On the other Lynx, they have to get the heavier plasma equipment onto the roof. Alice will lower it down once the roof has been secured.

Darkness descends over the Lynx's hold, and I look up and out of the open hold door, expecting to see that the atmosphere outside has got thicker with smoke as we get nearer to the city. That doesn't seem to be the case, however; I can't see any significant increase in the amount of smoke we are flying through. I take off my ballistic glasses to get a clearer look, and the air outside is hazy, not hazy enough to make it darken as much as it has, though. My head turns forward to try and get a view out of the front cockpit windows and it has definitely got darker than a minute ago when I was up there.

"What's happened to the sun, Buck?" I ask into my headset.

"Some dark clouds have moved over, Captain, looks like rain is moving in."

Again, I unbuckle and get up to the cockpit, to have a proper look for myself. The scene before me now is even more sinister, there are dark clouds cutting the sunlight from the city, casting it into shadow. The skyscrapers of the City of London and Canary Wharf are barely visible, in the smoky depths of the city and with the sunlight taken from them too, they now look like black scars rising up from the ground. The loss of the sunlight above allows the orange light from fires that burn on the ground all over the city to glow and that glow resonates as if the city is sinking into hell, which it quite possibly is!

The impending rain may well fight or even extinguish some of the fires that have taken hold and help salvage the city before it does crumble into hell, but I curse our luck.

Rain will hamper our mission on many levels; will wet ropes mean we have to abandon our fast rope descent to the target and be forced to land the helicopters onto the roof? That would add time to the mission and aircover would be lost as the helicopters land and take off, one at a time. Sergeant Dixon cannot afford to get any of his delicate electronics wet, and he will be working on the safe next to a hole in the roof. If the rain is heavy, it could come down on his position by the safe. Rain, especially heavy rain as any soldier will tell you, dulls almost every human sense, impairs your vision, hearing and even your sense of smell and your equipment gets slippery, harder to use. Don't get me wrong, rain can be an advantage in certain circumstances; the cover it provides can give a big tactical advantage if you are stalking an enemy or helping to cover a retreat, for example. For this mission, however, the rain, while it will mask our approach to the target, offers downsides far outweighing the up.

"Lieutenant Winters, receiving, over?" I say urgently into my headset as I retake my seat.

"Receiving, over," his reply comes through.

"Weather update, looks like rain at the target area, over?"

"Hold, over," the Lieutenant says; he must be checking. "Latest update, rain central London, estimated, 1410 hours, starting light to heavy, then constantly heavy, winds strong. The storm is now estimated 1450 hours, winds strong to gale force, rain very heavy and lightning expected, over."

"Received, the storm is getting earlier and earlier; please advise if moves forward again, over," I tell the Lieutenant.

"Received, over and out," he finishes.

The mission timing is getting tight, too tight, so everything is going to have to go like clockwork for us to stand any chance of completing the mission and leaving the Orion building before this storm hits. In any event, we are in for a soaking no matter how well the mission proceeds and we need to make sure Sergeant Dixon can work without the rain affecting him.

"Where is the tarpaulin?" I ask Josh.

"Tarpaulin?" Josh says.

"Yes, the plastic sheeting!" My frustration gets the better of me.

"I know what it is, I'm just thinking where it is?" Josh admits.

"Josh, think, we need it."

He looks around the hold as if he is hoping he might see it, but then says, "I know." He leans right down, looking under our seats, then thankfully reaches under and pulls out a newly sealed cellophane-wrapped green tarpaulin.

"I knew I'd loaded it, sorry," Josh says.

"No problem, sorry I snapped. Throw it down to me, okay?" I tell him.

"Yep, okay, Dad."

"Four minutes to target," Buck's voice comes through our earphones.

The smoke is getting thicker inside the hold of the Lynx, and it is stinging my eyes a bit and irritating my throat. We are flying into central London and the sounds of battle from below travel through the air and up to us as we go. Even with my earphones on, I can hear the constant gunshots and explosions from the ground. We haven't time to try and look down to see how the battle is developing; we have our own priorities to worry about, but even a glance out of the open hold door tells us the battle is ferocious and extensive. We fly straight over it and past the Apache helicopters that are dotted around at a lower altitude, their rotors cutting through the plumes of smoke, trying to support the ground troops.

"Are you set, Sergeant?"

"Yes Sir," he replies, now standing next to his seat, making sure the briefcase is secured properly to him.

"Is everybody else ready?" I ask the three men in the opposite seats and they all sound off in confirmation.

"Okay, prepare the ropes," I order.

Josh quickly swaps seats with Sergeant Dixon and then leans forward to grab the spooled-up specially made, core-weighted, thick rope. The thickness and the weights wound through the middle of the rope helps prevent the rope from flying around in the wind or from the downdraft from the helicopter's rotors, the thickness also aiding with grip and control on the descent.

We are getting close to our target, and I can see that without Buck's updates, the last big island junction of the A40 Westway before the Orion building is going past the open hold door in the near distance. The junction is empty; clearly, Operation Denial hasn't penetrated this deep into London yet—if it ever will!

"Two minutes to target," Buck's voice sounds.

Thankfully, the rain isn't more than a drizzle and providing it stays that way, we will be good to go down via the ropes. Not that I'm looking forward to the descent. I can remember the last time I fast roped. Take it slow and steady, I keep telling myself as my body trembles, the butterflies in my stomach having spread to my whole body. I need to calm down and quick, so I close my eyes for a second, then concentrating on my breathing. Slowly, my heartbeat comes under control, my composure returning somewhat.

"You okay, Captain?" Dixon asks.

"Yes, Sergeant," I lie.

"Coming up on target, one minute," Buck says and nearly sets me off again.

The Lynx flies over the North West corner of Hyde Park and I see the dozen or so railway lines leading into Paddington Station. Following the lines, I get my bearings as they lead across and into the Station. I look across the large span of Paddington Station's roofs and there, sitting behind them, is the dreaded Orion building. I never thought I'd think of the building this way, but then again, I could never have envisaged I would be flying in with two Special Ops teams to infiltrate it.

Buck takes us over Paddington Station, heading straight for Orion, taking the decision that the time to recce the area has been swallowed up by the incoming weather.

The whole Paddington Basin area is masked in smoke, which is still pouring out of the tall, smouldering Hilton Hotel a few buildings across from Orion. The other remnants of yesterday's fighting on the Edgeware Road add to the haze.

Slowing the Lynx down to a hover, Buck does at least take the time to circle around the Orion building. I'm standing right at the hold door looking down on the once-familiar building that I helped design, but it looks so alien to me now. The building looks lifeless and I suppose it is because I'm not counting the current occupiers that I know are inside, waiting, as life. The hope that I would see signs of power in the building is soon dashed, since it is impossible to see through the mirrored glass even in the relative darkness that surrounds the building, so we won't know until we get inside and flick a switch.

Gradually, the Lynx comes around and behind it, the second Lynx hovering into formation at our tail. I am sure Dan is in the same position as me, at his hold door, looking down at the forlorn building below. Our arrival hasn't gone unnoticed; down in the grounds at the front of the building, inside the perimeter fence, the Rabids are beginning to stir and wake up from their standing stupor. They start to look up to the sky, to the two helicopters, in the hopes that new prey is arriving, their thirst for fresh flesh insatiable. I can see them opening their dark mouths in anticipation and I imagine the deathly noises coming out of those holes, their twisted invitation to their victims.

Finally, the Lynx is at an angle that gives me a view inside the hole in the roof of the building, but darkness encases Sir Malcolm's office. I don't see any movement in the shadows inside the hole and that is the best I could expect; there is no time to delay any further.

"Take us down," I say ominously into my headset.

"Understood," Buck says and starts his descent.

"Okay, lads, here we go. This is it, so watch your speed and spot your landing," I tell them.

As we draw close to the roof, I say "Ropes," to Josh and whoever has the rope on the other side of the Lynx. Josh pushes out the lever bracket that holds the rope away from the side of the fuselage, his arm reaching out of the hold door as he releases the thick heavy rope. The rope tumbles down out of the helicopter, unwinding as it goes until it reaches its full length and is snapped to a stop by the protruding bracket above and its anchor to the side of the helicopter by the hold door. There is no spring back towards the helicopter to speak of, the well-designed weighted rope staying quite static and resembling a metal pole more than a rope.

This is it, I think to myself as I pull on my heat-resistant gloves as Buck gets into position, the rope dangling a foot or so off the roof and close to the hole. I prepare to exit, my legs and arms feeling numb and my stomach burning with fear and anticipation.

"Okay, hold position, Buck. Go, go, go!" I hear myself say and then I'm moving, ignoring my body's protests and hesitation to go. I take hold of the top of the rope with my gloved hands, swing my body out from the safety of the Lynx's hold and then I'm sliding down; my hands gripping the rope control my speed and my legs wrap loosely around the rope to direct my descent. I immediately know I am going too fast and my hands squeeze the rope tighter to slow me down, the heat vibrating through the thick gloves, making them feel warm on my palms and fingers, but they do their job.

I slow too much, coming to a near stop just short of the roof. Sergeant Dixon is already coming down fast from above, threatening to career into me. My hands release the rope and I drop the last few feet onto the roof, the extra weight of equipment causing me to land hard but my knees bend in reflex to cushion the blow.

As I step away from the landing zone, I quickly pull off the thick gloves, take hold of my M4 and immediately take up a covering position, the muzzle of the rifle sweeping the roof, looking for targets. Sergeant Dixon hits the roof hard too, behind me; he is carrying more weight than me, but even so, he controls his descent, landing like the well-trained pro he is. On the other side of the Lynx's underbelly, the rest of the SBS team are down their ropes in quick succession and the three get down just as fast as it took Dixon and me. They are already fanning out from the landing zone, clearing the way for the next team to descend, stalking behind their rifles until they find the optimal covering position and when each man has, he drops to one knee. I do the same and by the time all five of us have taken a knee, every zone of the roof has a rifle trained on it. My zone includes our entry into Orion, the charred black hole with rubble around its edges. It is only then when I am in position that I notice the rain is starting to come down harder and the light has decreased even more around me, the mix of smoke and heavy cloud cutting off so much of the sun that it feels like dusk already.

Josh, above us, releases the dangling fast ropes' anchors and the ropes drop down onto the roof and are quickly followed by the tarpaulin. As soon as he finishes, our Lynx tilts and flies forward, making way for the second Lynx to make its run. Trooper Collins, who is closest to the insertion zone and the dropped ropes, hastily clears the ropes and the tarpaulin out of the way, as the last thing we need is for one of the next team to land on one of the ropes and twist an ankle, or worse.

"Roof secured, cleared for insertion," I say into my headset as soon as I am satisfied.

Our relative reprieve from the loud whine of engines and buffering from rotors is short-lived as the other Lynx hovers into position. In that small window, however, there is no mistaking the sound of banging and rattling coming from the locked rooftop door that is away to my right, a chilling reminder that we are not alone. The door is in Dixon's zone and his rifle is trained on that door, but if, God forbid, the door gives way, there is no telling how many Rabids would flood through it from the stairwell and the seven floors below.

I try not to dwell on that scenario, but I do have to consider that eventuality, although I cannot think of a positive outcome if the door is breached while we are still here.

Behind me, the second Lynx approaches the insertion zone and the noise increases exponentially, as does the downdraft. I don't look around to see how it is doing or to see if the men are dropping down the ropes yet. My concentration is focused on covering my areas; the only time it wavers for a split second is when my eyes dart to the door and every time they do, I half expect to see the door bursting open and Rabids streaming out.

I instinctively know when the Lynx is in position when the noise and wind from the rotors are at their peak and sure enough, within a couple of seconds, Dan takes a position a few feet to my left, on one knee, his rifle trained at the ready. This time, the Lynx hovers over the insertion zone for longer as Alice releases the ropes and then has to lower down the kit for the plasma cutter. I trust in the team doing their jobs and continue to concentrate on my area, waiting patiently for them to finish and for the Lynx to move off. Soon enough, the noise coming down from above changes and then above me, the second Lynx moves away from the roof to take up its position, covering us from the air.

All ten men that are now on the roof stay in their positions until the second Lynx has moved off and the volume on the roof reverts back to a relatively normal level, my eagerness to get on making those few seconds drag out.

Even though the two helicopters have left our immediate vicinity, they don't stray far, well within rifle range—and the noise from their engines is still considerable. That noise doesn't drown out the thunderous drumming on the stairwell door and the door is visibly rattling under the constant barrage it is receiving from behind it; we need to get out of here as soon as possible.

"Okay, let's get this done," I say into my headset when the Lynx has gone and taking my cue, everyone starts to move.

"Dan, make sure that door is well covered," I order.

"Don't worry, Boss, I've brought a surprise for that task," Dan says.

My confusion doesn't last long as I follow the direction of his eyes over to the landing zone and see an M2 Browning, 50-calibre machine gun, sitting beside the plasma equipment, with boxes of belt-fed ammo for it there too.

"Nice surprise," I tell him, "get it set up."

Dan, gets to it, as does the rest of his team who move to their assigned positions to provide cover on the roof for my team, whose job is the safe down in Sir Malcolm's office.

Sergeant Dixon and I approach the uninviting hole down, both of our rifles trained on it. We stop short of the hole though, while we wait for the other three members of our team to carry over the plasma equipment. I'd nearly forgotten I'm still wearing the ballistic glasses. A raindrop runs down the front of them to remind me and I reach up to take them off; they are doing more harm than good.

Watts goes past us first, the rifle he was holding replaced by the boxed plasma cutter. He is closely followed by the two other men. One carries the gas bottle and tarpaulin, while the other has the generator. They put the equipment down near but not too close to the hole. We don't want it to get in the way of our insertion down and the equipment in place, they retreat to our position.

"We are going to take it slow and quiet, so clear your corners. Sergeant Dixon will only follow us in when the room is secure, understood?" I tell the team and each of them signals, affirmative.

The four of us spread out as we move on the hole, Watts on the left, then me, Simms on my right and Kim next to him in our little semi-circle. Dixon stays put as the main character covering us, his briefcase at his side. We keep low, all of our rifles concentrated on the dark hole as we inch in closer. I thought I'd left my nerves and fear back in the Lynx's hold, but they are boiling to the top again and I have to push them back down, refocusing my mind back on our task, something in which I am clearly out of practice.

With only a couple of feet to the edge, I signal to halt. My left hand reaches up to my body armour and pulls three glow sticks out. It is impossible to hear if any sound is coming from the hole, but if there is, it is drowned out by the loud incessant banging reverberating from the door behind, the whine of the Lynx above and the patter of heavy rain. There isn't a beam of light coming from the hole; were lights in Sir Malcolm's office on or off yesterday, and is the power on or off in the building? I can't answer either question.

I do hear the low cracks as I break the three glow sticks between my two hands, I give them a good shake with my left hand and give them a couple of seconds for their orange glow to develop. Deliberately, I swing my arm once to show my team I'm about to throw them, then take a second swing and release them towards the hole. For a split second, I think my nerves have got the better of me and my throw is going to miss the hole, even from this short distance... but it doesn't, my embarrassment is saved and the glow sticks sail into the hole, disappearing into the darkness. The main reason for throwing the glow sticks in is of course for the light. There is a second, however and that is to see if there is a reaction to them from any Rabids that might be lurking. There isn't any reaction, and nothing changes apart from the hole has a tinge of orange glowing from it and Corporal Simms throws a couple more sticks down for good measure.

Tentatively, not taking anything for granted, I rise to a stand and the orange glow from the hole increases the higher I get. I still can't really see into the office, so I edge forward, my rifle poised, and beside me the other men take my lead and do the same, all of us ready to shoot. Gradually, I begin to see into Sir Malcolm's office, and it looks just like we left it, apart from the darkness and scattered glow sticks on the floor trying to brighten the room. Sir Malcolm's desk is still pushed up against the door, my feeble attempt to stop a hoard of Zombies hasn't moved; it gives my confidence in the mission a boost.

"The office door is still shut; it looks like the room is clear and we are good to go," I say to the team.

"Affirmative; the office is clear," Corporal Simms confirms.

"Okay, Dixon, can you bring a couple of the ropes over, in case we need a quick exit?" I ask.

"Affirmative," he replies.

"I'll go down first, cover me," I tell the other three.

I move right to the edge of the hole and get down on one knee in front of it; putting my left hand down for support, I lean down into the hole as far as possible to give the office one last check before I go in. The office definitely looks clear so I turn around, put both hands on the wet edge of the roof and start to lower myself in, my feet reaching out as I lower, looking for the coffee table that is still on top of the sideboard housing the safe. My feet find the table and I transfer my weight onto it, making sure it is steady, then carefully step down onto the secure sideboard.

Before I give the next man the all-clear, I again scan the room, the orange glow twinkling as the rain comes down through the hole above, piercing the light. But apart from that, nothing moves.

Giving them the all-clear, get down off the sideboard to make way for the next man and take a position next to the sideboard, one hand on my M4 and the other steadying the coffee table. The quiet of the office is spoiled by the banging coming from the rooftop door which travels down through the hole above me and from the door to the stairwell which is next to Sir Malcolm's office. Thankfully, the Rabids seem to be ignoring the door next to the office, for now at least.

Three of the men are down in quick succession, Sergeant Dixon the last of those three, after passing his case down. Lance Corporal Kim stays up top to ferry the rest of the equipment over and pass it down, but the first thing he does is to tie off two of the fast ropes and drop them down. If we have to evacuate quickly, they could be invaluable.

Sergeant Dixon doesn't mess about and makes a beeline to the safe. He has no need to look for it; the sideboard's sliding door is still open, revealing its position. He reaches up and turns on his LED headlamp, getting to work dismantling the keypad.

"Do you want the tarpaulin up?" I whisper to him.

"No, the rain isn't coming down here," he whispers bluntly back as if I have broken his concentration.

Fair enough, I think to myself and press the button on my radio. "Dan receiving, over." I talk into the radio as loudly as I dare.

"Receiving, we have you covered up here, Boss, over," Dan tells me, reading my mind.

"How's the door holding up, over?"

"Uncertain, Boss, it is holding, for now, over."

183

"Received, over and out."

Kim finally comes down through the hole after passing down the last piece of equipment. He uses one of the ropes to assist his descent and he makes it look easy compared to the rest of our fumbling attempts. Deciding to let Dixon work, with Simms assisting him and Watts setting up the plasma, Kim can give them cover while I leave the office to quickly check how the barricaded stairwell is holding up.

"Kim, help me move the desk back from the door," I instruct.

He immediately complies and we take a side each, lift the heavy desk and shuffle it back a few feet, just enough for me to open the door and squeeze through.

"I'll only be a couple of minutes," I tell Kim as I leave Sir Malcolm's office.

Darkness encompasses the lounge area outside the office, the dull light coming in through the windows barely enough for me to see the dark blobs of furniture that are only feet away from me. There is no sign of any power in the building; perhaps I should have brought some night vision goggles, but we didn't think we would need them. This is supposed to be a fast mission in the afternoon, the light was not supposed to be a factor. I take out another glow stick and risk cracking it. As the glow starts to resonate, I avoid looking directly at the stick, not wanting it to affect my night vision that is starting to develop. Standing the stick up against the wall, I move past it and towards the barricaded stairwell door, and the orange glow builds as the chemicals mix and react. It is amazing how much difference a small glow stick can make in a dark room.

Checking around the lounge area as I go, I find it hard to compute where I actually am, it feels so unreal to me. I recognise the area, of course, as I've worked in it long enough. My office is just along from me, but the feeling I get is that this place is different now and I suppose it is; I am different too, everything is different, and the world has been turned on its head.

I press on, pushing those bloody thoughts out of my head. They could drive you mad, but now is not the time to try to quantify the meaning of life!

The dull banging and screeching that we could hear in the office is louder and clearer out here and the sounds seem crisper. I put it down to the fact that the office walls are dampening the noise as I get to the end of Sir Malcolm's office and to the barricade; I see that isn't the only reason, however. Above the piled-up boxes and furniture, on top of the filing cabinets that we used for the barricade, yesterday, it's hard to see in the darkness but the stairwell door is definitely cracked open a small amount. I'm shocked to see it but I'm certain it is open; the Rabids must have broken the door frame because it was locked. It looks like the only thing that saved us yesterday was Stacey suggesting we make an arch with the filing cabinets from the door to the wall. I look again at the barricade and the filing cabinets and it dawns on me that they have moved, only slightly but they have definitely moved, and I wouldn't trust it to hold back another attack.

Time to see how the safe is coming along, I think urgently to myself, but just as I'm about to leave, something in the stairwell hits the door and it bangs into the first filing cabinet, which in turn shifts the rest of them slightly. If confirmation was needed that the barricade could not be trusted, that was it; if the Rabids knew we were down here, they would be attacking that door no doubt and probably getting through it.

Getting back inside the office, I have a new apprehension about this mission. Kim helps me put the desk back against the door, a lame fortification at best, me hushing him as we go, nervous to make any noise. I then get him over to the rest of the team by the safe, so that I can talk to them quietly.

"We have got to keep the noise to an absolute minimum; the stairwell door is cracked open and it won't hold another attack, understood?" I whisper and they all nod. "How is it progressing, Dixon?"

"On track. I am just connecting the safe to the computer to override its lock," he whispers back.

I give him a thumbs up and then leave him to it, taking up a covering position with Kim.

"Dan, report, over," I say as quietly as I can into my headset.

"Unchanged; they are trying to break through the door. I think it's the noise from the helicopters agitating them, over."

"Received, I think we are close here, if it works, over and out."

"Received," Dan confirms his understanding.

I cut the conversation to a minimum; seeing the cracked door has made me seriously edgy to even talk, we are in a very precarious position, I've got to hold it together. The other members of my team seem to be pretty calm and getting on with their jobs as if it's just another day in the office. I remember that calmness and confidence from when I was a fully-fledged Special Forces Operative, living for the buzz of a mission, craving the adrenaline rush and camaraderie with my brothers in arms, when nothing else mattered. Those days are long gone for me, I am now a fully-fledged single father and my buzz comes from my children, Josh and Emily. I was late finding that buzz, too late, especially with Josh. I missed so much of his childhood, something I will always regret.

On the other hand, perhaps their calmness comes partly out of ignorance, as I'm the only member of my team that has actually had contact with these creatures, face to evil face, contact. On three or four occasions yesterday, I scraped through close calls with these Rabids, barely surviving, I know full well how formidable they are, and these men don't. They haven't come up against them, so they can't, no matter how many times they have been briefed and warned. I doubt they even believe an unarmed enemy poses any real threat to their skills and firepower; ignorance really is bliss and I hope it stays that way for all our sakes.

There is a lull in proceedings as we wait to see if Dixon manages to crack the safe's lock and I decide to join Kim covering the office door, my nervousness getting the better of me. The rain is starting to come down harder, bigger drops falling through the hole in the roof and in faster and faster succession. Luckily it is somehow keeping away from where Dixon is working. The angle at which it comes through the hole means it hits the sideboard and the floor in front of it. The sideboard must be sitting at a slight slope because the water collected on it runs down along the top of the sideboard to the opposite end of where the safe is, and flows down the side onto the floor.

Kim glances over to where Dixon is working and says something under his breath that I don't quite catch; maybe I'm not the only one whose nerves are starting to fray or is he just picking up on my uneasiness? I glance over. I can't help it, hoping I see the safe door swing open, but it doesn't. Are we going to have to start cutting away at the bloody thing with the plasma? I fucking hope not? The last thing we need now is noise, sparks, flashing light and more time.

My head turns back towards my covering position, still trying to ignore the door behind Dixon, the door to Sir Malcolm's private bathroom where he sits on his toilet with his brains splattered over the tiled wall...I can't deal with thinking about that right now. As my head comes around, a bright flash of white light washes through the orange light of the glowsticks and for a second, I think they have decided to power up the plasma to start cutting into the safe. I'm about to go look around to see and to ask Dixon if he has given up with his solution, then realisation hits me before I do.

However, the flash of light didn't emanate from over there, it came from above from the hole in the ceiling. A dull rumble of thunder reverberates over the noise of rain and Rabids banging on the door above a few seconds later, to confirm that the flash was lightning. The delay in the rumble tells me it is still some distance off at the moment, but I don't like it, not one bit.

Chapter 15

Kim looks at me with a face that says, 'oh shit', straight after the thunder passes. And I suspect I have the same look on my face, as it looks like the storm is going to be on us at any time. Above us, the hammering on the rooftop door increases, almost giving the impression the thunder hasn't stopped, the new noise adding fuel to the fire for the Rabids trapped behind it and their desperation to break through and find new prey.

"Boss, receiving, over?" Dan's voice sounds through my headset, making me jump.

"Receiving, over," I say as I look over to Sergeant Dixon in anticipation of his question.

"How much longer? The storm is inbound, we have multiple lightning strikes in the East of the city and that local one has set the Rabids off. I don't trust this door, we need to vacate A-SAP, over," Dan says urgently.

Sergeant Dixon looks over to me knowing I will want an answer for Dan, and he indicates five more minutes which I assume is until he knows if his method is going to work.

"Received, we are looking at five minutes, over." I decide to give Dan an honest but vague answer, not wanting to tell him it could be longer, a lot longer.

"I am not sure we have any longer than that, if that, over." Dan's voice falters.

"Understood, hold your position at all costs, we cannot afford to leave here until the safe is open," I tell Dan sternly, knowing the rest of his team on the roof will also be listening.

"Understood, Boss, over and out,"

Even if there is only an outside chance this goddamn safe has anything that will help cure this infection locked inside, we have got to retrieve it, no matter the cost to us few men. Countless lives could be saved in London alone and who knows, countless Rabids could be cured, if that is in any way possible?

Dixon is tapping feverishly at the keyboard contained inside the briefcase that is on the floor in front of Sir Malcolm's safe, wires crossing the divide between the two carries the code that will hopefully override the lock. Concentration is etched on his face, that is bathed in a blueish light from the screen he is staring at. Dixon's eyes dart up from the screen, over to the safe occasionally, and I follow them when they do, in anticipation that the safe door is going to pop open. But the flipping thing doesn't, not yet.

"Captain Richards to transport; receiving, over?"

"Receiving, over," Buck says.

"Status report, over."

"We are in a holding pattern, ready to give covering fire or to land and Evac, over," Buck tells me.

"Good, hopefully, Evac any minute. Stay ready," I tell him.

"Received, standing by, over and out."

Where else would the two Lynx be, I chastise myself? I just couldn't help checking that they were standing by. We have got to get out of here as soon as that safe opens.

Another flash of white light fills the office for an instant, and time seems to stand still as we all wait for the inevitable rumble of thunder that will follow, our faces turned up to the hole above and sky beyond in alarm. I am conscious that Sergeant Dixon is the exception. He hasn't allowed the flash of lightning to break his concentration or distract him from his task, his eyes don't leave the screen, determined to succeed.

I barely get to the count of one before the thunder hits and it isn't a rumble; the thunder is an almighty elongated crack as if the sky itself is splitting apart. My lungs hold my breath in as tension and fear of what might follow paralyses my whole body. The thunderclap was so powerful, I know there has to be a reaction from the lurking creatures.

"It's open." Somebody says in that moment of paralysis, but I don't register it properly, my mind fixed on listening to the booming noise and high-pitched screeches rising from the depths of the building and going all the way up to the door above us on the roof.

"Captain Richards, the safe is open!" Corporal Simms shouts in my direction.

I'm immediately pulled back to reality as I register what the Corporal has shouted at me, my wits finally returning, and I look over to the open safe just as another lightning bolt flashes. The intense beam of light catches Sergeant Dixon with his arm in the safe for an instant, like a camera flash catching a criminal in the act and then the beam of light is gone. My eyes struggle to readapt to the low orange light, the photo momentarily burned into my retinas. This time, the thunder almost immediately follows the lightning and the crack is impossibly more powerful and louder than the last, and it feels like the whole building vibrates under its wrath.

Self-preservation kicks in and my years of hard training take over and not a second too soon because the vibrations aren't coming from the thunder, they are coming from Rabids sent wild by the storm, inside the building.

Dixon is without ceremony emptying the contents of the safe into a holdall. He is grabbing whatever his hand touches first and throwing it into the bag as quickly as he possibly can.

"Stand by for Evac, the safe is open, Buck, make your approach," I shout into my radio, not worrying about my shout being heard now over the din of Rabids.

"Received," Buck responds.

A dull thud comes from the roof area above me, instantaneously followed by someone shouting, "BREACH" into their radio. Automatic gunfire rings out above our heads, from small arms, whose noise is then overpowered by the colossal and distinctive sound of Dan's Browning 50-cal.

The sound causes everyone, even Dixon, to freeze for a second as we realise our worst fears have happened and the Rabids have smashed through the rooftop door. Our mission has just taken a dire turn; the Evac position has been compromised with no viable alternative or fall-back position. The team on the roof is under immediate threat and fighting for their lives with limited ammo. If only that door had held for another few minutes…

Back on the rooftop, sheets of rain pour down onto the rooftop of the Orion building, soaking Dan and his team to their cores. It runs down their faces, into their eyes and over their weapons. Pools of water spread across the expanse of the flat roof, growing constantly as the roof's drainage system struggles to cope with the sheer amount of rain falling, and the wind is howling around them, threatening to blow them off their feet.

Even with the storm accosting him, Dan can see that the stairwell door across from him is taking a hammering from the Rabid creatures behind it, the door visibly rattling in its frame. It is only a matter of time until the door succumbs to the onslaught and gives way, Dan's hope of getting off the roof before that disaster happens diminishing by the second; even though everyone is ready to move for Evac, the two Lynx are close, hovering above, poised to descend at a moment's notice. The only thing holding them up is getting that godforsaken safe open.

Dan had nearly tried to convince Andy to abandon the mission, that the risk was now too high and that they should retreat and regroup when he had radioed him just now for a progress update. Andy had quashed that idea before Dan could even broach it and even though Andy might not be aware fully of their precarious position, Dan had to admit he was right. This mission has to be now, like he said, at all costs, storm or not; they might not get another chance. If they leave and the door is then breached, any team that came back to retrieve the safe would have to fight their way onto the roof and to get into the building, because the Rabids would spread onto the seventh floor through the hole in the roof.

Perhaps the door will hold for another five minutes, Dan thinks to himself, trying to stay positive as he looks around at his drenched team in their positions around the roof. He then glances up to the sky in front of him, stupidly, to double-check that the Lynx is still there. It is, hovering as steadily as it can in the wind and the rain, Alice poised at the hold door ready for action should she be needed.

Dan doesn't look around to check on the other Lynx which is up and away to his right, ready to land, nearer to the roof's Helipad. Dan's concentration reverts back to the door just as the first lightning bolt lights up the whole Orion building's rooftop, taking a snapshot of the rainswept scene, of him, his team, the door, everything, including the two Lynx above. The lightning is followed by an almighty crack of thunder and Dan ducks slightly as if the sky is about to fall on him. His concentration doesn't waiver from the door, however, and his quivering finger hovers over the trigger of his 50-cal Browning, which gives him some solace. The door's shaking and rattling escalates significantly, visibly moving in its frame, threatening to burst open at any moment as the Rabids behind it flare up, reacting to the crack of thunder.

Miraculously, somehow the door stays shut, but just as Dan starts to thank his maker for watching over them, the second lightning bolt blazes from the sky and almost simultaneously an explosion of thunder cracks over him.

The wooden doorframe splits in two down the middle, releasing the solid door to fly outwards, virtually straight. The door slaps onto the sodden rooftop, sending cascades of water flying into the air all around it. Rabids spray out from the door like a fizzy drink from a shaken bottle, many falling to the ground, unable to control the pressure from behind. The ones that fall are trampled on by the rampage that follows as a stream of Rabids surge onto the roof.

Dan's quivering finger fails him, shock and fear taking over his body as he goes into a near stupor, his body inexplicably fighting his brain which is telling him to pull the trigger and fire. He hears "BREACH" shouted into his headset and gunfire erupt from the rest of his team as they go to battle. Finally, after an age, which is, in fact, a second or two, his brain wins its fight and his finger squeezes the Browning's trigger.

Dan's hesitation has given the impossibly quick creatures a foothold onto the roof, as they fly out of the stairwell. The rifles the other men fire at the Rabids are largely ineffective, their bullets missing their targets and not powerful enough to do real damage when they do hit—and their magazines don't hold enough bullets. That doesn't deter these Special Forces professionals; they don't hesitate when the enemy presents itself, as Dan did, and even as they struggle to overpower the enemy, they still move forward, stalking towards the enemy, trying to push them back and stem the tide.

Although Dan's hesitation hands the Rabids a window of opportunity, the Browning's awesome firepower and ferocity quickly shuts that window. The 50 calibre bullets churn out at an unimaginable rate, rip through any flesh and bone they meet and then continue through to their next victims, the bullets not stopping until they hit something solid. The bullets' victims today are infected rabid people, but people nevertheless, young, old, male, female and different races. The bullets don't discriminate; they rip through them all. Dan almost feels sick as he sees dozens of his unfortunate fellow Londoners slain by his hand. He doesn't relent though; his hesitation takes them too close to catastrophe and he knows that any one of these victims would sink their foul teeth into him, given the chance.

Rabids suddenly stop attacking from the stairwell and a wave of relief flows over Dan. Not only because he can release his finger from the Browning's trigger and stop its slaughter, but since he is also running low on this linked belt of ammo for the gun. If it runs out while they are still streaming from the door….

Dan isn't naïve enough to think for one second that the Rabid attack has been thwarted and they have all been killed. He hasn't forgotten the amount of Rabids there were in the grounds of Orion yesterday; that attack was the tip of the iceberg, he is sure of it, and that it is only a matter of time before another starts. Reluctantly, Dan decides he has got to change the Browning's ammo belt now, while there is a lull in the Rabids' attack.

"Reloading, cover me!" he shouts to the rest of the men and he races to do just that.

Dan trusts they are ready to cover him as he goes about reloading the Browning and fights the urge to keep looking over his shoulder to the open door, even though every fibre in his body is telling him to. He has to change out the Browning's ammo as quickly as possible, to get another three hundred rounds into the gun because the forty or fifty rounds remaining on the current belt won't hold off another sustained attack.

Out of the corner of his eye, he sees fleeting movement through the rain but still, he resists turning to confront it, his body racked with fear as he pulls a new belt into the loading mechanism. Gunfire breaks out from either side of him as his team tries to defend. Dan is nearly done, the new belt is in and he grabs the gun's left grip while at the same time reaching up with his right hand to pull the open-top cover down, locking it into place. And then the same hand finally whips back the side-slide to load the gun.

Dan focuses ready to fire, just as a Rabid launches into the air at him, bullets hitting the Rabid's body from the right as his team tries to take it down—but they have no effect.

The Rabid is almost on top of Dan, its black pupils fixed on him as its mouth opens and its arms spread ready to envelop him. This time, Dan doesn't hesitate. He yanks down on the grip, lifting the muzzle of the gun, and pulls the trigger. The Browning bursts into life, sending dozens of 50-cal rounds ripping into the Rabid in mid-flight, stopping it in its tracks. They tear the Rabid apart, its body splitting in two. As it falls, bullets smash into its face and up through its head which explodes, ejecting its contents splattering backwards.

A second Rabid close behind the first is also obliterated from the same burst of bullets, and they both fall onto the ground as a mince of flesh, bone and red-black blood.

Dan is playing catch-up; however, his reloading of the Browning keeps him out of the fray for vital seconds, and a third Rabid, slightly to Dan's left, is missed by the burst of bullets. He keeps firing and tries to swing the long muzzle of the gun to get the Rabid in its sights, but it doesn't quite catch up. The Rabid is too quick, the arc of bullets all missing the terrifying creature whose evil dead eyes are fixated on Dan's position. Continuing to swerve left, the Rabid has done its job, it has drawn Dan's fire away from the stairwell, its main target; whether this is intentional or not, it looks like a disastrous error.

Dan sees his error as Rabids start to stream out of the door again and terror grips him; they are only meters away from his position. The first Rabid is still swerving left to avoid the fire from the Browning, but if he diverts that salvo of bullets away from it and at the door, it would be on him straight away. Just as Dan is about to divert the Browning at the door and take his chances with the single Rabid, tracer bullets fly over his head, their flashing red and green light directing the hailstorm of bullets that rip into the stream of Rabids in front of him.

The Mini-Gun, firing from the Lynx above, despatches the Rabids that made it out of the stairwell in next to no time. They are all left in a heap of flesh and Josh carries on firing down into the stairwell to make sure. *Thank you, Josh*, Dan thinks somewhere in the back of his mind, but he doesn't have time to dwell on it or feel relief; he has got to focus on killing his target. He hears gunfire from his team as they too try to take down the creature, but they all miss; the target is so fast and too far away for them.

"We have the contents of the safe, Captain," Corporal Simms tells me from below, but I barely register what he says as I look out, watching Dan and his team struggle to keep control of the roof. The coffee table on top of the sideboard feels unsteady under me as I stand on my tiptoes, the top of my head poking out through the hole and the rope gripped in my hand helping to steady me.

"Captain?"

"Ok, let's move," I tell him.

"Yes, Sir," he replies.

I take a higher grip on the rope and pull myself up as a hand pushes my boot to help me on my way. I am eager to get assistance to Dan as quickly as we can. Another bolt of lightning hits, its long fork shooting downwards through the torrents of rain and it's immediately followed by the obligatory deafening crack of thunder.

Taking a knee next to the hole, I look down the length of my rifle, providing cover for my team as they prepare to move. Across the roof, Dan opens up again with the Browning as another wave of Rabids attacks from the stairwell; even with my limited vision through the rain, I see that he is in trouble. A Rabid is trying to flank him on my side and more are coming at him from the stairwell. I aim at the Rabid flanking him and fire, in hope more than an expectation that I will hit it. I miss and try to aim again, but the creature moves too fast. Above and away to my right, tracer fire rains down from the Lynx's Mini-gun, I can't see Josh from my angle, but I know it must be him firing. I desperately hope that it will free Dan to deal with other Rabids.

Kim appears next to me and as soon as he does, I'm up and running towards Dan's position. He's let go of the Browning and has resorted to firing his sidearm at the fucking Rabid which refuses to go down. The creature, seeing its opportunity, has stopped flanking and is going for Dan head-on and is nearly upon him. Now closer to Dan, I slam my anchors on, pull my rifle up, aim—and just as the Rabid jumps at Dan, I shoot.

The Rabid lands on top of Dan, knocking him backwards off his feet, onto his back on the roof and they both go down, water spilling up as they hit the ground. For a second, I think I've hit it, but to my horror, it is still moving and attacking Dan who is beneath it, the creature's arms flailing at Dan and then its head goes in to attack.

"NO!" I hear myself shout as I sprint the remaining distance to my mate.

As I reach them, the Rabid's head is down into Dan's neck area and he is withering underneath it, his legs and arms kicking, still trying to fight. Without thinking, I immediately jump down on top of the Rabid and push my arm under its neck and pull back as hard as I possibly can. The Rabid resists my pull and I hear cracking sounds from its neck as I continue to pull with all my strength; suddenly, it releases and I'm falling backwards, with the Rabid's head locked between my arms, falling back with me. The creature whips and bucks its whole body trying to escape my grip. Its strength is astounding, unrelenting, and my wet grip starts to slip.

A dark figure appears above our struggle and moves down on top of us, the figure's left hand grabs the hair of the Rabid and I see a glint of light from the steel blade before it is plunged into the Rabid's head. The blade enters the Rabid's head right next to my right ear, the crack of bone and quench of flesh travelling loudly into my brain as it goes in.

Lance Corporal Kim starts to pull the limp Rabid off me and I quickly push the thing off at the same time. I'm both desperate to get to Dan and yet dreading it. As soon as the weight of the dead Rabid is off me, I scramble on my hands and knees over to Dan who is still on his back where he fell, his arms and legs twitching. I try to take that as a good sign, at least he is still alive, I kid myself.

As soon as I am on my knees over him, I see the damage the fucking evil creature has done to him. His eyes are wide open and desperate, full of fear as he fights to draw breath through his lacerated neck which is pumping out blood. Frantically, I rip open one of my Velcro pockets on my body armour, pull out a field dressing, quickly apply it to the wound and put pressure on.

"Buck, emergency medevac," I shout into my radio, as shock hits me, making my head spin.

"Delay that order, Wing Commander," I hear someone say above me and look up to see who the fuck has the balls to try and override my order.

"Who said that?" I bawl at the three men standing around me and Dan.

"I'm sorry, Sir," Sergeant Dixon says, "we can't take him with us."

"I'll be the judge of that, Sergeant; he is still alive!"

"No Sir, I'm sorry he isn't; he is infected, and we can't risk him turning on the helicopter and even if he didn't, they wouldn't let us land with him back at base," Dixon tells me. "We have the contents of the safe and that is the priority, we need to go, now."

My head turns back to my friend and I stare at him for a moment, seeing his fight to draw breath has slowed and his eyes flicker as if they want to shut, but he is too scared to let them. I know deep down that Dixon is right, Dan is beyond saving, yet I still try to think of a way to, even as he fades before my very eyes. In the end, all I can do is be with him for his final moments and I take his hand in mine, trying to give him some small amount of comfort. Fleetingly, I feel Dan's hand lightly squeeze mine before it goes horribly limp and then as more lightning flashes overhead, his eyes stop flickering and his pupils dilate. My head drops and sadness fills me as I know he has gone, the loss hard to take in.

Gunfire erupts above me from the Browning; one of the men has taken up Dan's position of defending the stairwell.

"Captain, we have to get out of here," Dixon says.

Reluctantly, succumbing to the inevitable, I release Dan's hand, which drops to his side as I push up off the soaking roof to stand. I pause, looking down at him knowing I have a ghastly decision to make; do I make sure Dan doesn't turn into one of these heinous creatures and put a bullet in

200

his head or do I leave him here on the roof? Is there any chance that a cure will be found to turn the dead back to life, and is Corporal Simms carrying the answer on his back in the holdall containing the contents of Sir Malcolm's safe? My gut tells me that it is near impossible and that as much as it pains me to accept, Dan is dead. Even if a cure is found, it is a long way off and I know that Dan, who loved life and lived it to the full, wouldn't forgive me if I left him here on this godforsaken roof to turn into pure evil. My hand is already on my Glock as if it is telling me what I have to do, and I pull the pistol out.

"Do you want me to do it?" Dixon asks from beside me.

"No," I tell him after a pause, "I'll do it for him."

Dixon raises his rifle and moves off, joining Simms and Kim, leaving me alone with Dan. His dead eyes still stare up to me and at the sky beyond. I bend down, pushing them closed, and then move around so I am standing behind his head. I raise the pistol, aiming at the top of his head.

"Rest easy mate," I tell Dan and I fire a single bullet.

Chapter 16

Turning to leave my friend where he lies, the loss weighs heavily on me, as Dan is the second real friend I've lost in action and I still haven't got over the first, Rick, and that was years ago. I feel bile trying to rise up in my stomach as nausea and grief threaten to take hold of me, I have to force them back and get my head back on point. Josh is flying above me and Emily and Catherine are waiting for us to return, I've got to focus on them for now; there will be time to grieve later. The mission is eighty percent complete but losing concentration and taking your eye off the ball for the last twenty percent, when you think you're in the home run, is a fatal error to make. This mission isn't over yet.

"Alders, receiving, over," I say into my radio.

"Receiving," he responds from above.

"Make your approach, let's get out of here, over," I order.

"Inbound, over and out."

Immediately, Alders breaks from his position and the Lynx starts to manoeuvre down towards the Helipad.

"Josh, receiving, over."

"Receiving."

"Keep covering that stairwell; the helicopter landing is going to rile them up so be ready and hold the position until it takes off and Alice can replace you, understood, over?"

"Understood," Josh replies.

Watts has taken Dan's position on the Browning, while Dixon and Kim are close by with their rifles also aimed at the door and I cover the rear with my rifle aimed at the hole, down into the building.

"First team, prepare for evac; that includes you, Simms, look after that holdall," I order. "Downey, you're with us, Kim, you go with the first team." Downey is a medic; always keep a medic close by.

Alders lands the first Lynx cautiously, which considering the high winds and torrential rain, is understandable; he handles it well. The first five men quickly embark onto the Lynx and seeing Simms get on with the holdall is a relief. As soon as they are all onboard, Alders powers the Lynx's engines and steadily takes off.

Watts constantly has to fire bursts from the Browning throughout the landing and take-off into the stairwell, he seems to be controlling the attacks. One Rabid escapes its fire but is quickly taken down by the other men. When the second Lynx lands, the Browning won't be covering our Evac; we will hold position until it's on the pad and then make a break for it, trusting that Alice has us covered when Alders' Lynx is in position.

Alders' Lynx rises into the murky forbidding sky that constantly has flashes of lightning running through it both near to our position and further out, over the city. Hell of a time for a savage storm like this to hit, I think to myself—right in the middle of our mission and Operation Denial that has tens of thousands of troops on the ground, trying to save the city. I discipline myself as I think that at least our mission is nearly done, we aren't home and dry yet.

Alders' Lynx nears its new covering position above us, and I see Alice preparing in the open hold, getting ready to provide cover for our Evac. As it closes in, Buck gives way, surrendering his position to Alders and then he starts to make his descent down to the Helipad, away to our right.

"Alice, receiving, over."

"Receiving, Captain," she answers.

"We will wait for your go-ahead and feel free to have a test fire," I tell her, knowing she hasn't used the door gun yet.

"Received, stand by."

Watts' firing of the Browning has slowed right down and I'm not sure if I should be relieved or alarmed by this. My gut tells me that it should be alarmed and that the Rabids are biding their time, waiting for the opportunity to strike.

We hold our position patiently, waiting for Buck to make his landing, knowing he has his work cut out for him with the atrocious weather conditions. Suddenly, Alice opens up with her door gun above and she hits the mark immediately, the tracer fire going straight through the open door and into the stairwell below. And my confidence unwittingly grows.

"Downey cover the rear," I order as Buck's Lynx gets close.

He takes up my position and I get up and move closer to the Helipad to watch Buck's descent and get ready to get my team on board. The Lynx descends slowly and steadily as Buck constantly makes corrections to the descent, as the wind tries to blow the Lynx off course. It is nevertheless coming down nicely, sideways towards the Helipad.

Directly above the Lynx, the sky flashes and as if in slow motion, a lightning bolt forks all the way down and strikes the middle of the Lynx's rotors. Shock and panic take over my body as the power of the rotors fails, grinding to a halt almost instantly and the helicopter drops like a stone from about ten meters up.

"Josh!" I shout as I break into a sprint towards the falling helicopter as if I can help him somehow. The bottom of the Lynx hits the side of the helipad, crushing and twisting its metal frame upwards. And for a second, I think it is going to stick there, miraculously held in place by the twisted metal frame. The left side of the helicopter is in mid-air though, and it starts to list over; it is going to plummet over the side of the building with Josh on board.

My feet hit the steps of the helipad as the Lynx approaches the point of no return, its list speeding up as it horribly tilts away from me. Suddenly the helicopter jolts as part of its fuselage breaks away from the helipad's frame; it is about to drop.

"Jump, Josh," I shout at the top of my voice in a frenzy, even though I can't see him.

My heart stops as I see Josh at the hold door, pulling himself up on its frame, his face grimaced in panic. "Jump!" I shout again. The Lynx shudders constantly as parts of the metal frame break and the helicopter starts to fall away from the building. *Fucking jump Josh, it's now or never* I think to myself as the helicopter goes into free fall.

Josh manages to get onto his feet just as the Lynx slips from its perch and he falls forward, out of the hold door, not managing a jump as the helicopter plummets out of sight and down the seven floors to the ground below. There is a sound of glass smashing as the Lynx tears into the side of the building, pulling windows and glass with it on its way down before it crashes into the tarmac below.

At first, I think my eyes are deceiving me when I see Josh clinging onto a part of the helipad's mangled frame that has been bent out from the mainframe by the force of the crash and the Lynx's fall. I scramble across the broken frame to get to him and pull him to safety, the remnants of the frame creaking as I go, as if it will give way and follow the helicopter's drop.

"Grab my hand," I tell Josh as I reach out to him.

Josh's chest is on top of the fragments of jutting-out steel and his hands grip to them as his legs dangle in mid-air below. He looks too frightened to move and his head keeps looking down at the remains of the Lynx below, where an orange glow is building from a fire taking hold of the wreckage. It is only a matter of time before the fire spreads to one of the fuel tanks and when that happens, the jet fuel will explode, taking the other fuel tanks with it.

Josh is right over the wreckage; he has to get out of the path of the fireball that will inevitably rise up when the fuel ignites.

"Josh, look at me," I say calmly, "Josh?"

He does eventually look at me. "Take my hand, let's get you off there."

Josh's right hand relaxes slightly and then he quickly releases the steel and grabs my outreached hand. "Good lad," I tell him and start to pull him up and over to me, from his precarious position. His left hand pulls himself to help me and his legs and feet soon start to help too as they get higher, reaching the steel.

We both climb across the mangled part of the pad.

"What happened?" Josh manages to say, bent over and shaken as we reach the undamaged part of the helipad.

"A lightning bolt strike," I tell him, catching my breath.

"Did the Wing Commander get out?" Josh asks, clearly disoriented.

"He didn't have a chance, I'm afraid."

"Bloody hell," he says sombrely and starts to cough heavily, still bent over as if he is going to be sick.

"Captain Richards, receiving, over?" Flight Lieutenant Alders' voice comes over my headset.

"Receiving."

"Sir, I can't land on the helipad, it's too damaged, so I will get into position off the East side of the building to pick you up, over."

"Hold position, and stand by, over," I order.

My wits start to return after the latest catastrophe and I start to weigh up our options, the priority is getting the holdall back to base. I struggle as I try to add up how many of us there are left to get back to base, my cluttered mind hindering me. Eventually, with a little help from my fingers, I count twelve people including the pilot Alders, who need transporting. That's too many for the Lynx to carry; it is rated to carry a maximum of nine people, so even with favourable conditions, which we are very far from, it would be a no go. Surely Alders knows that?

"Alders, receiving, over."

"Receiving, Captain."

"The Lynx is rated to carry nine people isn't it, over?" I ask.

"Yes, but if we dump equipment, it will handle twelve, Sir," he replies, forcing me to think again.

We have just lost one helicopter and a good man that was trying to land, and now I am considering letting Alders hover off the side of the building, in a thunderstorm for the remaining men to jump onboard and overload his helicopter while we will inevitably be under attack by Rabids, which they will as soon as the Browning stops shooting. His offer is very tempting nevertheless; the last thing I want is for us to be stranded here—my son, stranded—but in the end, I have to make a decision and the mission takes priority.

"Alders, return to base immediately, over."

"Captain, I can't leave you here," he protests.

"Picking us up is too risky; the holdall has to get back. Return to base now, that is an order, understood, over?"

The radio goes silent for a moment and the Lynx above doesn't break from its position.

"Returning to base, Captain, I will come back for you if I need to, you can count on it, over."

"Thank you, Flight Lieutenant, but I trust Lieutenant Winters is already making arrangements, over," I say in hope.

"Received, good luck, over and out." Alders signs off as the Lynx breaks position, swoops around and then powers forward with urgency in the direction of RAF Heathrow.

Silence ensues as me and my team watch the Lynx fade away into the rain, all of us, I am sure, with a feeling of foreboding and dread as to what will happen now.

Yet more gunfire erupts, which in a weird way I welcome because it snaps me out the feeling of helplessness growing inside me and back to action. Lieutenant Winters hasn't responded to my reference to him. I know he has been monitoring our communication for the entire mission, that is why I haven't updated him, but I would have expected to hear of him now.

"Lieutenant Winters, receiving, over?"

Still nothing; have comms failed at base? Was my assumption wrong and he hasn't heard a thing that has happened, or is it because of the weather?

"Lieutenant Winters, receiving, over?" I ask again, now worried that we really are stranded.

"Receiving, Captain," he finally says.

"Bloody hell, Winters, I thought comms had failed, over!"

"Sorry Captain, I was onto flight command, trying to arrange an emergency Evac for your team. The good news is that I've managed to get transport arranged, but the bad news is it's a forty-five-minute ETA, over."

"Negative, Lieutenant, we haven't got the ammo to hold out for forty-five minutes, we are running low as it is, so get it here quicker, over," I tell him, as I look over at the empty ammo cans on the floor by the Browning.

"Sorry Captain, I was trying to do just that, that's why I was off air. They can't get it to you any quicker. I had to screw them down to forty-five minutes. They are overstretched, it's chaos there, Sir, over."

"Keep on to them, we need evac A-SAP, Lieutenant, over."

"I will do my best, Captain, over and out."

Fuck, things are going from bad to worse, I think to myself and they are sure to get worse still; the fuel tanks on Buck's Lynx haven't ruptured yet and the Browning still has ammo, neither of which will last.

The rain comes down, lightning flashes, thunder rumbles, the Browning erupts and my brain strains to figure out how we are going to hold on for another forty-five minutes. We haven't been here for that long now, yet we have lost two men, one of them my best friend. A Lynx has

209

crashed, and our ammo is depleted. I'm struggling to formulate any kind of coherent defence.

Chapter 17

Josh seems to have got over his close escape from the plunging Lynx. I know it will hit him at some point. The torment of his experiences over the last two days, especially yesterday in the Tower of London—where God only knows what horrors he witnessed as his regiment was torn to shreds—will hit him. Post-Traumatic Stress Disorder will creep up on him over the next few days as he has time to sort through his memories and starts to file them in his head. The shock of what he has seen will start to bed in, he will start to relive the horrific events and the guilt of surviving when so many of his friends and comrades did not, will start to pull him down. I know this from my own experience of PTSD, but unfortunately, he doesn't possess the coping mechanisms I have been taught and honed over many years to deal with the stress. Even my well-practiced methods don't mean my demons go away; they never do, they are always there haunting me, as Emily will attest to.

Right at this moment, I have got to make sure that Josh and the rest of us have a chance to deal with our demons, somewhere down the line. We have got to stand our ground on this rooftop for another forty-five minutes. The only other option is to take cover inside the building and that would mean surrendering the roof to the Rabids, surrendering our only evac position. That is not an option, we make our stand here on this desolate piece of ground, we make our ammo last and we fight the enemy.

"Ammo, check!" I shout as Josh and I join the rest of our team across from the mouth of the doorway, the Browning silent for a moment.

"Just reloaded, last can," Watts spits out to me from behind the Browning, his concentration focused ahead of him. Dixon on his left flank and Downey on his right flank have their rifles aimed in the same direction and both update me with what they are still holding.

We need to conserve the last remaining can for the Browning; it will be vital to cover our evac when it finally arrives.

"Okay, listen up. Watts, conserve your ammo, only fire if you absolutely have to. Dixon, take first shot, then you Downey, then me and then Josh. I will throw down grenades if they build up. We gotta make the ammo last forty-five minutes, understood?" Just as I finish, Dixon fires twice, taking out another Rabid.

"Understood, Sir," Dixon says, his gaze not wandering.

Rabids only try to attack sporadically, in ones and sometimes twos. They are all despatched quickly by Dixon, with the help of Downey when needed but I don't have to fire my poised M4. My gut still tells me that it is just to test our defences, sacrificing a few of their kin to do it. A larger more determined attack is coming, I can feel it, so what are they waiting for?

My question is quickly answered, the crashed Lynx's fuel tanks finally blow, and it happens.

The blast from the left, behind us, is dulled by the seven floors of the Orion building that separate us from the explosion. The decibels it creates are further saturated in the pouring rain. The boom is still loud enough and together with the flash of orange light from the detonation, it is the trigger the Rabids have been waiting for.

They don't catch us by surprise, and we haven't been distracted by the explosion; we are prepared for the assault. Dixon fires first, shooting early as we see the first of the Rabids' heads appear above the pile of bodies on the stairs. Dixon's shot is excellent, straight through the forehead of the beast whose head whips back and it drops, yet another body added to the malingering pile.

Following straight behind the first doomed creature are two more, and this time, Dixon and Downey both fire their weapons. One is hit, but it's only a body shot, which it doesn't even register, and it doesn't slow it down. It breaks out into the open air before one of Dixon's rapid-fire bullets splits its head. The second evades Downey's shots completely as it springs up onto the side of the stairwell wall, grabbing onto the door frame near the top and seemingly to defy gravity, it springs into the air from there and comes hurtling towards us.

As the third in line to shoot, I do, firing at the flying creature as gravity does finally take hold of it and it arches down towards the rooftop. My automatic fire hits the Rabid in multiple places but it isn't until it hits the ground that I get my headshot and kill it.

Dixon and Downey are now almost constantly laying down rapid gunfire into the doorway as Rabids keep coming. Josh joins in the defence and takes down his fair share of targets while my concentration stays on the flying Rabid.

With my Rabid down, I release my M4 to hang at my front and grab two grenades, pulling the pins as I do. The three men firing are just about keeping the horde at bay and Watts has resisted getting in on the action, conserving his ammo as ordered. I wait for a gap and throw the first grenade through it and down into the stairwell, shouting "GRENADE!" as it goes. Before the grenade explodes, the second one is following down, and I have taken back hold of my M4.

Two explosions meld into one as the grenades go off, and as the blast escapes through to the roof, it brings with it Rabids. The force of the blast throws three catapulting out of the stairwell, but a blast that would stun or kill normal people doesn't faze the Rabids they hit the rooftop and spring up immediately. Their flesh torn and burnt, they dive at us; one comes directly at me before I have time to aim my rifle. I manage to step sideways out of its path and spin to bring my rifle around to bear on it. As I'm about to shoot it, Josh's rifle opens up from beside me, filling the Rabid with bullets. His fire quickly finds the Rabid's head and it drops, just in front of me. Josh doesn't pause to evaluate his kill and neither do I; we are back on task fast, our fire back at the stairwell, defending our position.

Dixon and Downey are concentrating their fire on the door too, having despatched the other two Rabids that were blown out from the stairwell. The Rabids keep coming and I'm getting very concerned with how much ammo we are expending holding them back. Watts has reverted to using his rifle from behind the Browning, to pick off any Rabids that are missed. I don't see any other option but to use more grenades to try and stem the flow of these fucking relentless creatures.

I pull the pin on one grenade and throw it down, trying to put more force into the throw and aiming higher into the stairwell in an attempt to get it further in and reduce the risk of the explosion blowing any Rabids out again. It's pot luck though. The grenade goes off with no Rabids blown out and I throw another down. My theory is that a succession of smaller explosions won't blow any out and do enough damage over the spread to stop them coming, or at least slow them down.

A total of four grenades explode inside the stairwell, smoke billowing out of the top of its doorway and into the dark rainy sky. Thankfully, following the fourth grenade exploding, the Rabids' attack ends, at least for now.

214

"Nicely done, Sir," Watts congratulates.

"Thanks, but let's not count our chickens. Stay ready; they will come again!"

That I am sure of. They will keep attacking, they can smell prey nearby. We need to get the fuck off this roof. We still have thirty minutes until evac and that was only estimated, it could be longer. I hold out no hope that it will be quicker. Not with how this mission has panned out so far.

"Lieutenant Winters. Receiving, over?"

"Receiving, over," he answers almost immediately.

"Latest ETA on evac, we are in the shit here, over!"

"Still no better, Sir, they are prepping for take-off, over."

"Prepping for take-off? Are they taking the piss? Order them into the air now, over!"

"I'm sorry, Sir, I've tried everything I can to speed things up, over."

"For fuck's sake, at this rate, there won't be anybody here to pick up. Apart from Zombies that is, over."

"I will try again, Captain. Please hold, over and out."

"Please hold," Dixon interjects. "Is this guy for real? Does he think we are trying to get a taxi to the airport?"

Thankfully, he doesn't say it over the radio for Winters to hear.

"I am sure he is doing all he can," I say, trying to calm the men, even though anger boils inside me. How can they leave us out here with our arses out? If we still had the contents of the safe, you can bet your bottom dollar Colonel Reed would have had birds in the air immediately. I will have to thank him next time I see him, I promise myself. So much for trying to do the right thing. "Okay, let's do an ammo check, while we can."

"Captain Richards, receiving, over?" Flight Lieutenant Alders' voice comes through my headset, taking me completely by surprise as he should be almost back at base.

"Receiving, Flight Lieutenant, over."

"Evac, ETA, five minutes, over," he tells me, but I struggle to understand what he means.

"Explain yourself, over," I tell him.

"I'm on my way back to pick you up, ETA, five minutes, over."

"You can't possibly have got back to base and back here that quickly, over."

"I haven't been back to base, I've put down in Richmond, dropped off most of the team and the holdall and turned around, over."

"Alders, you had your orders, the mission takes priority."

"It is, Sir, it will just be a bit late. The holdall is safe and none of us was just going to leave you behind, especially Alice. She was quite insistent, weren't you Alice?"

"You got that right, Sir," Alice says, "we are coming to get you!"

For a moment, I think about ordering them to turn around and complete the mission as ordered. The moment is only fleeting though, and my relief is shared by the rest of my team on the roof, that is plain to see.

"We will be ready, thank you," I tell them.

"Well that's a relief," Josh says, smiling.

"We aren't off this roof yet, son, stay alert." Josh's game face returns immediately, and he goes back behind his raised rifle.

Alders is going to have to pick us up from the north side of the building. That means the Lynx's door gun won't be able to cover the stairwell, I think, running through how we will evac. The south side has the burning Lynx at its base, giving off heavy black smoke and it could still explode further. That smoke is also affecting the east side, which is a no-go anyway because of the mangled helipad frame. We don't want to be climbing over that, we need a swift exit and the west side has all the buildings communication antennas and arrays lined up, high into the air.

The north side is the only viable option and the Browning is going to have its work cut out, covering the evac, as is the person who is going to be behind it.

It dawns on me that there hasn't been any lightning recently. The rain is still pouring down by the bucket load and the wind is still strong. Does that mean the thunder and lightning have passed, and perhaps our luck is changing? I bloody hope so, but I curse myself for thinking it and probably jinxing it.

Dixon fires off two shots in quick succession as if to chastise me for even thinking our luck is changing. The Rabids aren't done with us yet, and I hear Dan's voice in the back of my mind taking the piss for letting my mind wander, so I redouble my concentration.

"Take the right flank, with Josh, Lance Corporal," I order Watts, behind the Browning. "I'll take over, here."

Watts' chiselled face looks surprised and aggrieved by my order as if it is some kind of personal slight against his competency, which it is not. I see that he is about to make some sort of protest and tell me that he has it covered, but I tell him that he has his orders before he can. Watts stands aside and relinquishes the Browning to me, not looking too happy, and joins Josh on my right.

"Alders, receiving, over?" I say into my comms unit.

"Receiving, we are three minutes out, I can see the building, over."

"Received. Evac point is the North East side of the building to your left of the rooftop door, over."

"Received and understood, over."

"Get into position as quickly as possible. The noise of that Lynx will kick things off here, over."

"Received, over and out."

"Right," I say, "this is it. When the Lynx arrives, I will cover the Evac. Evac point is over there," I say, pointing to the right side of the building behind the stairwell door. "Josh and Watts, you're first to go. When you're on board, cover Dixon and Downey's retreat. The Lynx's door gun won't be accurate enough. Then I will make a break for it with your cover, understood?"

Everyone says "Yes Sir," apart from Josh.

"I'm not happy with that plan, Dad."

"It's the only way to do it. You have your orders."

"Dad, it leaves you too exposed!"

"Someone has to cover the evac, Josh. It's manageable unless someone has a better plan?"

Nobody does and silence ensues.

"Okay then, standby for Evac," I tell them.

In the distance, the sound of a helicopter starts to pierce the constant patter of rain falling onto the rooftop. I risk a quick look around behind me to where it will be approaching from and see the Lynx's lights floating in the air, through the rain and not too far away.

"Here it comes!"

Everybody tenses up and my stomach lurches. Josh is correct in his evaluation of the evac, I am going to be very exposed. He knew it as well as me, as did the rest of the men. Desperate times call for desperate measures, no matter how positive I tried to spin it for Josh. With each member of the team that breaks for the Lynx, the more exposed I will be until I will be here alone, with no backup. Just me and the Browning and then, when it's time for me to break for it, I will be leaving the power of the Browning too.

Noise from the Lynx's engines and rotors is now clear to hear. A feeling of relief is there amongst the one of anticipation and fear. I seriously doubt we would have held out for another twenty to twenty-five minutes waiting for the transport arranged by Winters. Whatever happens in the next few minutes was inevitable, even if we'd had to wait, so I'd rather do it now with the Browning loaded with a full chain of ammo.

"Dixon, before you go, throw two grenades down, okay?"

"You got it, Sir, and good luck."

The Lynx swoops in fast over our heads, before pulling its nose up and air braking suddenly out across from the north side of the building. A glimpse up shows me Alice gripping on at the open hold door, while Alders performs his sharp manoeuvres and a welcoming empty hold behind her.

Like clockwork, the noise brings the inevitable Rabid attack from the dark depths of the stairwell. I see Rabid heads and eyes first above the mounds of minced flesh on the stairs and in front of the doorway. Multiple targets present themselves as if they know this is their last chance to feed.

Dixon opens up first, shooting almost constantly at Rabid targets as they surge up and towards the open air. He is closely followed by Downey firing in more short-targeted bursts, and then Watts has to join in too, firing off single shots. I resist the nearly overwhelming urge to pull the trigger and unleash the Browning's fearsome power as I see the eyes of the baying creatures attacking, thirsty for blood.

With the onslaught in front, I cannot afford to watch Alders as he positions the Lynx ready for our evac. My eyes flick away from the fight and across the rooftop, checking the Lynx's progress, willing it to get into position quickly. At least then, Josh can retreat, get onto the transport and get the fuck out of harm's way.

That in itself will be a massive weight off my mind.

Each time I do steel a glance away from the attack and over at the Lynx, it is closer, and Alice gets bigger as she shouts directions out to her pilot. Rainwater starts to fly at us sideways across the rooftop as the downdraft from the spinning rotors of the Lynx starts to take effect, affecting our atmosphere. Alders seems to be taking an age to get into position, the noise from the helicopter increasing constantly. This isn't actually the case. I know that in the heat of battle, things happen very quickly until it's time to wait for something, especially for help when you're under fire, and then time extends.

Dead bodies are piling up inside the stairwell and around the doorway, and I see them all as dead as human dead bodies, not dead Rabids or dead Zombies. They are dead people. They were infected with an evil virus which turned them into horrific deadly creatures. Now they are dead, the virus is dead with them and it weighs heavy on me that we are forced to kill so many people, indiscriminately.

What other choice is there? We have to slaughter them, as they attack—and slaughter them, we do. Dixon and Downey are firing constantly to keep them at bay. The deafening noise from the incoming Lynx now that it is almost in position is like a drug to the Rabids and revs them up even more.

"Alders is in position!" Josh shouts at me.

"Okay, Josh, give me your last grenades and then move now, you two!" I shout back at Josh and Watts.

Josh gives me two grenades and then immediately makes a break for it, running across the roof, his rifle swinging from side to side in his hands across the front of his body, and water splashes up as his feet hit the sodden roof.

Watts waits a few seconds; his rifle's aim not wavering from the doorway. As Josh reaches halfway to the Lynx, Watts shoots out a burst from his rifle into the stairwell before dropping his aim, pulling his rifle in and turning to run after Josh.

I see Josh climb onboard the Lynx, Alice taking his hand to help pull him in and a wave of relief washes over me. The feeling is short-lived, however, as I turn my full concentration back to the onslaught in front of me and place my finger fully onto the trigger of the Browning.

Dixon and Downey move across the front of the Browning's muzzle as they get into position for their retreat, shooting as they go.

"Move it!" Dixon shouts to Downey, who releases his last few shots and then makes his break for the Lynx.

Suddenly, there is nothing to shoot at, nothing moving in the dark stairwell. There are no dead eyes or gaping mouths to aim at. Dixon shoots a look in my direction, confusion etched on his face. Is that all of them? Have we won the battle and managed to kill the hoard of Rabids that were so determined to taste our flesh?

"Go!" I shout at Dixon, who drops his rifle down and turns, ready to run.

The moment 'go' leaves my mouth, the sound of a stampede echoes out at me from the hellhole across from me. Dixon hears it too and is caught in stasis mid-turn, trying to decide whether to carry on and go for the Lynx or reverse his turn, to fight whatever is coming.

"Go, I'll cover!" I shout again at him, making his decision for him. Fear rushes through my body as I immediately regret telling him to go.

Dixon sprints across the roof, making it halfway across to the Lynx in no time. That's it, I say to myself, Dixon is nearly there, time for me to make a run for it. I glance over again to the Lynx and see Josh at the door, shouting desperately and waving me to come, to run to him.

Chapter 18

My hand relaxes slightly around the grip of the Browning and my index finger goes to move from its trigger as I go to make my run to the waiting Lynx. Josh is waving at me to run, frantically.

Time slows and all the noise around me is extinguished as my brain computes what my eyes are seeing. Heads are bobbing, with wide evil eyes piercing the murky darkness of the stairwell as a new attack is rushing towards me. There are more Rabids than I have seen before coming up the stairwell, trampling over the bodies as if it is one last push for them to finally break out, out of their dungeon. Some Rabids aren't quick or strong enough and they fall down to be trampled into the mush of flesh below.

Every fibre of my body wants to run to the Lynx, to Josh and the others. My brain calculates that it will be a fatal mistake, that there is only a second until they do break out into the open air. I would be engulfed with Rabids as soon I attempted to run, there is no one in a position to cover me.

Adrenaline washes into my bloodstream, and my hand instantly tightens around the grip of the Browning and my index finger pulls sharply on the trigger.

I barely register the roar from the Browning as it lights up and sprays bullets out of its chamber, into its barrel and out of its muzzle, which instantaneously becomes red hot. The Rabids at the front of the attacking horde don't stand a chance and are cut to pieces, as are the ones coming up behind them. As they fall and go down, ripped apart, others replace them, undeterred by the fate of their kin. These too are despatched by the Browning with ease; they are all coming from the same place and it can't miss, its power is too great.

That power is finite, however, and it cannot last. I try to ease my rate of fire, try using shorter bursts to conserve the ammo contained in the chain being fed into the gun. A chain that is nearly half used already. I desperately hope that the attack will slow or even better, it stops again for them to regroup. The Rabids keep coming though; perhaps this really is their final hoorah, and they are not going to stop until they are all either dead, or I am.

My mind manages to imagine Josh, even in the middle of my desperation. It sees him trying to jump down from the Lynx so that he can run back across the roof and help me. It sees Dixon and Watts holding him back, even when he tries to fight. They won't let him go and in some imaginary way, I thank them for it.

There is no sign of the attack easing. The Rabids are still hurtling into the Browning's hail of bullets without hesitation. I have no idea how many I have cut down, but it is a lot and my ammo is depleting rapidly.

I only have one option that I can think of; use the two grenades Josh gave me. Throw them in front of the door and hope the blasts blow the fuckers back down the stairs to give me the little time I need.

My right hand on the Browning, keeping it firing, my left hand reaches for the first of the grenades that I'd placed by the feet of the Browning. Picking it up, I raise it to my mouth and pull out the pin with my teeth. The pin slips out and I spit away.

Throwing the grenade into a good position is not going to be easy, especially left-handed. Bodies and body parts litter the ground in front of the door, two, three and even four bodies deep. All I can do is get the distance right, where it ends up in the mangled mess is going to be a lottery, the best I can hope for is that it stays on top. The first one arcs through the air, but I don't look to see where it ends up because I am reaching for the second grenade whilst still firing the Browning. I throw the second one, trying to do it as quickly as possible so that the blasts happen as closely together as they can.

I keep my finger on the trigger of the Browning, firing constantly, using as much ammo as possible, even if I don't see a target. Any ammo remaining after the grenades go off will be wasted anyway because I won't be here to fire it.

Grenade number one explodes and I duck down, taking as much cover as I can behind Dan's hastily constructed firing point. The blast is considerable. I must have been lucky where the grenade landed, and I hope the second explosion is equally fierce. My hand stays on the grip of the Browning and I keep firing blind, trying not to move its aim away from the door. The heat from the blast hits my raised gloved hand but doesn't threaten to burn it, and I wait for blast two which will be my signal to make my run.

Seconds after the first, grenade two explodes. My luck hasn't held though. The second blast is dulled, the grenade must have nestled down into the bodies. Nevertheless, it is now or never, my right hand releases the Browning, my legs push off and I spring up from behind the firing point.

As soon as I'm up, I know I'm in trouble and my legs nearly falter. Rabids are at the door already and coming through. How, I don't know, but they are. The only consolation is that they look dazed and uncertain; could it be the smoke and mist from the explosions is hampering their vision? That won't last. They are still flooding out and they are right in my path to the Lynx.

I run parallel to the Lynx in the vain hope that I can run around them. Gunfire erupts from the Lynx, from whom, I can't afford to look but it does take some of them down. The noise from the new gunfire also has the effect of attracting the Rabids to it—or at least some of them—and away from me, but that is taking more of them into the path between me and the Lynx.

Shit, I keep running away from the door with nowhere to go and with Rabids spreading across the roof. A chilling screech pieces my ears from behind, I daren't look back but I can feel them behind me. Not all are going towards the gunfire. The damaged helipad... can I take shelter on that somehow, get out of their reach or find cover for a new firing position? No, I quickly decide, they would be on me before I had a chance to find anything up there.

I sprint to the only possible harbour there is, the hole in the roof, and the depths of the building below.

Rabids are close behind me, I can feel them, they are gaining on me. I see the hole coming up in front of me and I never would have thought that dark abyss would ever look so inviting.

Meters away from the hole, a Rabid is right behind me. I see it out of the corner of my eye, the dark figure almost upon me, ready to pounce. Adrenaline pumps into my legs, forcing them to go faster. They are no competition for the speed of the Rabid though, and the beast jumps at me.

I drop down below its jump and slide along, through the water that covers the entire roof, aiming for the gaping hole that is just in front and hoping the speed of my slide will carry me far enough to reach it. The Rabid sails over me, flailing its arms down to try and grab me. The creature misses and without me to stop it, it flies over the hole, then hits the edge of the building with a crunch before bouncing off and disappearing over the edge.

Snatching a look behind me, I see another coming at me. My momentum is more than enough to reach the hole, but I don't try to slow. I let my slide carry me into the hole. As I reach the edge I swivel and grab hold of one of the fast ropes that still hangs down and use it to control my descent back down into the building. My wet boots hit the sideboard hard and slip from beneath me on the polished varnished top. Falling forwards, I try to stop myself by gripping the rope harder, but it doesn't stop me going down; the wet rope and wet hands nullify the friction. My stomach hits the edge of the sideboard, bringing me to a sudden stop and winding me, I let go of the rope and fall down onto the floor, gasping for breath.

Trying to pull myself together, curled up on the floor of Sir Malcolm's office that is bleaker than ever, the orange light waning, the glowsticks well past their peak. I'm aware of something at the hole above me, peering down. Quickly gathering myself, my hand reaches for the Sig in my shoulder holster, I pull it out and roll onto my back, raising the pistol up in both hands.

A silhouette drops right at me, its shadowy form unmistakable. As it comes down into the dull orange glow, its mouth is gaping open and a loud screech vibrates down into my ears, threatening to make them bleed. The orange glow reflects into the Rabid's eyes and I take my shot, aiming right between its dark pools.

The screech is immediately cut off as my bullet hits its mark. I roll to the side, out of the falling body's way and I just make it in time. It smacks into the floor next to me with a thud. The dead Rabid's head bounces back off the floor before it comes to a stop down on Sir Malcolm's rug, with one lifeless eye looking in my direction. I'm transfixed by that eye for a moment, a moment I can't afford.

I don't register the second Rabid coming through the hole above until it is too late. There is no time to react and bring the Sig to bear on it. The beast lands right in front of me and on top of the dead Rabid, its head whipping around, fixing its cursed eyes on me. Shock rips through me, making my mind flounder and my body goes rigid.

Mustering some function back into my limbs, my arm feebly tries to bring the Sig up, to try and get some kind of shot away. My arm just isn't quick enough, it's not even close. The Rabid's legs push it sideways straight at me, its twisted face full of hatred and its vile mouth opening.

A welcome rush of adrenaline finally courses through my failing body, energising it, giving me some strength back. I manage to get my arms up to meet the onslaught, just in time, the Sig dropping to the floor. Off-balance, the Rabid has no trouble pushing me backwards onto the floor, but my arms lock into position. Sitting astride me, the Rabid's neck stretches as it tries to get its snarling evil face into me; my arms hold firm though against its shoulders, trying to push it back.

Drool from its wide mouth hits my face but I ignore it; my only thought is to keep those teeth as far away from me as I can. The Rabid's strength is overpowering, its determination to feed relentless, I redouble my effort to keep pushing it back. Its head goes back slightly, relieving some of the pressure from my arms before it springs forward again, letting out an almighty scream from the depths of its throat. Inches away from my face, the scream is almost overwhelming, penetrating me to my core and the smell from its noxious breath is nearly enough to knock me out, it makes me urge.

I do not buckle or give in, my determination to fight coming from deep within me. I have to fight and survive for my children, there is no other option.

We are in a stalemate, my arms holding firm against the Rabid's strength, neither of us backing down. The Rabid quietens down and stares at me, looking deep into my eyes as if it is looking into my soul. I stare back into its black eyes, looking for some semblance of humanity, if there is any remaining. Darkness is the only thing I see.

The pressure is suddenly released from my arms as the Rabid straightens its back and rises up from my arms. At that moment, I gamble, quickly lowering my right arm and reaching for the Glock in my side holster. As I pull the pistol out, the Rabid screams down at me again and swings its right hand towards my face as if it is going to punch me. Instinct makes me pull the trigger.

Recoiling from the force of the bullet that hits it somewhere in the left side of its body, its swinging hand hits me on the left side of my face. The hand scrapes across my face and I feel the Rabid's nails dig into my cheek, tearing across it.

Panic and terror engulf my entire being as I feel my skin tear. I pull the Glock's trigger, again and again, I keep firing, filling the Rabid's body with bullets. The Rabid jolts on top of me as the bullets rip into its body until I abruptly pull the Glock up and shoot the fucking thing through the bottom of its jaw. The bullet blows the top of its head off on exit and the Rabid drops back away from me, dead.

In a daze, I quickly get to my feet and scramble over to the door of Sir Malcolm's bathroom and yank it open. The darkness inside is almost total and the stench of death fills my nostrils. I search my body for the penlight that I know I have on me somewhere. Pressing the switch, the torches light illuminates the bathroom. Sir Malcolm's dead body, the cause of the stink, is where I left him splayed on top of the toilet, I take no notice of him. Entering the bathroom, I close the door behind me and lock it; more fucking Rabids are bound to come, following the gunshots. Going over to the marble sink on the left, I look into the mirror above it and shine the light onto my face.

Blood seeps from three long gashes on my left cheek, my head spins and dizziness threatens to take hold and make me faint as my blood rushes out of control.

Dropping to my knees, I put my head down between them, getting blood back into my brain whilst forcing myself to control my breathing.

Gradually, my breathing slows and the dizziness subsides. Dark thoughts go through my mind in the silence, bent over on the floor. I am infected, I know it, I can feel this virus in my cheek, ready to burrow further into my bloodstream. Images of Josh and Emily pass across my eyelids. I have let them down, especially Emily, still so young and so dependent on me. I feel immense sadness that I won't be there for her and to see her grow, and it fills me, tears seeping through my closed eyes.

Despair nearly takes over me, but then Josh and Emily start to give me hope and strength; am I going to give up on them so easily? Never!

Lifting my head, I look over in the direction of Sir Malcolm, immediately seeing what I knew was there. I scramble across the floor and grab the bottle of Sir Malcolm's best single malt Scotch whisky, his last tipple before shooting himself. Discarding the top, I pour it straight onto my gashed cheek. The sharp sting is instant, but it doesn't deter me, I pour again, whisky running down my cheek and neck and soaking into my top. Now I put the bottle to my lips and take a large swig, the whisky biting, burning my throat before it slides into my welcoming belly, warming it.

Getting to my feet, I pull the toilet roll from its holder and return to the sink, plonking the bottle and roll down. Under the torch's light, I look again at the gashes and pick up the bottle to have another large swig. Using my fingernails, I retrace the lines of the gashes, digging deep into my own skin, ignoring the pain. I want to get the blood flowing outwards.

Blood seeps more readily out of the gashes after my surgery and I pour more whisky over them. The sharp sting feels deeper now, or is it just my mind playing tricks?

Unfurling a good wad of paper from the toilet roll, I drench it in whisky and press the sodden paper into my cheek, pressing hard and keeping it there despite the burning sensation. The smell of whisky is strong, anybody coming into the bathroom now would think I'm trying to drink myself to death, not trying to save myself.

A deep burning throb pulses in my cheek, I scan around the sink for some painkillers. Sir Malcolm always had some around for the arthritis he suffered with, in his hip. Nothing. Picking up the torch, I check the cupboard under the sink, and bingo, packets of ibuprofen piled next to his other drugs. I take two tablets swilled down with water and I lower the wet paper to check my wounds in the mirror. My cheek is swollen and the gashes quite inflamed, worryingly so. Despair flares up again and my head drops; this isn't the first time I've been injured, not by a long chalk, the gashes don't look normal.

Trying to stay positive, I pick up the torch again to see what else is in the cupboard. There are various packets of drugs; Sir Malcolm must have had other ailments I was unaware of. I have no idea what most of them are for, but I do recognise the antibiotics. They won't have any effect on the virus if I am infected, but at least they will stop an infection from the wounds. Putting the antibiotics onto the top, I look again at the other packets. There are two different packets that look like the antibiotics and I decide to take them along with the antibiotics; one of them might be antiviral, so what have I got to lose?

Turning away from the mirror, the concoction of pills taken, I slump down onto the floor again. This time, however, I sit with my back resting on the cupboard below the sink, the paper still pressed onto my cheek. I have done all I can, I think to myself, and I unclip my M4 which is still strapped at my front and put it onto the floor beside me. The burning has gone off, so I pour more whisky onto the paper, have one last swig and then press the paper back against my cheek. I

231

haven't noticed if any Rabids have entered the office next door; I haven't been listening and I'm almost beyond caring.

Now I can only wait to see if I am infected. Time will tell, although I don't know how much time. I hope Josh is halfway back to base, back to relative safety and to be reunited with his sister. My head flops back against the cupboard. I think I will rest my eyes for a minute.

Chapter 19

Josh runs across the roof, directly at the waiting Lynx and the welcome sight of Alice waiting at the hold door to help him on board. Water droplets spin through the air in every conceivable direction, gravity having lost the battle against the helicopter's rotors, at least for now.

Alice grabs his outstretched arms and pulls him into the relative calmness of the Lynx's hold. They don't exchange any pleasantries, Alice immediately raising her rifle again, aiming back across the roof to provide cover. Josh spins around, taking a position next to Alice and he does the same ready to help Watts who is approaching fast.

Downey is quickly onboard too, but Dixon is hesitating; something is wrong, Josh thinks frantically. He sees his Dad shout at Dixon who then, thankfully, lowers his rifle and starts to make his run. Josh allows a small amount of relief as Dixon comes; his Dad should be close behind him. Dixon passes halfway but his Dad doesn't move from his position. *Now, Dad, run now!*

A blast of noise travels across the roof as the Browning erupts. Dixon slows, debating whether to turn around and go back to help. He decides against it though, as it might do more harm than good, and this was the plan. So he carries on and boards the Lynx.

Feeling helpless, Josh can only watch his Dad in his fight. He gets more and more anxious as he knows the

Browning must be running low on ammo and there is no sign of the fight ending. He sees his Dad start to struggle with grenades and it tips him over the edge.

Josh goes to jump down from the Lynx. Someone has hold of his body armour, pulling him back. Dixon has been waiting ready to intervene, expecting Josh to have a rush of blood, to go and try to help his Father.

Anger gets the better of Josh and he turns to fight off whoever is holding him.

"Let me go!" Josh growls in Dixon's face.

"I'm sorry, Josh, I can't. Stick to the plan, give your Dad a chance."

Two explosions go off in quick succession.

"Stand by!" Watts shouts.

Josh and Dixon immediately end their face-off, their focus returning to the fight across the roof.

Josh sees his Dad spring up from behind the Browning to make his retreat to the Lynx.

"Yes. Dad, run!"

Rabids shoot across the roof, almost out of nowhere, cutting off the path to the Lynx, the explosions seemingly having no effect.

"Covering fire!" Dixon shouts. "Alice, get on the door gun."

Rabids are already coming at the Lynx even before they start shooting, but more come when the firing starts.

Josh can't focus on finding targets to shoot; he is fixed on watching his Dad run for his life. He is running away from the Lynx and it's obvious he isn't going to be able the reach it. There are too many Rabids between and more piling onto the roof constantly.

"Take us up, Alders," Dixon instructs, seeing the same as Josh, knowing they are no good where they are. A higher altitude will give them a better position of attack and they will be better placed to hopefully evacuate the Captain.

As the Lynx rises steadily, Josh sees more clearly the trouble his Dad is in. There are two Rabids right behind him with more following. Josh does now aim his rifle, trying to get the lead Rabid in his sights. He doesn't; it is too far away and moving at speed, so he has as much chance of hitting his Dad as hitting the Rabid.

"He is going for the hole; he is going into the building!" Josh shouts as he realises his Dad's only option. "Get us over there, Alders!"

The Lynx tilts and turns, Josh's view is cut off. He desperately moves around the hold to try and see what's happening. He is too late; his Dad has disappeared when he gets eyes on again.

"Where's he gone; did anybody see?" Josh shouts, panicked.

"He went into the building," Alders confirmed over the radio. "Two targets followed him in."

"Get me over the hole, I'm going in!"

"Negative, put us into a covering position, away from the hole," Dixon says, overruling Josh.

"Are you fucking joking? Get me over the hole! If you want to sit up here, that's up to you!"

"Josh you're not thinking clearly, we need to draw them away from the hole and regroup. If we go over that hole, they will pile into it."

"We've got to help him."

"We will, Josh," Alice interjects.

"The first thing is to stop them coming onto the roof; what explosives have we got?" Dixon asks.

"Only grenades," Watts says, "we left the C4 by the safe. But I have an idea; we collapse the walls on the stairwell, with the door gun. Its 50-cal, it will do it and it will divert them away from the hole while we do it."

Dixon thinks for a second, looks at Josh and then orders Alder into position.

"Watts, take the door gun. Everyone else. start clearing that roof, use grenades if we have to, just get it cleared!"

How many Rabids followed his Dad into that dark pit, Josh wonders; is it already too late to help him? *No, stay positive. There is still hope. If nothing else, Dad is a fighter.* Perhaps this is the reason his Dad spent so much time away in foreign lands fighting when Josh was young, becoming almost a stranger. Was it fate, to prepare him for these dire days, so he could protect Emily and save Josh from the White Tower? They say God works in mysterious ways. God or not, if anyone can survive down in that building, it is his Dad.

Alice relinquishes the door gun to Watts as Alders brings the Lynx into position. Josh has already started taking pot shots out of the hold door, his face a ball of determination and concentration.

The wind blows through the hold since Dixon slid open the opposite door. The wind brings with it rain and the smell of acrid smoke, but it means they can clear the roof from both sides of the Lynx. With Dixon and Downey on the opposite side, Alice takes a position behind Josh, raises her rifle and starts looking for targets.

The 50-cal door gun bursts into life, the noise tremendous even with the team's headsets defending their ears. Watts aims for the bottom of the first side of the wall that protrudes up from the roof, to hold up the small roof that covers the stairwell below. The stream of 50-calibre bullets hits the breeze blocks like a chain saw cutting through wood. Watts steadily moves his aim across the whole side of the wall, cutting a line through it.

The assault has the added effect of stopping more Rabids coming onto the roof. Whether it is because the bullets go through the wall and cut the Rabids down on the stairs, or they have paused until it stops, it's hard to know.

With the first sidewall of the structure cut, Watts instructs Alders to move around. The back wall is quickly cut through, leaving the moment of truth, cutting through the last side. The Lynx moves around and as it does, the rest of the team continues to clear the roof of Rabids, shooting constantly.

Watts opens up on the last wall, shooting the breeze blocks, hoping to see the structure collapse. The gun stops its assault, but dismally, the structure is still standing.

"Shoot up the sides," Alice offers.

A grin crosses Watts' face as he adjusts his aim and does just that. He peppers bullets up the side of the wall, which starts to shudder. The middle goes first, caving inwards, closely followed by the top and bottom of the wall, which is pulled down by the middle. There is no cloud of dust to speak of, the soaking rain extinguishing it. Still the roof stands, however, held up by the two other walls that refuse to collapse. Their refusal is short-lived, Alders has to hover around, but a short burst from the 50-cal takes the other side wall down. It collapses down into the stairwell and almost perfectly brings the back wall down with it, the roof helping to pull it into the stairwell. A pile of breeze block rubble now fills the stairwell with the roof almost entirely covering the top. That danger is blocked.

"Why didn't you do that at the fucking start!" Dixon jokes at Watts' expense.

"Because you didn't ask me to," he retorts.

"Good job, now get that gun clearing the roof," Dixon orders.

Gradually, the roof is cleared of moving Rabids; the 50-cal does the majority of the killing, but the whole team gets their fair share. No grenades are used, as they aren't needed. Alders moves the Lynx around as directed until every one of the Rabids is dealt with.

The slaughter complete, the roof is littered with bodies. Rabids still move, crawling or flailing around, stranded in position where they fell. They pose little threat if the team is careful to avoid them. Josh, understandably, is eager to get down onto the roof and presses Dixon.

"Okay, take us down," Dixon finally instructs Alders. "Watts, cover us, stay on that gun. We are going to take it nice and easy down there. Watch your footing; just because these fuckers are down doesn't mean they are dead, we don't want anyone else bitten."

Alders manoeuvres the Lynx back into its original position. He hovers off the north side of the building, lowering to allow them to disembark.

Josh ignores Dixon's instructions about taking it steadily. As soon as the Lynx is low enough, he plunges off the side of the helicopter. Landing on the roof with a splash, he doesn't wait for back-up, he is off and running. Swerving around the carnage spread across the rooftop, he takes the shortest route possible to get to the hole.

"Bloody hellfire!" Alice hears Dixon moan as Josh sets off; she doesn't take any notice though as she jumps down and sets off after him.

Dixon and Downey are down on the ground soon enough, but they are more cautious, stalking behind their rifles looking for threats, covering the two overzealous younger members of the team. Nothing attacks; the clean-up has been comprehensive, Dixon made sure of that. He foresaw Josh bolting to his father, and he doesn't blame him for it, not one bit.

All that remains on the rooftop are dead Rabids and Rabids with catastrophic injuries, rendering them little or no threat. That doesn't stop these two men going through their processes, scanning, checking blind spots, methodically moving, drawing on their training.

Reaching the hole, Josh's stomach lurches horribly as he looks down into Sir Malcolm's office. Two bodies lie on the floor in the dim office, neither of them moving. Is one of them his dad? The room is too dark to make out if it is or not, Josh trembles as he kneels, straining to see.

"I don't think either is him," Alice says as she stoops next to Josh.

"I can't tell, it's too dark, so I'm going down."

"Hold on," Alice says as she cracks three glow sticks one after the other and throws them down.

"It looks like you're right, so where the hell is, he?" Josh questions as the orange glow is revitalised from the new sticks. "I'm going in, cover me."

Without waiting for an answer, Josh starts to climb down into the building. Dixon and Downey arrive on the scene just as Josh starts to disappear.

"You two cover," Dixon orders Downey and Alice as he goes to follow Josh down.

Josh stands on the floor next to the two bodies. One of them is face-up, a Rabid, its eyes fixed open, dead. The other is face down and Josh is almost afraid to turn it over. The body clearly isn't his Dad, but he is afraid nevertheless; what if he has got it wrong somehow and his mind is playing tricks on him?

Josh forces himself to bend down and turn the body, so he can be sure.

Two dead Rabids are good, but where is his dad? There is no one else in the office and no other bodies. The office door is shut with a desk pushed up against it so he couldn't have gone out there, if he had, the desk would have been moved.

"Where is he?" Dixon asks as he gets down, looking around the room in confusion.

"There is only one place he can be, in the bathroom," Josh answers, looking over to the bathroom door.

Dixon grabs Josh's arm as he goes to move towards the door. "Let's do this right, Josh, we don't know what is behind that door, understood?" He looks Josh straight in the eye.

"Yes Sir," Josh replies.

"Good lad. Get your rifle light fixed," Dixon tells Josh as he goes to get his mounted.

Both men approach the door, their rifles aiming out in front. Even with the two lights shining onto the door, it looks dark and ominous, the dark wood appearing to soak up the majority of the light.

"On my mark," Dixon tells Josh as Josh goes forward, his hand reaching for the door handle.

Dixon steadies himself, pulling the butt of his rifle snugly into his shoulder, aiming, ready to tackle whatever surprises are about to be released.

"Mark."

Josh, his rifle raised in one hand, swiftly pulls down on the door handle with the other and swings the door open. In the same motion, he steps back towards Dixon, ready to fire.

Light from their raised rifles shines into the bathroom, catching a slouched dead figure seated on the toilet. Neither of them is sure who the figure is, but the dark suit trousers and loafers tell them it isn't Josh's Dad.

Dixon's body tenses as he sees another figure on the floor. He lowers his aim suddenly to throw light on it, ready to shoot.

"Dad?" Josh says involuntarily as he is drawn to the figure sitting on the floor, their back against the sink cupboard. Josh knows it is his Dad, but he can't see his face though. His head is bowed down, his chin against his chest, his arms unmoving, palms up each side of him on the floor.

"Dad!" Josh is more forceful, scared that his Dad is dead, and he goes to rush into the bathroom but is stopped.

"Nice and easy now, Josh," Dixon tells him, again taking hold of his arm.

Josh knows why Dixon is being cautious, he doesn't want to deal with that, he tries to ignore the possibility. He does move into the bathroom slowly now, however, towards his dad. As he enters the smell of death is stomach-churning. Josh pushes through it and another smell accosts his nostrils, a strong smell of whisky. Has his Dad been drinking, is he asleep from the influence? That can't be, surely?

Josh nears, but his step falters as his Dad's head starts to rise up from his chest. Josh is shocked by his appearance, his face almost grey, drained of blood and sweaty. His eyes are darkly glazed and half-shut. Most shocking of all, however, are the three trailing cuts across his left cheek, running down towards his chin. The horror of those wounds is not lost on Josh; he has been clawed by one of the two dead Rabids on the office floor. His Dad is infected.

Now Josh does think he is going to be sick, his head spinning, he can't breathe.

"Josh, is that you?"

Is Josh hearing things? He must be, he thinks to himself; can the Zombies talk now?

"Dad?"

"Josh, what are you doing here, you should be going back to base, to Emily?"

"I came to find you, Dad. What happened?"

"I got scratched, I think I'm infected. Sorry, Josh."

"You got nothing to be sorry for, how do you feel?"

"Terrible, son, I feel terrible, thirsty."

"Downey, get down here pronto, we have a medical situation," Dixon orders into his radio.

Josh grabs a glass from the sink, fills it with water and goes down to his Dad, offering the glass to his cracking lips. Andy manages to drink some of the water down but then starts coughing and retching.

"Pills on the side; give me two of each," Andy manages to say.

Josh does, not knowing what else to do, he puts them in his dad's mouth and raises the glass again.

"Thanks, son."

"Shit," Downey says as he arrives at the doorway next to Dixon, a look of shock on his face.

"Anything you can do?" Dixon asks him.

"I brought some rabies antiviral shots with me. I doubt they will do any good?"

"Well, why did you bring them?"

"All I could think of in case I got bit, silly really," Downey says, slightly embarrassed.

"Give him one," Josh urges.

"I really don't think it will do any good."

"Do it!"

Downey unclips the strap from around chest and shrugs off his medi-backpack. He goes down on his haunches, putting the pack in front of him, unzips the top and rummages inside. He rises holding a pair of latex gloves, a sealed packet and a small plastic wallet, with the top open showing four syringes. Putting on the gloves, he slides a syringe out.

"Put your head back against the cupboard please, Captain," Downey asks, bending down in front of Andy. He covers his nervousness of being so close to an infected person well.

Downey inspects the wounds, rips open the sealed antiseptic wipe and cleans off the wounded area.

"Hold his head still," he asks Josh as he prepares the syringes. "This is going to hurt, Captain, try not to move."

Andy says something unintelligible under his breath, his dry lips barely able to move. Downey lines up the injection in between the top two cuts on Andy's cheek and then pushes the needle into the flesh. He is careful not to go too deep and risk the needle popping out of the inside of the cheek. The plunger goes all the way down, pumping the serum into the cheek.

Josh loses his grip on his dad's head as the injection goes in. Andy, enraged by the searing pain, pulls his head free and growls harshly at the perpetrator. Downey stumbles backwards, almost falling over, shocked by the reaction and afraid Andy was going to bite him.

Josh, shocked too, moves his hands away and gets up.

"Sorry, that hurt, a lot," Andy manages to say.

"It's okay, Dad, don't worry; it looked painful," Josh tries to comfort.

"That's just the first injection, three others are supposed to be taken over the next fourteen days," Downey says, recovering somewhat.

Andy's head flops down uncontrollably. It then comes up again, his unrecognisable eyes looking for Josh.

"It's time for you to go, Josh, you're going to have to leave me here."

"No, Dad, we will take you out of here, somewhere safe and I'll stay with you, help you fight it."

"I'm not going anywhere; you have to get back to Emily. There is no other way, you know that."

"He is right, Josh," Dixon says. "We have to move out, now."

"Leave me those injections and any other supplies you can spare."

Josh has to accept the inevitable. Dixon and Downey unload themselves of all the supplies they can, as does Josh, finally. They put the stuff into separate piles on the floor, ammo, medical, food and a pile of other stuff like batteries. The food pile is small, only a few ration packs, energy bars and some chocolate. Downey puts the wallet of injections down onto the floor next to Andy's M4, making sure he knows they are there.

"Help me take my helmet off," Andy asks weakly. Josh does and puts it onto the floor with the rest of the kit. "Dixon, can you take Sir Malcolm out of here, put him on the couch?"

Dixon and Downey go to move the body out.

"Josh," Andy says, his head moving around slightly as if he has trouble seeing his son.

"I'm here, Dad."

"Go to your sister, don't let anybody separate you. Colonel Reed gave me his word we could leave after this mission."

"I will."

"Tell Emily I was killed quickly. Tell her the truth when she is older if you feel you have to. She won't handle it yet. Look after each other, whatever happens. But it won't be easy, especially now.

"I know how you feel about her, but see if you can reach your mum, forgive her, okay?"

"Yes, Dad, I will, I will make sure Emily is safe and well."

"Thanks, son, I love you both, tell Emily for me."

"She knows that, but I'll tell her."

"Fight this, Dad, you have to fight it, promise me," Josh says taking his dad's hand in his, it feels so cold.

"I promise. Now go."

Josh places his Dad's hand back down on the floor by his side and reluctantly gets up. Dixon is back in the doorway waiting for Josh. Downey has already gone back onto the roof with Alice. Josh has a thought and unclips the light from his rifle, switching it off. It's only a matter of time until the batteries in the torch on the sink-top drain.

"Dad, I'm putting a torch into your hand for when you need it; can you feel it?"

"Yes Josh, I've got it."

"Keep fighting, Dad, I love you. Contact us if you can okay?"

"I will look after your sister, Josh. Now get out of here."

Josh gets up again and turns away from his Dad, whose head is dropping to his chin again. Dan flashes into his mind, lying on his back on the roof with his Dad standing over him, pointing his pistol. Josh cannot contemplate doing the same for his Dad or anyone else using that remedy. Josh and Dixon's eyes meet for a second, Josh knows what he is thinking but nothing is said and thankfully, Dixon turns to leave.

Josh pauses at the door, taking one last look at his Dad before he leaves and pushes the door gently closed behind him. Tears well up in Josh's eyes, he feels like he is shutting him into his tomb and the guilt of having to leave him behind is too much to bear.

Epilogue

Alders gains height from the roof of the Orion building, finally able to leave the godforsaken place behind. The rain lashes onto his windscreen, the wipers just about managing to handle clearing enough water to give him sufficient visibility. The risk of a lightning bolt hitting the Lynx has passed, along with the thunder. There is just the heavy wind and rain to deal with now.

With both of the hold doors shut, the helicopter is starting to warm up, bringing welcome relief to four soaked passengers sitting in near silence in the hold. There is no silence in their heads, unfortunately; along with the remnants of the battle ringing in their ears, dark thoughts start to fester.

Josh has gone into himself and sits in total silence, trying not to let the shock of the mission—knowing his father is infected and being forced to leave him behind—envelop him completely. His mind fights to not fall off an edge, as he knows that is the last thing his dad would want. He has to be strong for Emily and he will be. She will need him more than ever now.

Alice tries to comfort him, to reassure him with little success. She doesn't give up though, she keeps talking to him from time to time and tries to make him eat something. She understands it will take time for him to come around and she will be there to help him.

The Lynx makes good progress despite the weather and it is soon touching down in Richmond to pick up the rest of the team and the holdall. With everybody on board, the Lynx is overcapacity and the hold is full. Alders is confident the helicopter will handle the extra weight and he is careful when he takes back off. The Lynx's engines strain and protest but they take the helicopter up to resume their journey back to base.

The precious holdall is pushed under a seat, the whole team hoping the fucking thing was worth it.

To Be Continued

The Series 1 Trilogy Completes With

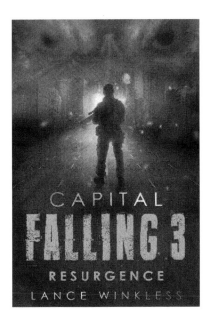

CAPITAL FALLING 3 - RESURGENCE

Terror is spreading. Chaos abounds.
The future has never looked so bleak . . .

The drama builds to an explosive finale, as the series one trilogy culminates in **CAPITAL FALLING 3 - RESURGENCE**.

As military operations to save London from the Zombie Apocalypse meet with ruin, the Rabid virus appears unstoppable. Heart-breaking losses continue to mount while the city crumbles — along with hope. Will those who've survived find refuge, and can fate, itself, be escaped?

Ferocious action escalates, sentiment spikes as the streets run red, and black smoke rises. White-knuckle thrills await the reader. Just don't lose your grip . . .